A TWISTED TALES NOVEL

SUGAR WOOD

BRYNN FORD

Sugar Wood
Copyright © 2021 Brynn Ford
Published by Brynn Ford

Cover Design Copyright © 2021 Pretty in Ink Creations
Interior Formatting by Nada Qamber at Najla Qamber Designs
Editing by Silvia Curry at Silvia's Reading Corner

More from the Author
www.brynnford.com
brynnfordauthor@gmail.com

This book is dedicated
to the ever-present struggle

CONTENT WARNING

This steamy dark romance is a twisted retelling of Hansel & Gretel, and features an MMF relationship. Heed the warning—this is a dark story and parts of it may be upsetting to some readers. Please use your best judgment in deciding whether this book is for you.

Visit www.brynnford.com/sugar-wood
for a list of tropes and triggers in this book.

PLAYLIST

Stream on Spotify
spoti.fi/3lfCznq

Beautiful Crime by Tamer
Throne by Saint Mesa
The Devil Within by Digital Daggers
Run by AWOLNATION
I Come With Knives by IAMX
Hollow by Cloudeater
Mercy by Hurts
Desire by Meg Myers
Where the Dark Things Are by Kerli
Stardust by IAMX
Flightless Bird, American Mouth by Iron & Wine
Mr. Sandman by SYML
Vendetta by UNSECRET ft. Krigarè
Twisted by MISSIO
Out of the Woods by Anthem Lights

CHAPTER 1
Glory

NO MORE. NO *more. No more.*

The two words are a silent plea repeating in my mind. My consciousness is splintered, and each touch of his rough hands over my skin wedges it deeper.

No more.

His fingers lift the button of my jeans.

No more.

His hands push them down to expose me.

No more.

He reaches between my legs and caresses my dry flesh with calloused fingers. He groans against my ear and tells me he loves me.

No more!

I scream the words inside my mind, but out loud, my voice falters, whispered and cracking. "Stop…"

He ignores me like he always does.

"I don't want to."

"Shh, princess. You know you don't mean that."

His fingers stroke and I cringe, fighting to stay present. If I let myself float away from the moment, drift on a black sea inside my mind, he'll do it as he always does. He'll fuck me, and I'll come back into awareness with pain between my legs and a new hole in my heart.

How many holes can he make before my heart disappears altogether, leaving a hollow void inside my ribcage?

The bliss of slipping away calls to me as he strokes, manipulating my body. I close my eyes and see an image of my gray, dying heart full of holes, dry and flaky, floating inside an empty cage of bones. It pumps once, twice, then disintegrates, the ashes drifting away, particles escaping between the bars of bone.

I want to drift away with them.

I want to be free from this.

I thought I'd escaped it when I left for college—coming home for winter break was a mistake, though I didn't really have a choice. I only have access to my father's money if I return to him, if I let him hurt me. It took me a year after graduating high school to convince him to let me leave for college, but I'd promised him I'd come home on breaks…not because he's a loving father who wants to keep up with his daughter.

He wants me home for *this*.

I've been free of him for three and a half months, and naively, I thought it would be different now. I'm nineteen; I'm an adult, a college student. I'd left home, though I could never really leave him.

Our name followed me like a curse—Glory Tolliver, the spoiled heiress of the Tolliver's Treats empire. My father's maple confections were loved around the world. He'd built his factory in our small town in Vermont and had made a fortune.

Once upon a time, I was set to inherit it all…that was, until he married my stepmother, Maura, when I was twelve.

That was only one year after my mother died. That was the year this started, and no one knows.

No one knows, except for me.

Not even my stepbrother, Huxley, knows, though he knows everything else about me. I refuse to tell him for fear he'll see the truth about me. The truth is that I'm worthless, nothing more than a spoiled brat with a pretty face and a tight cunt for my father to abuse.

His heavy hands on my hips jerk me back to awareness, away from the image of the pieces of my ashen heart floating away like dust in a window's sliver of sunlight.

"No," I try to use my voice but it's meek, like it always is, "I don't want this."

He shushes me, bending me over the island counter, and my palms land on the cold, dark granite. Sickness rolls through my stomach and my non-existent heart tries to pump adrenaline through my veins, but it's only pulsing weakness.

I'm weak.

I'm weak?

I jolt as he moves against me, preparing to take what he wants from me, and it terrifies me more now than it ever did before. When I was a child, it was simpler somehow. I had no choice then. He was my father, and he was God in this house. But now I have a choice...I have a voice.

But how do I speak when I've been silent for so long?

My eyes fall upon the black wooden knife block holding various blades on the island in front of me, and I scan the row of steak knives. I could grab one and threaten him with it, though I know that wouldn't stop this. He'd laugh at me. Worse, he might take it from me and turn it against me. I swallow hard as a lump of fear rises in my throat.

"I've missed you," he says with such care that it makes me sick.

He doesn't care.

Nobody cares.

My cell phone rings and my head snaps toward it as he abruptly stills behind me. I left it on the island counter, and I could reach it if I stretch. It buzzes against the granite as the cheerful ringtone plays. I rise onto my tiptoes and reach for it, stretching my arm as far as I can, my fingers splayed and grappling over the speckled countertop. My ass brushes against him as I reach, bending deeper over the counter, and he lets out a disgusting groan as he prepares to enter me.

My fingertips sweep the edge of my cell phone and I strain to grip it. My knuckles bend as I dig my nails into the edge of my floral phone case, and I let out a breath of relief when it slides toward me. I quickly flip it over and see Huxley's name on the screen—my stepbrother, my constant savior.

"What are you doing?" my father asks me.

I slide my thumb across the green button to answer the call, but as soon as I say, "Hux?" it's torn from my grip.

My father rises and backs away from me, and I spin to see him holding my phone to his ear. "Hux, good to hear from you!"

I can hear Huxley's voice travel through the line, but I can't make out what he's saying.

"She's here, she's fine," my father tells him. "We're just having a little father-daughter bonding time."

If I still had a gag reflex, I would vomit.

He reaches out, trying to run his finger through a strand of my bleached blonde hair, but I smack his hand away. His response is a simple tilt of his head. I quickly pull up my underwear and jeans and button them, hoping this is the end of it for tonight.

But I know it won't be.

He makes small talk with Huxley as he steps forward, plants his palm on the top of my head, and shoves me down until my knees buckle and I drop to the floor in front of him.

No more.

No more!

I put my hands on his thighs and dip my head lower than his hand can reach, pushing away from him with force. I spin away and rush around the massive island, fear gripping me as I see the frustration harden my father's eyes.

He's more terrifying now than he ever has been before. Perhaps it's the time away where I've been free of him that makes his presence so frightening now. Regardless of the reason, I'm scared, and for the first time, I feel an urgent pull within me to seek help…to get out of this, to get away from him.

I can't do this anymore!

I steel myself, take a deep breath, and call out for the only person who's ever really been there for me. "Hux!"

I don't say another word beyond the single syllable cry for help—it's enough to get my stepbrother's attention, assuming he can hear me through the phone. I stare into Beau Tolliver's nasty green eyes and breathe deeply as I stand my ground and wait. Hopefully, I'm waiting for help to come and not more violence at my father's hands.

"She's fine," he says into my phone, a look of malice spreading across his salt-and-pepper-bearded cheeks. "You know how she gets…I think being away has been rough on her mental health." A pause. "Sure. You can come on over, son. How far away are you?" He pauses and listens, then cocks a thick eyebrow at me. "Ten minutes. Sure. We'll see you then."

He ends the call and slowly lowers my phone to the counter, setting it facedown on the black, speckled granite, though he doesn't release me from his gaze.

"Why did you do that?" He speaks to me slowly, as if I'm stupid. "He's worried about you now. And you've left us with only ten minutes because you couldn't keep your mouth shut. That's hardly any time for us at all. Come back over here so we can finish what we started before he gets here."

I straighten my spine, swallowing a painful lump in my throat. "No." The word feels foreign slipping from between my perfectly painted pink lips…but it also feels powerful.

"Glory, I won't ask you again."

My voice is quiet, as it has always been. "And I won't tell you *no* again."

"Good," he says, bending to pull up his pants, though he doesn't buckle them. He moves along the edge of the island, and it startles me.

He didn't understand my words.

"I won't tell you no because I'm not doing that with you. Never. Not ever again." I swallow in an attempt to steady my wavering voice.

"If you want that check for next semester, you'll be my sweet little princess like you've always been."

I shake my head as he rounds the counter, coming closer, and as I move around the short side, I come face to face with the block of knives. There's an impulse, an instinct, an urgent need that shoots through my arm, making my palm twitch to wrap around the smooth handle of a protective blade.

I blink and when I look down at my hand, I'm holding one—a knife—but not one of the small steak knives. My palm is wrapped around the handle of a massive butcher's knife, and my hand aches from my tight, twitching grip.

My father raises his palms in surrender, though we both know he'd never do that. "Glory," he chuckles, "let's not waste our time playing games. Huxley will be here any minute now."

"Get back."

He creeps toward me, and I take a step backward—a mistake. He could see my weakness in that movement. I always show my weakness.

I want to be strong.

I need to be strong.

I move toward him, my pristine, white sneakers creeping forward over the tiled floor.

His eyes widen as he takes a step back, and that single step shifts something. The demon energy that was flowing from him seeps through my pores, wrapping around the ashes of my heart and setting them on fire.

I take another step toward him, and he backs away.

I inhale with the burning rush of power that explodes through every ashen particle, setting off tiny explosions of rage as each speck bursts with its own memory of one of the hundreds of times he's abused me.

Words whisper from my lips as I move forward without conscious thought. "You're sick."

"Glory Ann Tolliver, you put that knife down. Right now!"

I flinch, a natural response to him yelling and the use of my full name. I shake my head as the instinct to obey my father tries to take hold, but then something strange happens. Anger drives down on the part of my mind that splinters, hammering a wedge deeper and deeper into the crevice, until suddenly, it breaks and a filter of crimson slips in front of my eyes.

The filter clouds my mind and silences the world around me. It moves my feet beneath me; it grips the handle of the blade tighter…It thrusts my arm forward.

My arm twists.

My father falls.

The blade slices and slips and stabs.

I feel trapped inside myself, lost to some strange possession that controls my actions. It's calming, in an odd sort of way. My mind feels free of the shame that comes with allowing my father to abuse me when I'm old enough to stay away.

I let out a heavy sigh and let the filter shield me from what I'm really doing, from the screaming and bleeding and sounds of slicing flesh as my body takes control, finally allowing me to protect myself.

The filter frees me, and the only color I see is red.

THREE WORDS ECHO inside my mind, bouncing past misfiring synapses and failing to make understanding as my body moves without conscious thought.

No more. Run.

No more. Run!

My lungs ache, my cheeks burn from the cold, and my feet are snow-soaked. The red-hued filter is lifting, and I'm coming back into awareness. The sensations of the world around me are painful and warning as they creep into being.

"Glory!" I hear Huxley call my name and I slam to a stop.

I blink once, then again, gradually bringing myself back to reality. I'm no longer in the mansion, no longer in the kitchen, no longer with my disgusting father. Somehow, I'm outside, surrounded by trees and darkness.

Sugar Wood Forest.

I've awakened from a violent daze to find my physical being clustered among the tree trunks from which our family business taps its maple. I whirl around, guessing at the direction from which I came, thankful to see that I haven't gotten far. I can still see the floodlights shining down on our back patio and Huxley's shadow as he runs past them.

I look down and red flashes across my vision once again, though this time, it isn't the filter.

It's blood…the blood of my father.

There's a trail of red sneaker prints stamped in the snow, revealing my path from the mansion.

"Glory!" I hear Huxley yell again.

I watch his shadowed form and see him running toward me, following the trail of bloody footprints across the snow.

What do I do?

I lift my palms to see that they're coated in thick crimson and it feels like fire on my skin. Everything within me burns, but I'm fixed on the spot, wondering if I'm hidden among the trees and as still as their trunks that rise high and dark around me.

My voice is a whisper again, barely audible. "Hux…"

I've slipped so easily back into the weak shell of the girl I was before. But for a moment, I was strong…a moment that I had no control over made me strong. Though now the drop-off from the adrenaline rush washes my strength away, wiping me clean of the demonic energy that had set off explosions of violent power inside me.

I fall to my knees, sinking into inches of snow, and I start to cry. My pathetic sobs echo through the trees, speaking louder than I ever could with my own words.

"Glory." His voice is so close now.

I lift my head slowly and see him approach. My bloody palms are turned up as if I'm holding something.

He stops just in front of me, his eyes scanning me and registering the reality of my appearance. "Glory? Shit, what happened?" He lowers to his knees in front of me and I feel softer in his presence.

"Is he dead?"

"I don't know…" His tone wavers with worry, or maybe it's just from the cold, winter air. "I think he must be. I saw him and went frantic looking for you, so I didn't check. Who did this? Was someone in the house?" His head whips from side to side, scanning the woods beyond us for a potential threat. "Shit, Glory." He grabs my arm and tugs it toward him, twisting it and inspecting it for injuries before doing the same with the other. "You're hurt?"

I shake my head slowly. "No…no one was here. Hux, I…" I can't say it.

"Who did this?" he demands an answer.

It's because of his insistence that my troubled mind compels me to respond immediately—I'm groomed to respond to men and their orders. "I killed him. I did it."

"No, you didn't. You wouldn't do that. Someone must have been here."

"My father tried to—" I swallow hard. "He tried to hurt me and I snapped. I stabbed him. I killed him. He's dead."

There's such relief in those words.

I killed him.

He's dead.

How can there be such relief in murder?

"What do you mean, he tried to hurt you? What did he do?"

I meet Huxley's deep brown eyes, always so kind and caring toward me. "He did what he's always done to me."

The silence around us is deafening. I feel like it should be louder, as though there should be sirens and shouting, gunfire and the whipping blades of a helicopter searching for me above the trees.

I killed my father…I murdered Beau Tolliver.

But there is no sound other than the echo of the snowflakes landing on the ground. Somehow, I can hear every single one of them crashing to the earth.

"What did he do?"

I can't say the words. I *won't* say the words. I can't tell Huxley what's been happening to me for years—the things I've let my father do because I was too afraid to speak, too scared I'd lose my inheritance.

I don't even care about the inheritance anymore, not since I moved out and found out what it felt like to be free. I only needed enough money to pay for my classes so I could finish my degree, then I could become self-sufficient and leave him forever.

That's what I told myself anyway, when the nagging feeling to take next semester's tuition and room and board checks and *run* overcame me. Maybe that's what should have happened. I should have let him have his way with me tonight, write me the check, and run away to find somewhere to hide away in the world where he could never find me.

But I killed him instead.

"Glory, tell me…what did he do to you?"

My voice is soft. "I can't tell you. I can never tell you. No one can know." My hands are shaking, though I don't know whether it's from the cold or my nerves. I drop my head, unable to look into his eyes.

Arms close around me and he draws me into his embrace, wrapping me in warmth and protective calm. "It's okay." His palm cradles the back of my head, a shielding hold that encourages me to lay my head on his shoulder and bury my face in his neck.

I breathe in and his familiar scent calms me. He always smells like vanilla-flavored coffee, sweet and bitter all at once—just like him. I let myself sink into his hold. I let him hug me, caress my hair, whisper that everything's going to be okay.

"Are they going to arrest me? Am I going to jail?" Tears tumble from my eyes, and I cry into his bomber jacket.

He grabs my shoulders and pushes me back, his hands slipping up to hold my cheeks. "No, Glory. No one's going to arrest you. I won't let that happen."

"I killed him!" I scream, my voice echoing loudly through the silent forest.

The powerful sound of my typically meager voice blends with the night, fading gradually before disappearing among the trees, as if the branches themselves could carry it deeper into the woods, so deep that no one could ever find it.

"You said he tried to hurt you," Huxley reasons. "Self-defense, right?"

I swallow as flashes of red come to mind, showing me

faded and blurred images of the knife slicing into my father's flesh repeatedly. I cut him, stabbed him, too many times to argue anything but overkill, and that alone makes me guilty.

I shake my head. "I don't know how many times I stabbed him…more than I had to. They'll think I did it for the money. They'll think I killed him for the inheritance."

I watch his expression, my gaze skimming up along the line of his cheekbones, pronounced in the way his jaw is set with tension. I glance across his furrowed brow where a stray strand of his natural, golden blond hair has fallen despite his careful styling. My eyes draw a line down his symmetrical nose to his soft lips, noting the day-old scruff that's peeking in around them.

Slowly, his appearance shifts from gentle savior to plotting determination. I watch as his brown eyes flicker; the wheels turning in his mind, working through the reality of this situation.

He was always so thoughtful. He never made a decision without completely thinking it through. He's helped me out of trouble more times than I can count. I know I haven't been the easiest stepsister to have. I know I've never been worthy of the care he shows me, but he's always come to my rescue.

He's in his last year at Princeton, and I couldn't be prouder of him—but he almost didn't go because of me. The six-hour drive between us almost kept him from following his dreams—graduating from an Ivy League college before going on to law school.

I'm so damn lucky he's here right now. I didn't know he was coming home for winter break, and neither did my father. Sometimes I wonder if Huxley can feel my pain from afar, as if he somehow knows when I'm about to be hurt and comes to save me before I can even call for him.

He's saved me so many times before, and he doesn't even know how much it means to me…how much *he* means to me.

When his head begins to bob slowly in a nod, I know he's got a plan. He's figured something out, some way to help me out of this nightmare.

"Okay," he says. "Here's what we're gonna do. We're gonna clean up, wash away all the blood, and get rid of the evidence. We're gonna bury him here in the forest, and then we're leaving. We're driving back to Princeton tonight, and as far as anyone knows, you've been visiting me all break, staying at my apartment. Okay? If we go deep enough into the forest, we can bury him and no one will ever find him."

I don't argue with him, I don't question him, I don't ask for clarification. I nod and agree to do what he says because I trust him. I trust Huxley with my life because he's never let me down before.

He's the only person I can count on, so I give him my faith, relieved that even in this living nightmare, I'm not alone.

I have Huxley.

He's going to fix this.

CHAPTER 2

"ONE MORE," I groan as Glory and I roll my stepfather's lifeless body in the tarp.

Three rotations and he's as well wrapped as the two of us can get him on our own. We both rise, panting from exertion, but our exhaustion tonight has yet to reach a peak.

"You should shower and change," I tell her. "Wash all the blood off you and bring me your clothes. We'll burn them in the fireplace."

She nods, her face almost impassive as she blindly takes my direction. Even in this shitshow of a situation, my chest rises with pride to know how I have her trust. I *should* have her trust. I've worked hard enough for it over the years. Glory was never easy to love with all the trouble she got into as a teenager, but I loved her all the same.

I loved her more than I should have.

That was one reason I knew I had to leave for college when I was eighteen, though I hated leaving her behind to clean up her own messes. Somehow, she'd managed to get through the last three years without me before leaving for college herself this fall.

Still, there was always a voice nagging in the back of

my head telling me I shouldn't have left her alone. It told me that something wasn't quite right here between Glory and her father. I liked Beau well enough when my mother had first married him, but something just felt off about him. It's why I called and checked on Glory so often. It's why I called her tonight, because it just didn't feel right to me that she came home for winter break, knowing that no one else would be here.

My mother was doing a sales pitch for Tolliver's Treats at a new major distributor and she won't be back until tomorrow at the earliest. And I'd already told Glory I wasn't coming home, so I couldn't wrap my head around why she'd want to come home alone to her father. Maybe that would seem okay to other people, but it didn't feel right to me. I should've trusted my instincts all along. Maybe then I would've seen it and I could've done something about it.

She'd always cringed at his touch.

She flinched at his words.

She faked smiles and resisted hugs.

And she obeyed his every command, as if she were afraid of the consequences of not obeying him.

Fuck.

All the signs were there, and I ignored them in favor of being her savior, her rescuer, the one who came to help her when things got really bad.

But I didn't know how bad they were until tonight. I only realized it when we were rolling the tarp…when I noticed his pants were unbuckled.

I hope the conclusion I'm drawing is wrong, but the nausea in my gut tells me I'm right.

If we lived in a perfect world, she'd get off with a hand

slap for killing a man who would do something so vile to his own daughter. But our world is far from perfect. I'm trying to find a way to justify self-defense in my mind, but *fuck*, what she's done to him…I can't begin to guess how many times she stabbed him. The scene is gruesome, and they're going to prosecute her for this overkill.

They'll dig into her past and try to convict her based on all the trouble she's been in, not to mention her mental health issues. And it won't do her a damn bit of good that he was Beau fucking Tolliver. He owned this small town and the whole world knows who he was. I'm not convinced in the least that she won't go down hard for this, and come hell or high water, I'm not letting that happen to her.

She's stronger than she gives herself credit for, but I don't think she would survive prison.

Glory uses her toes to kick off the heels of her once perfectly white tennis shoes, then removes her socks and places them on the tile floor. It's a smart move. She won't track the blood farther through the house this way. She grips the hem of her fitted black T-shirt and peels it up over her head.

I pinch my eyes shut and turn my back on her, as if modesty is required in our current predicament where she's covered in her dead father's blood. I couldn't say when she became so comfortable around me that it doesn't bother her to strip naked in my presence, and though she's done it a hundred times, it still catches me off-guard and I have to force myself not to look.

She may be comfortable with it, but I'm not. It pushes a boundary I know I can't cross, because if I do, I'll never come back from it. I have my Ivy League reputation to maintain, and I don't think an affair with my stepsister will be a good extracurricular activity to add to my law school applications.

I hear the items of clothing drop to the floor as she strips behind my back, and I swallow my rising curiosity. I clench my fists at my sides and take in a breath that shudders through me, causing an ache in my balls that I can't relieve.

"I'll go take a shower," she whispers, and I wait until I hear her gentle footsteps pad across the tile floor before I turn around.

Her bloody clothes are folded neatly and placed on top of her soiled tennis shoes. The neatness and care with which she placed her ruined clothing almost makes me feel bad that I have to destroy them. Glory is a beautiful mess and an organized disaster. The enigma of her personality keeps my heart in a vice, squeezed so tightly that it can't beat for anyone but her.

It's painful to want her knowing I can never have her. She doesn't need me that way. She needs me to be her stepbrother, the guy who always made sure she was safe, taken care of; the guy who always put the pieces back together after her wreckage. She needs me to take care of her, to make sure she's protected and safe.

If she ever let me in as more than that, I wouldn't be able to protect her from myself.

But I *will* protect her from going down for this.

I head outside while Glory showers, walking around the fence that encloses the in-ground pool. I trudge through snow to the shed at the far back of the yard, near the forest tree line. Inside, I find an old, wooden sled and drag it out, hoping it will hold up well enough to move Beau's body. I pull it closer to the house—as close as I can get to the patio by the sliding glass door—and head back inside.

By the time I've rolled duct tape around the tarp, locking his body inside, Glory has finished her shower. She comes into the kitchen with nothing but a T-shirt and her underwear, and my heart stops at the sight of her.

She pauses as our eyes lock, tucking a strand of wet hair behind her ear. "I'll get dressed after I help you clean up."

"You don't have to help me clean up."

She walks toward me. "Yes, I do. This is my mess." She opens the cabinet beneath the kitchen sink behind me. "Do you need me to help you move him outside?"

"No, let me handle that."

She straightens, putting a spray bottle of cleaner onto the counter as I bend, grabbing hold of the looped handle I made out of duct tape that wraps all the way around the body. I use it to drag him, watching the end of the wrapped tarp where his feet are tucked inside to make sure I'm not dragging a trail of blood behind us. We must have done a good enough job of getting him on the tarp without making too much of a mess on the outside of it because he drags cleanly.

Through a struggle, I manage to get Beau outside and onto the sled. Then, I go back in to help Glory. We scrub the kitchen clean, following every possible path she might have walked while covered in his blood, and wipe it all down with harsh chemicals.

We go over it again and again, making sure everything looks exactly as it had when she'd first come home, then I send her upstairs to put on some warm clothes.

She comes back down wearing jeans that hug her in ways I shouldn't notice, pulling an oversized, cream-colored cable-knit sweater on over her fitted, soft pink T-shirt. She slips on some fuzzy boots that look warm, but impractical for a wilderness walk with the oversized foot and flat sole. She throws on a heavy, hunter-green parka with a fur-lined hood, and I feel satisfied that will keep her warm, at least.

I zip up my bomber jacket, noting the small, dark stain on the sleeve. I'll need to throw this jacket on the fire later and burn it like I burned her bloody clothes—but for now, I need it for warmth. I pull my gloves from my pockets and slip them on before grabbing the rope attached to the sled. It's heavy now, adorned with the bright blue, crinkled tarp filled with Beau Tolliver's remains.

We stop at the shed again so I can retrieve a shovel from inside, and I hand it to Glory. She takes one hand from her pocket and grips the handle, though she looks odd holding it.

She's not the princess everyone thinks she is, but it's true that she's never done a day's worth of manual labor in her life. I don't know that I've ever seen her break a sweat outside of a planned workout, and those usually took place in her matching sports bras and leggings with her make-up and hair done.

She's not pretentious or spoiled, but she looks the part— which is why her little outbursts that get her into trouble get blown out of proportion. She simply loses control of herself sometimes.

We all do.

"You ready?"

She nods. "How far out do we go?"

"As far as we can. We need time to dig a hole and we need to make it difficult for him to be found."

"Okay," she agrees.

"Brush away our footsteps with the shovel, and make sure all the bloody ones you made earlier are covered, too."

I tug at the reins, dragging the sled behind me as I head for the tree line with Glory at my back. We enter the forest. Silence surrounds us except for the treads of the sled gliding over the rising snow. Moonlight peaks through the bare branches, allowing us enough light to see just in front of our steps, but as we march deeper into the forest and the trees become more densely packed, the light dims until it fades away, almost entirely.

"This is creepy," Glory whispers. "How are we going to find our way back without our footsteps?"

Shit. I didn't think of that.

I stop and turn my head to look around us, realizing how easy it would be to get lost in this labyrinth of trees. I drop the rope and pull out my cell phone, relieved to find that I still have service, though the signal is weak. I don't know how far in I'll lose that service, but we need to go a lot deeper into the forest than this.

I can only see a faint glow of the floodlights from the back of our house from this distance, so I think we're far enough in that we don't need to hide our footsteps until we make our way back.

"Stop covering our tracks," I tell her. "We can follow them back to this spot on our way home."

She nods and we trudge ahead, walking in silence for what must be a mile. Somehow, the snow falls quicker, heavier, though the path of trunks is denser and the bare branches above should block the path for it to reach us as it falls. I change our direction, knowing it would be foolish to take a straight path out from the house, and we walk another ten minutes or so before I finally decide we should stop.

"I think this should be far enough."

Glory whirls around to look behind her. "Hux, we need to hurry. The snowfall is starting to cover our tracks."

I look back to see she's right, and I instantly feel stupid for somehow thinking that would be a reliable way to find our way back home. "Shit. Give me that." I hold out my hand for the shovel, feeling new urgency to finish this.

I find a spot nestled between two trees—a spot wide enough that I know I shouldn't run into too many roots there, though the bases are close enough to make for an inconspicuous burial site.

"We should've brought two shovels," she says. "I could've helped you."

"You don't need to help me with this. I'll take care of it." I start by shoveling away the snow, working until I've exposed a rectangular, body-sized patch of earth beneath.

"You don't have to do everything for me."

"I know I don't…I want to."

It takes a full five minutes for me to pile away enough snow to see the earth beneath, and as soon as it's clear, I slam the blade of the shovel down into the sod. I dig and dig and dig, and it doesn't take long before exhaustion starts to set in.

This is going to be a long fucking night.

CHAPTER 3
Glory

I'M SHIVERING LIKE mad. I don't know how long he's been at it, but it feels like hours have passed since he started digging. It's all but done now. My father is in the hole, and Huxley works on covering him with dirt.

I wander and pace as he works, ashamed that once again, my big brother is cleaning up the mess I've made. He always comes to my rescue, and I love that about him—I know I can always count on him—but I don't feel deserving of it. I don't feel I've earned his care.

Exhaustion sets his features as he works, pausing for a moment to swipe the back of his hand across his brow. It's freezing out here, but he's broken a sweat, nonetheless.

I can't look at him for too long because he looks different. Older, stronger…more attractive. I shake my head and turn away to avoid staring at him and bringing myself even more shame for thinking of my stepbrother as handsome.

Instead, I look out into the dark forest, all blackness sweeping between the trees except for the small circle of light from our cell phones, which we've propped up around the grave with their flashlight features on.

The grave.

I should feel something about that word. I should feel something now that my father is dead…that save for my stepmother—who I don't really care for—I'm an orphan.

But all I feel is relief.

My eyes trace shadows in the silent forest.

Odd.

In the distance, I see a vague, tiny cloud of white smoke move across the darkness. It floats away into the night, but a few seconds later, I see a faint pinpoint of orange light, almost like a spark, before another small cloud of smoke puffs out and drifts away.

Then there's a shadow…a dark silhouette of a human that shifts and moves behind a tree trunk.

My eyes must be playing tricks on me.

Are they?

I turn to look at Huxley, my lips parting to tell him, but he's working so hard to clean up my mess that I feel guilty bothering him.

It's probably nothing. I'm probably imagining things.

Still, I'm curious enough to find out if the little white smoke clouds are real or whether I'm hallucinating. I slowly walk between the trees, my feet crunching the quickly piling snow. I glance behind me after a few steps, reminding myself that I can follow my tracks back to Huxley, and it's only then that I realize how high the snow has piled since we left the house—and our path back might be covered.

I whirl around and march back toward Huxley. I scan the snow on my way, searching for the tracks we made, and quickly descend toward panic. I can't see any tracks other than my pacing—none that will lead us out and away from this spot. When I reach the grave, I bend and pluck my cell phone from where it's laid as he shovels another pile of dirt onto the growing mound. I take it with me as I look, holding the light toward the ground and searching all around me.

I turn back and look at Huxley a few yards away. "I can't find our tracks."

He stops, looking up at me, my cell phone light casting an eerie glow around him. His eyebrows pull into a straight line. "Shit. Well, the sled was pointing…" He looks down at it and cocks his head. "Did you turn it?"

I shake my head. "You did. You pulled it close to the hole and turned it to drop him in."

He runs a hand through his golden blond hair. "It's… it's fine. We'll figure it out."

"Are we lost?"

He huffs out an agitated breath. "I said we'll figure it out. One thing at a time, Glory. Just let me finish this."

I'm trembling and it's not just from the cold, it's from fear. It's two o'clock in the morning, pitch-black, and all I can think about is how we might freeze to death if we can't find our way back in the dark.

I wonder if that makes me selfish on top of everything else. I murdered my father tonight, and we're burying his body, trying to cover it up. And here I am, fearful of the darkness and the cold and how we'll survive the night in the snow.

I deserve to freeze to death for this.

Huxley finally finishes filling in the hole with sod and begins to shovel snow on top of it. He levels it out with the flat back of the shovel, smoothing it over the surface, and somehow, he manages to make it look as though the spot is undisturbed…as though we were never here and there isn't a body buried beneath. I'm impressed by it, though that's strange to think in this circumstance.

I'm impressed by *him*.

He straightens and inhales a heavy breath, swiping his coat sleeve across his sweaty brow, a perfect image of strength and power. He exhales, fog escaping from between his lips. Stress extends across his features and the guilt of what I've put him through—what I've *always* put him through—makes shame sink deep within me.

I move to him, quickly closing the short distance between us, and I throw my arms around his neck, hugging him close. "Thank you, Hux. I'm so sorry. I'm sorry I keep fucking things up and you have to keep saving me."

He's stiff for a beat, but after a moment, I feel the tautness of his muscles loosen and relax. He sighs and the shovel drops from his palm, plopping into the snow beside us as he wraps his arms around my waist and squeezes me tight.

"I will always save you," he murmurs. "Always. And for what it's worth, as fucked up as this is, I'm proud of you. I'm not proud of the violence, I'm just…I'm proud that you finally realized your worth and fought back."

I didn't do it because I thought I was worth something. I know that I'm not. I just lost control of myself entirely, but I don't want him to know that—he'll think I'm insane.

Maybe I am.

There is a small part of me that feels his pride, though… the way it wraps around me like his arms do, embracing me fully, fueling me with warmth and care.

He pulls back slowly, grabbing hold of my shoulders

and dipping his head to meet my eyes. "I think I know what he did to hurt you. How long has he been raping you?"

I flinch.

God, the impact of that word is jarring.

It's the right word, but hearing it out loud makes it too real.

I shake my head. "I can't talk about this. Not now."

His features soften, his head tilting to the side. His hand comes up and cradles my cheek, his touch giving me a jolt of his warmth, even through the glove that covers his palm. "I understand," he says. "It's over now. He's never going to hurt you again."

I nod.

"I'll always protect you."

His thumb brushes against my chin and I feel the tenderness of his touch everywhere. It's not just a brush across my chin, it's a stroke down my hair, a caress over my arm, a tight embrace around my belly.

For the first and only time in my life, I feel peace. I'm safe in Huxley's presence, shrouded in the darkness and surrounded by silence so loud that it makes the world seem distant and unreachable.

THE PEACE STRETCHED on through the first hour, but as we approach the end of the second hour with no end to the tree line in sight, we've both devolved into frantic shells of ourselves, frightened that we'll be lost forever and desperate for warmth.

"Maybe we should go this way," I point off to my right.

Huxley huffs, "Why? What makes you think that direction will lead us home?"

"I don't know...I just know that walking straight isn't

working."

"Maybe we should just stop."

"And freeze to death?"

"No. We'll wait until sunrise. Maybe then we'll be able to see something and can find our way back."

"This doesn't feel right. I don't think we're anywhere near home. I don't think sunlight is going to show us the way, either. Hux, we're lost. *Really* lost."

"I *know* that. Don't you think I fucking *know* that? Fuck!"

His shout echoes through the night, bouncing back as an eerie cry for help. Except, there's no one around to help us.

"Let's…let's just go a little farther, okay? Let's try this direction." I point off to my right again. "Let's walk for ten minutes and if it doesn't get us anywhere, then we'll stop and wait until sunrise."

"Shit. I really fucked up here."

Huxley's cell phone died, though we still have the flashlight on my phone. The battery is draining quickly, and there's no service to make a call. Even if it did have service, would we dare? If we alerted anyone to our location, we'd have a lot of explaining to do, and then it wouldn't just be murder that they charge me with. It would be murder, moving a body, covering up a crime…and Huxley would get arrested for his part in it, too. We're truly helpless now, and I don't know what the fuck to do.

The only thing I do know is that I'm not letting Huxley think that he fucked up, that this is his fault. If I hadn't lost myself to a fit of dissociative rage, then we wouldn't even be here.

"It's okay. We're gonna be okay. This mess is my fault,

not yours," I say.

Instead of trying to assure me otherwise, he falls into silence, and it causes a small stab of pain in my chest—a pain I deserve.

"Come on." I take his hand, pulling him with me as we change direction.

We stop after another ten minutes or so of silent wandering through the night. We let the sounds of the whistling wind pushing through leafless tree branches wrap around us and whisper dreadful things.

You're lost.

You're alone.

You'll never escape this forest.

You'll die here.

I put my hand on my chest and turn to face him. "Hux, I'm—"

The light on my cell phone goes out, the battery finally dead.

"Fuck."

I feel the disconnect from reality wash over me. It's rushing through my mind as the only way to separate myself from this nightmare and avoid outright panic. I press my eyes shut against the emotional numbing that's rippling through my veins.

But then he grabs hold of me, pulls me against him, and holds me close. A jolt of electricity tries to break through and overcome the detachment taking hold of me. My eyes pop open again to a mirage, a hallucination—or at least, I think it must be.

Off in the distance, I see smoke—not the tiny white puff I saw before, which rolled away into the night. This is a billowing tower of subtle gray lifting and rising.

"What is that?" I whisper.

He releases me and lets go, his hands still gripping my shoulders as he turns his head to look behind us.

"That's…smoke. Like chimney smoke."

I feel reality creep back in to flush out the numbness. "You see it, too?"

"Yeah, I see it."

His palms slip down my arms, one falling away as the other grips my hand and squeezes. "Come on. Let's follow it before it goes away."

I have some apprehension, an anxious tingle climbing up my arms, but the cold follows it, reminding me that it won't be much longer before hypothermia sets in.

We have to move.

We trudge through the dark forest, stumbling and tripping as we tromp through thick snow without a light, our feet landing on roots and branches beneath. We come upon an incline, and it's a gentle sloping at first, but after a minute, it steepens.

We won't let that stop us.

Time is running out for us and desperation punches adrenaline through my veins. Though the hill sharpens to vertical, we push on.

Together, we climb.

CHAPTER 4
Glory

THERE'S A HOUSE at the top of the hill. We can see it now. Gray smoke puffs from the chimney, hinting at warmth inside. It gives me strength to push forward despite the way I shiver, despite the harshness of the cold seeping into my bones and weakening my muscles. Huxley and I make it to the top of the harsh incline, both fighting for each breath as our tired bodies carry us through the thick snow.

Huxley reaches the top first and turns back to reach out his hand to me. I take it and let him pull me, helping me make the last few steps up the hill before the land levels out. We don't stop moving. Though the upward climb is done, the snow is thick in the clearing surrounding the small brown house.

I recognize the inherent danger in showing up unannounced to someone's secret home in the middle of the forest, but the danger we face in the elements is far greater. I don't let go of Huxley's hand as we march forward, leaving our tracks in the snow. I look at the bright, round moon overhead, shining down at us like a spotlight. It's haunting in the sudden stillness, and an unnerving quiet settles around us.

"It's not snowing anymore," I whisper. Somehow, it feels wrong to speak any louder as we approach the house.

I glance over at Huxley to see him nod, a tight smile showing tension through his cheeks. His eyes are firmly on the house in front of us…a house in the middle of the vastness of Sugar Wood Forest.

It seems odd to me that there's a house here.

Our family owns a significant acreage of this land, though I don't really know how far our ownership extends from our home—and I don't know how far away from our home we've traveled.

Regardless of what I know and don't know, we've found this strange house and we're desperate. We need warmth and we need it now. Though the front windows are dark, I can see the faintness of light somewhere within, perhaps coming from someone's bedroom. Surely, if anyone's home, they're asleep at this time of night.

We trudge forward, heading straight toward the door. I'm ready to pound my fist on it, but Huxley steps in front of me, pushing me behind him protectively. He knocks on the door…but we're met with no response. He knocks again, and again, and still, no response.

"They must be asleep. Maybe they can't hear us?"

He nods and knocks again, pounding his fist against the brown wooden door. We wait and wait, both shivering and bouncing to ward away the cold.

"There's a light on in the back," I tell him, moving toward the window where I saw it. "Maybe if we go around back and knock?"

Huxley looks apprehensive, but there's no room for apprehension when we're this cold.

"Stay here," he tells me, and I nod before he disappears

around the side of the house.

A few moments later, I hear him knock against a back door or the wood siding maybe…I don't know. But when I hear the third tap of his fist echoing in the distance, the front door shoves open, swinging out toward me, and knocking me backward. I gasp in surprise as I land on my ass in the snow, which instantly sends a chill up my spine.

Looking up, I see the shadowed silhouette of a man in the dark doorway. There's a spark, the flickering embers of a cigarette, then a white puff of smoke drifting from him into the night. It's the same spark and smoke I thought I'd seen out in the forest when Huxley was burying my father.

I'm stunned into stillness as the man in front of me moves forward, revealing himself as the glow of the moonlight bathes him in a peculiar light. He tosses his cigarette into the snow, and it lands beside me. He's shirtless, wearing only a pair of tattered, well-worn jeans that hug his rugged hips. He squints down at me as he steps closer, and I can see the darkness in his eyes. They match his dark hair, which is thick and wavy, long enough to frame his chiseled jawline.

He blows out a final puff of smoke from the corner of his plump lips and his eyebrows—as dark as his raven hair— dip together in the middle.

"What are you doing out here, little bird?" It doesn't sound so much like a question, as if he doesn't care for my response.

Who is this man?

He takes a step closer, and I flinch, then quickly scramble to my feet. As I open my mouth to speak, to yell for Huxley to come back, the dark man moves swiftly into my space, turning his hand to slap his palm over my mouth while the other sweeps around behind me and grips the back of my head.

He pulls me in close. "Shh," he hushes me. "Don't say a word."

My eyes are wide as I watch him.

"It looks like you're in some trouble, little bird."

I shake my head against his hand.

"And you two made a mistake coming out here."

My heart beats wildly, reminding me that it is, in fact, still solid, that it still exists, that it's not ashen particles floating away like smoke in the night. The man's eyes catch and hold mine for a single beat before he moves. Both his hands come down at the same time to grab my shoulders and he turns me roughly, shoving me inside his house.

"Hux!" I shout, and it's the only sound I manage to make before the dark stranger slams the door behind him and locks it.

I'm locked in.

I stumble backward awkwardly, my heels tripping over a rug, my ass colliding with a wooden table, its legs screeching across the hardwood floor as my weight shifts it.

"Get back," I say, but my voice is weak.

The man doesn't say a word as he stalks toward me.

"We were lost," I explain. "We were out too late in the dark and we got lost. We just…We were hoping you could help us."

Still, he doesn't speak.

I back away, and he follows.

"C-can you help us?"

He keeps moving toward me.

My breaths quicken with fear, sensing the inherent danger we put ourselves in the moment we stepped foot on this man's property. I don't think he wants to help us. I don't think this is a good man. I think I should be afraid.

Huxley pounds on the front door, screaming for me, and the man glances toward the sound over his shoulder. I take advantage of the distraction, turning and running down the dark hallway, heading for the only room with a light on at the back, thinking maybe I can lock myself in or escape through a window.

And then what?

Back into the freezing forest?

I make it to the room with the light and rush inside, but he's right behind me. I reach for the door, ready to throw it shut, but he slams his massive palms against it and shoves it open. I back up as he comes toward me, and for the first time, I see him clearly in the light.

He's…beautiful.

Beautiful and dark and dangerous.

My hands clench into fists at my sides, a cold sweat breaking out on my palms. "Please, we were just cold…"

My eyes dart down to the fair skin stretched taut across sculpted abs. My gaze traces the lines, taking in the full picture of a strong, brooding man—a man looking at me with anger spreading across his cheeks which are speckled with black stubble.

My distraction is what does me in. In a flash, he comes after me, his hand darting out so fast that I don't have time to react before it latches onto my throat. His fingers curl around my neck, slipping around to the back to grip just beneath the base of my skull. He tugs me into his hard body with a sharp yank, and I slap my palms against his bare chest to push back.

"No!" I shout, but it's far too late for protests.

He moves behind me as he turns me around to face the door, his grip on the back of my neck so tight that I imagine bruises will form at the imprint of his fingers. He shoves me forward, marching me out into the hallway and back into darkness.

I hear Huxley frantically tugging at the locked door, and it rattles on its hinges. I reach my hands back over my shoulders, trying to grab hold of his wrist to fight him away, but he's strong, so much stronger than me. He forces me into a dark room across the hallway, but it's only dark for a moment.

Sudden light bathes the room as he flips a switch behind us...and I desperately want to go back to the darkness.

This isn't a bedroom.

It's a prison.

Two paces into the room and metal bars draw a line across the space, creating a rectangular cage. Like a beast with its hungry mouth open wide, the cage door stands ajar. And the man holding my neck is ready to feed me to it.

Shoving me through, he walks me into the prison cell and slams me into the far corner. I bring my arms up protectively just before I hit, and they jam between my chest and the corner where the walls meet, my fists balled beneath my chin. He moves in close, his frame molding to my back, pinning me in place.

His body is warm against mine. I'm frozen, and in my desperation to melt, I feel a strange sort of relief drip down my body like liquid heat. I want him to stay, enveloping me in his warmth.

But he doesn't stay.

He steps back, and I whirl around in a flash, adrenaline

quickly reminding me that I'm in danger here. I lunge, preparing to make a run for it, but he's quicker. He crouches in front of me and snaps something metal around my ankle too quickly for me to process. I look down and see the cuff he's placed around my ankle, but before I can shake it off, he secures it with a padlock.

I panic. I scream and pull my leg to the side, jerking against the heavy chain attached to it—a chain that's bolted to the floor.

"Huxley!"

There's a crash, the sound of glass shattering, and the dark man and I both turn our heads sharply to look toward the hall. He turns on his heel and stomps away, leaving me in the cage with the door open. It doesn't matter that the door is open because I can't leave the space. I test the length of the chain and it's a goddamn tease. I can take one step outside the cage and that's the farthest I can go.

I start to scream for help, but I swallow my sound as I hear fists colliding, skin slapping skin, bodies hitting the wall, hitting the floor, grunting and shouting, as Huxley undoubtedly fights the mysterious man.

My eyes widen, my heartbeat flurries, my breaths quicken with anxiety. I become as still and quiet as a statue as silence falls too suddenly, and I strain my ears to listen.

There's a thump, then the undeniable swoosh of a body being dragged across the floor.

Drag, stop.

Drag, stop.

Drag...

The stranger comes into view, bent over, his arms

beneath an unconscious Huxley as he drags him backward along the hallway.

I gasp and my hand slaps over my mouth.

No, no, no...

Huxley saves me...Huxley always saves me.

If he can't save me now, then we're both doomed.

CHAPTER 5

I HEAR GLORY beg faintly as the fear in her tone shakes me back to awareness. "Please, let us go."

I'm on my back and the floor is hard along my spine. I blink, rolling my head as consciousness returns slowly, but then all at once, I jerk awake, sitting up in a flash.

I gasp in a breath as I turn my head to find Glory standing beside me. It takes me a moment to process what I'm seeing because it's so fucking bizarre. Her small hands are wrapped tightly around metal bars that cage us in a small room.

I climb to my feet and my body tilts as my vision blackens for a moment. I reach out to catch myself before I fall, though my hand lands on nothing. But then Glory is at my side, grabbing hold of me, her arms wrapping around my waist to steady me. I fight dizziness, blinking against the swirling room, and I manage to reach out and wrap my fist around one of the bars. I tug on it, pulling myself upright so Glory doesn't have to bear the weight of me.

"Hux," she says.

The way her fear sinks inside me makes me sick. It starts a fire in my gut that burns bright and hot, setting off an explosion of protective energy.

I put my arm around her shoulders as I balance with the other against the bar, looking out at the man who has made us captives. "Let us out," I demand. "Open this goddamn door or I swear, I'll fucking kill you."

I finally get a good look at the creep who caged us, and I'm not quite sure how to process what I see. I expected to see someone strong and solid based on the way he fought me when I broke in through a window. I didn't expect to see lean muscles and a sculpted frame. His dark brown eyes are narrowed on us, studying us, and his raven hair is tousled and messy from our fight.

He doesn't appear to be all that much older than me— maybe by a few years—and that strikes me as odd because I can't understand why an attractive guy in his twenties would live alone this deep in the forest. I'm only guessing that he lives alone, of course, but the odds seem good since he's got a goddamn cage inside his house that he probably wouldn't want anyone else to know about.

He doesn't say a word, only tilts his head to the side, watching us both with dark, curious eyes—penetrating eyes that burrow deep and burn inside me.

"Let us out," I say again, my voice slow and commanding.

"Who are you?" He has a low voice, a gruff tone, an authoritative timbre. "Why are you here?"

"Please, just let us go," Glory pleads. "I told you, we were lost. We just needed some help."

"Tell me your names."

I squeeze Glory's shoulder, hoping she'll understand to keep her mouth shut. If he doesn't already know who she is, I don't want him to find out. If he learns her name, he'll know she has money.

"You don't need to know our names," I tell him. "Just let us out and we'll leave quietly."

"No," he says with finality, then turns and leaves the room.

He doesn't shut the door to the hallway because he doesn't need to. We're locked inside this fucking cage.

I let go of Glory and grab hold of the bars with both hands, giving them a good, solid shake, testing the strength of them. They vibrate in my hold as I wrench my arms against them, but they're sturdy and don't show any sign of weakness. "Fuck!"

"What are we gonna do?"

I spin, quickly scanning the room, my gaze landing on a wooden door at the back of the cage. "Did you try that?" I ask, already moving toward it.

"It's not a way out," she says as I twist the doorknob.

It opens away from us, into the room beyond it, which I quickly see is a small bathroom, basic in every sense of the word. There's a toilet, a sink, a single shower, no mirror, no windows. White tile floor, white painted walls…except they're decorated with simple crayon drawings, as if a child had been in here and colored on the walls.

More importantly, there's another door opposite the one I came through. My pulse ticks hopefully, sending a burst of adrenaline through my veins as my hand lands on the knob and twists. I tug the door open toward me, hopeful for an exit, but my heart sinks heavily. The exit is sealed behind more metal bars.

I grab hold of one as I step closer, peering into the space beyond the bars. It looks like another bedroom, though it's bare. There's a mattress sitting atop old, stained carpet, but otherwise, the room is empty.

I turn, looking around the bathroom, searching for something, anything that might be useful…but there's nothing. We're trapped and there's nothing we can use to defend ourselves with.

"What do we do, Hux?"

I shake my head in disbelief.

How did we wind up here?

How did we shift so easily from one nightmare to another?

"I don't know…" I tell her honestly. "I don't know what to do."

I reach into my pockets, suddenly thinking that my cell phone must be there. It's not, and it wouldn't matter if it were. It was already dead and who knows if there's service here, anyway.

"He took everything out of your pockets and mine," she says, something metal rattling against the floor as she steps toward me.

I follow the sound to her feet and see a cuff attached to her ankle. She's chained to a hook that's bolted to the floor. "Christ," I mutter, dropping to my knees in front of her. "What did he do?"

I tug on the padlock that secures the cuff and find that it's solid. I grab hold of the chain, running hand over hand down the length until I come to the bolted hook. I pull hard, testing its strength. It's solid, too. "Shit." I drop the chain and it crashes heavily to the floor. I comb my fingertips through my hair, tugging at the ends in frustration.

"Why is this happening? What does he want with us?"

"I don't fucking know!" I snap.

She flinches and takes a step back.

I stand and rush to close the space between us, wrapping her up in my arms and pulling her close. She's rigid, her arms pinned at her sides.

"I'm sorry," I whisper against her hair. "I just…I don't have answers. I don't have answers, and it fucking scares me. I always know what to do." As my hand comes up to cradle the back of her head, she softens, tugging her arms free from my grip to hug me back, to hold me as close to her as I hold her to me. "I won't let him hurt you. I'm gonna find us a way out of this." Yet, even as the words leave my mouth, I know my promises may be false.

I don't know if I can stop him from hurting her.

I don't know if I can find us a way out of this.

The not knowing is more terrifying than anything because I've never not known what to do.

I always know what to do.

I always save her.

But in this…I might not be able to save myself.

CHAPTER 6

Ambrose

I ALMOST WONDER if this is partially my fault. Perhaps they sensed my energy when I watched them digging in the forest hours ago, and unknowingly followed it back here to my home.

Earlier in the night, I had seen these two nearly three miles away. I'd come upon them by accident and stuck around to watch them for thirty minutes or so because their presence had been unexpected and their actions piqued my interest. That deep in the forest, in the dark, in the freezing Vermont winter with a snowstorm blowing through…finding them there seemed almost serendipitous.

I'd watched as the boy hacked at the frozen ground, managing to dig out a body-sized hole by sheer force of will. I'd dug out enough of my own to recognize what they were trying to do, and that captivated my attention. These two wholesome-looking young adults were out burying a body in the forest in the middle of the night.

Whose body was it?

How had they died?

What did these two have to do with that death?

The girl had seemed agitated, constantly moving and

fidgeting, playing with the light on her phone. At one point, I thought she'd seen me, but then she went back to her boyfriend or whoever he was and stayed by his side. Every time it looked like she was offering to help, he'd pushed on, insisting on doing the work himself.

Chivalrous, I suppose—a trait I don't possess.

I'd left after watching them for a while…before they'd finished their dirty work. Their presence had distracted and confused me, and I'd left my axe behind, which was fucking dumb on my part. Normally, I wouldn't worry about it, except for the fact that I've been found in an unfindable place. Clearly, I've become too comfortable, too complacent, thinking that no one would ever find me out here.

I head down the hallway toward the dim light, back into my bedroom. I grab a black hoodie from my closet and pull it on before perching on the bed to lace up my black boots. Then, stomping down the hallway, I head for the front door.

As I pass the open door of the room where I've trapped them, I dare a single glance at the two caged birds, and the sight of them makes my pulse quicken with anxious energy.

Why the fuck did I trap them?

Why didn't I just send them away?

The sight of them makes me pause with my head turned in their direction, but they don't immediately notice me. The boy has his arms wrapped around her, keeping her close. There's so much affection and protective energy in the way he holds her, and I can feel it rippling through him, traveling outward in waves that strike me in the gut and make my stomach clench with a strange mixture of jealousy and need.

I've never known a feeling like that—a feeling of being

protected and cared for.

I need a cigarette.

The boy turns his head just as I'm about to move and I expect him to shout at me, yell for me to let him out. But curiously, he doesn't. His brow furrows, his forehead creases in heated resentment for his current predicament, and the passionate hatred in his brown eyes sparks in the air between us.

I can't fucking look at them.

I stalk toward the door, grab my heavy black bomber jacket, and throw it on over my hoodie. I zip it in the front, tug my hood over my head, and walk out the front door, locking it behind me.

The snowfall has stopped, but there's a solid five inches of fluff in the clearing surrounding my home. It doesn't faze me. I trudge forward, stomping through the snow as I head for the tree line.

I walk for a solid mile before I stop to pull a pack of cigarettes from my coat pocket. I take one out of the pack and light it up before continuing.

I've walked this path so many times before that I don't even have to think about where I'm going. It's muscle memory. The cold air doesn't bother me much—it's the same temperature as my frozen, dead heart—but the snow around my ankles soaks through my jeans, making each step feel heavy. The dampness around my ankles makes the traumatized neurons in my brain fire with the memories of my haunted past.

I sink into the unwelcome recollection of the cold winter nights when my father would march me into the forest, wearing nothing more than my tattered pajamas—a simple T-shirt and long flannel pants.

He would take me out miles into the deep, then leave me behind. He'd put his watch around my wrist and set it with a thirty-minute alarm, then demand that I stay put until the alarm went off, and when it did, I was to find my way back home.

He tried to convince me that he was doing it for my own good—to teach me survival and navigational skills—but of course, that was bullshit. He didn't teach me a damn thing. He was hoping I'd die from exposure before finding my way back, so he didn't have to deal with me anymore.

But I always found my way back.

I still wonder sometimes why I fought so hard to survive. It's not like I was welcomed back with pride and praise. He'd just throw me back into the goddamn cage and leave me there for days. And I can't fucking figure out why I've filled that same trauma-feeding cage with new souls to rip apart.

Because they found you…and you didn't want to be found.

I veer off course without conscious thought, my feet carrying me the long way around to the place where I left my axe. A quarter-mile later, I come to a stop in front of the thick trunk of a familiar tree. Its base is wide, and it almost sits separately from the surrounding trees, as if its thick roots have pushed them all away as it grew…as if the rest of the forest were scattering from its looming presence.

I remember when I first found this tree when I was fourteen. I'd fought back against my dad for the first time and managed to get away from him before he could hit me. I ran as far and as fast as I could into the forest because I didn't know if he was angry or following me. I didn't look back. I just ran until I was tired, and then I wandered.

I wandered until I felt the pull of this tree.

Though autumn leaves had been scattered and piling across the forest floor that day, most of the maples still held on to their dying leaves, unwilling to let them go just yet.

But this tree—the one I'm standing before now—was completely bare, leaves piled thick around its base. There were no signs of disease or infection, it was a healthy tree. But somehow, it seemed eager to shed its leaves, eager to change seasons.

I felt so much the same—eager to leave my childhood behind, to take control, to fight back. That was the first time I felt like I might be able to take my power back.

And one year later, I did.

Now I stand on their graves, over the spot where, ten years ago, I dug and buried them beside this very tree, and I feel their evil trying to claw its way up from the ground. I don't believe in God, so I sure as fuck don't believe in the Devil. But I'm more than familiar with the sickness of humanity and the twisted energy it leaves behind. That energy breeds and searches, coiling around whatever new host it can find. I can feel it now in the roots of this tree, stretching far from the base beneath my feet, reaching out, infecting this forest, infecting me.

The trees speak in their silence, the wind kicking up and rustling through the bare branches above. I look up, moonlight peeking through the dark clouds, illuminating the claw-like branches as they sway. I can see how the wind blows through them, rippling still branches into movement, and my head tracks its direction, watching as it blows back south toward my home.

That home is infected, too.

And the two I've trapped within it will feel the effects of that soon.

I trapped them there like my parents trapped me.

I take a long drag off my cigarette and slowly blow out the smoke from the corner of my lips. I toss it down into the snow and stomp on it, making sure the light burns out before I turn away and head deeper into Sugar Wood Forest. I collect my forgotten axe and grab an armful of the wood I'd chopped earlier before turning back.

I should've sent those two away when they knocked on my door, but perhaps it was already too late for them by the time they'd arrived. They were already infected by the forest. They were already fading into sickness by the time they'd arrived on my doorstep. So, maybe it's good that I've sentenced them to death by trapping them in the cage that's been open and waiting for ten years.

Sugar Wood has made us all sick, and I can't let them infect the rest of the world.

CHAPTER 7

HUXLEY

I SLEPT A couple of hours, but mostly I've been restless. The wood floors are hard and the obvious anxiety from being locked inside a fucking cage in some psychopath's house kept me from letting down my guard.

I'm thankful that Glory was able to find some rest, at least. She's sleeping soundly now, her body curled against my side and her head on my chest. Perhaps her touch is another reason I can't sleep. My heart has been pounding painfully since she laid her head on my chest. She must have been able to hear it beating.

I rub my hand over her back as she rests, unwilling to let her go, though my mind screams to get up, to move, to figure a way out of this mess. But I can't bring myself to give up this moment because even in our shitty situation, I'm selfish enough to favor holding her close over taking action.

There's a loud thud from outside and it startles me. It startles Glory, too, her body jerking her awake.

She shoots up and looks around the room. "What was that?"

I watch her shoulders slump as the realization hits her all over again that we're still trapped here, that it isn't a dream. Another loud thud sounds, and I sit up, too.

Light floods the home from the hallway, showing us clearly that the sun has risen. Though there's no window inside our cage room, plenty of light seeps in through the large windows at the front of the small home, and it filters into our room.

I reach for Glory, running my hand down the back of her head.

She turns to look at me, her green eyes scanning the features of my face. "Did you sleep at all?" she asks softly, and the genuine concern in her voice guts me.

"A little."

She sighs. "I was hoping I'd wake up to find this was all a dream…a nightmare."

"I know. I was hoping the same."

"Has he come back?"

I shake my head. "No. At least I haven't seen him come down the hallway." I shift, sitting up straighter with my back against the wall. "I think he's outside." Another loud thud echoes, confirming my thoughts. "Sounds like he's chopping wood or something."

She turns sideways to face me, her knees bent and legs fawned. "What are we gonna do?"

I let out a long breath and rub my hands over my face. "I honestly don't fucking know."

"I'm sorry. This is all my fault. If I hadn't lost control of myself with my dad, we would never have been out in the woods. This never would've happened. I'm such a fuck-up."

She buries her face in her hands and it makes me boil with rage to hear her talk about herself like that. I grab her wrists, maybe a little too harshly, and yank them away from her face. Her head snaps up and her eyes widen in surprise at my roughness, but I have her attention.

"You're not a fuck-up, Glory. Yes, you've fucked up a few times in your life, but your mistakes don't define you. And regardless, what you did to your dad…that wasn't a mistake. He hurt you. He hurt you in the most disgusting way imaginable, and he deserved what you did to him."

"But we wouldn't be here if I hadn't—"

I jerk her wrists, tugging them toward me, pulling her closer as I lean forward. "If you hadn't, *I* would have. I would've killed him if I'd found him…doing that to you."

She visibly swallows, her tender throat bobbing, drawing my gaze to the curve of her neck. Her skin looks so soft, so smooth, and I find myself wondering if she's sensitive there… if my lips would tickle her skin or trigger desire…

"Hux?" It's like snapping myself from a trance to drag my eyes away to meet hers. She looks at me with a slight tilt of her head and hooded eyes. Her voice is a whisper when she speaks again. "You…Your eyes are different when you look at me now."

My fists clench unconsciously, but they're wrapped around her wrists. She gasps as I squeeze, and the way it makes her plump lips part is almost inviting.

What the fuck is wrong with me?

I swallow my longing for her because I'm certain it has no place in this cage. "I don't know what you mean."

She looks down and shakes her head. "Don't try to make me think I'm seeing things. I know what I see when I look at you."

"What do you see?"

"Well, I don't see my stepbrother. Not exactly. I see a

man who's come to my rescue over and over again, even at his own risk."

"I care about you." I let my hands fall away from her wrists and grip her cheeks instead. "I'll always rescue you, Glory. Always."

She leans forward and I feel the shift between us as something visceral, as if something unseen stirs inside her and reaches out between us, clawing into my burning flesh and pulling me closer. Before I know it, her lips are only a breath from mine and I have no idea what's fucking happening here.

I try to convince myself that this is only desperation, that it's only need for a greater connection in the midst of a dangerous crisis, a need to solidify a physical bond to strengthen each other when we're feeling so powerless.

But I know it's something more. It's aching, repressed cravings for more rushing to the surface. It's years of denial for me and years of loneliness for her. It's need I can no longer deny myself, knowing I can never deny her.

When her eyes flutter shut, it feels like a door slamming closed on our past, on our platonic bond as step-siblings. It feels like permission…

No.

It feels like a request, a demand to touch my lips to hers and take the last of our innocent relationship, swallow it down, and let it spark a fire in my gut that I know will burn us both to ashes.

Her tongue sweeps innocently across her lips and fuck, that makes me lose control. Gripping her cheeks, I slam my lips to hers, kissing her with a fierce passion I've never shared with anyone.

She whimpers against my lips, the sweetest sound of letting go as she parts them for me. Her tongue seeks mine as ferociously as mine seeks hers, and fuck, she tastes better than I ever imagined she would. She tastes sweet, just like maple candy.

Her body leans into mine as she grips my shirt, and I imagine she can feel my heart beating wildly beneath her touch. One hand slips down to her neck, wrapping around the side of it, my thumb slipping over that soft, smooth skin.

I kiss her as though I could consume her, deeply and with hunger. For some reason, I always imagined her returning a kiss with gentle innocence, with curious and soft exploration, but she's shattered my delusion. She holds nothing back, and it makes me wonder if she wanted me as much as I've wanted her—if we've always wanted each other and have just been pointlessly denying ourselves.

She moves quickly, shifting to straddle my outstretched legs. I groan as her body sways into mine, as she presses a palm to the wall above my head to brace herself as she bends and deepens our kiss.

Good God, I never expected—

My head snaps, turning toward the door and breaking our kiss as I see him enter like a black shadow in the night. Glory gasps as he approaches, her hands falling away as she quickly pulls her leg over mine, moving behind me. I get to my knees and move in front of her to shield her body with mine.

He moves in front of the cage, coming in close, crouching to his haunches. Sweat dots his brow, and his hands rest on the handle of a large axe, the blade seated heavily on the floor between his legs. There's something odd swirling behind his dark eyes, something I can't quite place.

"Is the entertainment for your benefit or for mine?" he asks with a tilt of his head.

I brood, choosing silence.

"Tell me your names."

"No."

"Tell me your names, and I'll think about letting you go."

"Fuck no. You don't need to know who we are, and we don't need to know who you are. Let us go and we'll disappear. We've got our own damn secrets to hide."

The man smirks, an unamused lift of the corner of his lips. He runs a hand through his thick black hair, and I'm fixated on the darkness of his eyes.

"You two are my secret now," he says. "But I haven't decided whether it's a secret worth keeping…or burying."

Glory whimpers, her hands coming up to grip my biceps as she presses her face into my back. Her need for me strengthens my resolve, gives me pride, makes my chest rise in indignation against this man as her savior, her protector.

He leans sideways, trying to peek around me at Glory. "What's wrong, little bird? Does being locked in a cage frighten you? Or does it set you free? Does it give you permission to do things you've always wanted to do but never let yourself?" He looks at me. "Was that the first time she's kissed you? Or has she kissed you before and feared this one might be the last?"

"That's none of your business."

"Everything you do is my business now."

His eyes burrow into mine, the darkness within them setting off a rush of…something. Anxiety? Anger? Passion? I can't find the words to describe what washes over me, but it's an unsettling feeling.

"I have a delivery to make," he tells us. "I'll be back in a few hours. Use the shower if you want, you both look like hell. If you behave yourselves, I might feel inclined to feed you when I return."

Glory shoves to her feet and darts out from behind me, rushing to grip the bars in front of him. He stands to meet her eyes, though his height forces him to look down upon her. "Don't leave us in here, please! Just let us go home. I promise, we won't say a word about you to anyone. We just want to go *home*. We don't even know your name. We won't tell a soul. *Please*."

God, the way her voice trembles…

The man steps closer, looking down at her in a way that makes my fists clench, though I don't know whether I want to punch him or hold her more.

"My name is Ambrose Bishop," he says, his gaze flickering across her face, drawing a line down to her heaving chest. "Now you know my name…and that's too much information to let you go."

The knowledge is more confining than the cage because it's damning. He can't let us go now with the knowledge of his name—he told us intentionally and the truth of that hits us violently, like a silent blast of energy through the metal bars.

He doesn't intend to let us go.

Ambrose Bishop swivels and strides from the room to the sound of Glory's scream.

CHAPTER 8
Ambrose

I MAKE THE drive to the Tolliver's Treats factory once a week to deliver chopped wood from the forest. They burn through it fairly quickly these days to boil the maple for their candies. They only use it for a few wood-burning stoves that make their premium treats—if they boiled all their maple that way, I'd have half the forest chopped down in a few months.

The rest of their candies are mass manufactured, but Tolliver's has always advertised the premium treats as *special*, as if boiling maple by burning the same wood they tapped it from makes it better somehow. It doesn't.

This used to be my father's job, but I took over without a single question from anyone when he died. I've done it for a decade now in his stead and for all anyone else knows, my father has simply moved on to other employment…or maybe they can guess that he's dead. I don't fucking know. No one in this place gives a shit and we all mind our own business.

The floor manager signs-off on the delivery and hands me my weekly check. I turn to stalk out of the factory before the bitch sees me, but it's pointless to try and avoid her because she always sees me.

"Ambrose," she calls, stomping across the cement factory

floor in her inappropriately high heels. "A word, please."

Maura Tolliver, the second wife of Beau Tolliver and the balls of their company. She's here more often than he is, and she rules with an iron fist. Their company expanded to sell around the globe when he married her seven or eight years ago, and it's because she's a ruthless bitch when it comes to her business.

She's a ruthless bitch, period.

I shove my hands into my coat pockets and turn to look at her as she glides toward me. "I'm busy, Maura."

"We both know that's not true." She comes to a stop in front of me. "My office. There's something we need to discuss."

I dare a glance back at the floor manager, who lifts her eyebrow and pinches her lips together to suppress an awkward smile. She thinks I'm still fucking Maura—they all do—and if I gave a shit about what other people thought of me, I might be embarrassed by it. But my mind doesn't have the capacity for caring anymore.

Maura turns with an expectant lift of her eyebrow and tromps away, swaying her pert, thirty-seven-year-old ass in her ridiculously tight pencil skirt, thinking it will entice me to follow. It enticed me to follow a couple of years ago, but dealing with her now is tiresome. Still, I follow, because the power she has over me frightens me. I know too much, and I've done too much for her to ignore her whims.

I follow her up the open, metal steps to the second floor, the whir of machines and the buzz of the factory floor still echoing all around. We walk across the loft landing to her office. She unlocks the gray door and waits for me to enter before shutting it behind us, cutting off the never-ending factory sounds and locking it again.

I expect her to round on me, use me and abuse me like everyone else has in my pathetic life, but strangely, she doesn't, and it sends a shiver down my spine.

She slowly crosses, almost somberly to her wooden desk floating in the center of the space, and she lowers into her chair behind it. "I need your help with a very important matter."

I let out a gruff sigh and drop into the chair opposite her desk. "What is it this time?"

"This is a discreet matter. It hasn't come out in the press yet. I returned home around noon, and I've been with the police the last few hours discussing this *terrible* thing that's happened."

"What are you talking about?"

She sighs, feigning something that resembles sadness. "My husband, my son, and my stepdaughter are all…missing. I came home from my business trip and discovered an empty house, though our vehicles were all there. Beau's shoes were at the front door where he always takes them off. My stepdaughter came home for her holiday break and her car was there, but she was gone, too. And more suspicious was the fact that my son's car was in the driveway—he wasn't supposed to be coming home at all. But they're nowhere to be found and we can't get a hold of them by phone or text. The police suspect foul play."

I give her unflinching eye contact, noting the emotionless way she shares this with me. "You must be devastated." Sarcasm bites my tone.

She fakes a somber expression. "I am, yes. It's devastating not knowing where they are."

"Cut the shit. What do you want from me?"

She pushes to her feet and circles round the desk, each slow click of her heels against the hard floor echoes menacingly and makes me tense. She slips between me and the desk, leaving little space between us, and she leans her ass back against the edge.

"I need your discretion with this." She reaches out to grab my hand, holding it between her palms as if she cares about me, though I feel nothing. "I need you to find them."

"What makes you think I can find them?"

"You've tracked down people for me before."

"Not missing people."

"I know you can help me with this. I know you *will* help me." She moves my hand beneath her pencil skirt and pushes it up her thigh. "You know I can make your life very difficult if you don't help me. We always help each other, don't we?"

I pull my hand away with a snap and stand so forcefully that my chair tips over.

She rises and steps closer. "I need you to find them and make sure they don't return."

"*What?*"

She pushes into my space. "You heard what I said. Find out what happened to them…and make sure they remain missing. For good."

She reaches down to cup my flaccid dick. I grab her by the throat and shove her back until she slams against the edge of the desk, letting out a strangled puff of breath. She smiles against it, and it puts me off even more. She thinks she can still manipulate me the way she did years ago.

"You want them dead?"

"You know I love it when you're rough with me," she purrs.

I release her and step back, nearly tripping over the fallen chair. "I don't want to help you with this."

"It doesn't really matter what you want, now does it? I've told you what I want you to do, so you'll do it. What other option do you have? Tell the police what I've asked you to do?" She laughs through her words. "Of course, you're not going to the police, because I'd tell them every sordid detail of your crimes."

"Crimes you paid me to commit on your behalf."

"Between you and me, Ambrose, I think you're the only one who would be charged. Who would believe that I hired you to do *anything?*"

No one would believe me.

No one is on my side.

I've always been on my own…alone.

That's why she latched onto me when I was young and stupid, and now I'm stuck, doing her fucking bidding. At first, I did it with the promise of sex, affection, *attention*. Now, I do her dirty work because I have no choice—because she holds all the cards with the evidence against me for the things I've done for her.

But I want out.

I want to be done with her.

I grit my teeth. "There's more at stake for you here, Maura. You're after the inheritance, aren't you? The Tolliver family fortune? So, what do I get for it? If I make sure they never return…"

Her jaw tenses and she twists her lips, looking at me sternly. "Five percent."

"Five percent of what?"

"Of our business. If Beau is dead, I'll have full authority to make decisions about Tolliver's Treats. That is, if Glory and Huxley are dead, too."

"You really want me to find your family and *kill* them?"

"Yes," she confirms. "And we'll need bodies…or at least parts of their bodies to confirm they're dead."

"But why kill them all? Why do they all have to be dead?"

"Because that princess stepdaughter of mine is next on the will after Beau."

I cock my head to the side, gazing at her discerningly. "And what about your son?"

She lets out a long, slow breath, as if this is hard for her, though we both know it's not. "He'll have to be killed, too. I don't know where they are, but they've all gone missing at the same time. I have to assume somehow, their disappearances are all connected. If you find Beau and Glory, you'll probably find Huxley, too. And if he knows, he'll tell the truth." She puts her hand over her heart in a fake, exaggerated motion. "My son always was too good for this world. I've accepted that he'll have to die, too."

I chuckle humorlessly. "You need medication."

Her eyes narrow. "For once in my *fucking* life, I'm doing what's best for *me*. Honestly, Ambrose, we're all just a bunch of animals. Morality is the worst thing that ever happened to this world. It's meant to be survival of the fittest."

"You live a sad, pathetic life in your lonely little world."

She grins. "I'm not sad and my life is quite joyous. I have power and I do what I want. What more could I ask for?" She pushes off the desk and saunters toward me again. "Do this for me, and I'll give you what you've always wanted."

"Oh? And what have I always wanted? Enlighten me with your insight."

"Independence. Freedom. Peace. I'll give you a bonus of

fifty thousand dollars, and as soon as I liquidate the company, I'll give you your five percent. It will be millions, Ambrose. Enough for you to live out the rest of your days doing whatever the fuck you wanna do. I'll even give you cash if you want it, so you can live your simple, off-grid lifestyle. I'll let you go, and I'll never call on you again. You can disappear for all I care."

"You mean, you'd let me go?"

I'm trapped here by the secrets she keeps—the things I've done for her that I'm not proud of, all the crimes I committed at her request.

If I had the promise that she'd let me go along with all of the secrets, along with the knowledge of the horrible crimes I've committed…If I had enough money that I'd never have to do any of that again, enough money to run away, disappear, build my house tucked away somewhere in the woods in a place where no one can find me…If I could live in tranquility without ties to Sugar Wood Forest, my parents, this fucking factory…

It would be everything.

"Are you willing to kill for everything you've ever wanted?"

Before I can think through a response, I find that my head is naturally nodding, though I feel a hint of sickness roll through my gut. I am willing and that doesn't sit well with me.

She grins and steps back before turning, moving to circle her desk. She bends, pulling open the bottom drawer and sifting through junk until she finds what she's looking for, dragging it out. She stands slowly and brushes some dust off what looks like a picture frame in her hands.

"I suppose I should have this on my desk so the police don't suspect I'm heartless. I'm sure you know what my family looks like from the media."

"I don't watch television and I'm not on social media."

She looks at me with shock. "Well, what the fuck do you do with your free time?"

My forehead wrinkles at her rushed judgment. "I read. What the fuck do *you* do?"

She shrugs. "Didn't peg you for the intellectual type."
Fucking bitch.

She comes over to me, standing beside me and turning the frame so I can see it. I sigh and turn my gaze to it. I recognize Beau, of course, because I've seen him in the factory with Maura.

But then…

A shock of lightning strikes through my heart as my eyes fall upon two blonde smiling teenagers who look far too familiar. My palms sweat and I scrub them against my jeans.

"My stepdaughter Glory Tolliver, and my son Huxley Hill. He never wanted to change his name when I married Beau."

"That's…This is…These are the people you want me to find and kill?"

"Yes."

I should feel some relief for the fact that, inexplicably, I've already found two of them. Rather, the two of them found me.
How had they found me?

It's as though the universe sent them to me, directed them to crawl beneath my boot, and ask to be squashed. But seeing them in this photo washes some strange sort of unease through my veins and I feel…uncomfortable.

"Do we have a deal, then?"

A lump rises in my throat, and I swallow it down. "Fifty grand bonus and five percent of the liquidated assets? Complete freedom from you and your bullshit…forever?"

"Those are the terms."

"I want ten grand up front, in good faith."

She looks at me, searching my eyes for confirmation that I intend to complete the task. I don't know what she sees there. I want the money. I want the freedom she's offering me, though the discomfort I'm feeling over this punches through every other beat of my heart.

You were going to kill them anyway…weren't you?

You told them your name.

There was never any other outcome.

I choke out the words, "Consider it done."

I leave the factory fifteen minutes later with my pockets full of cash that I hold fisted in my grip until I reach my truck. I climb in and slam the door shut, pull the cash from my pockets, and shove it all into my glove box.

Fuck.

I can be free from Maura Tolliver and have everything I've ever wanted. All I have to do is find Beau Tolliver and murder the little blonde birds who strayed too far from their nest and wound up in my cage.

Little bird.

I press my eyes shut to be met with images of golden blonde tresses swirling in my mind—plump pink lips with green eyes, brown eyes with a chiseled jawline and the hint of stubble.

I shake the image of them from my mind as I shift the truck into gear and roll forward.

I can't think of them as people. I can't allow their faces to puncture my mind with sympathy. I have to do this so I can finally be free from this insidious, infectious place.

I have to kill them to be free.

CHAPTER 9
Glory

MY ENERGY IS depleted.

I'm physically exhausted.

I'm hungry.

Emotionally, I'm detached for my own mental safety. If I think about where we are and what might happen to us for too long, the thin threads of my sanity threaten to unravel.

At least there was hot water so we could take turns getting warm and clean in the creepy bathroom. I took a sort-of shower—half-in and half-out of the stall since I couldn't pull my jeans all the way off my chained leg.

Huxley opens the door to the bathroom, coming back out to join me in the cage after his turn in the shower. He steps over my outstretched legs, then lowers to sit beside me, both of us with our backs to the wall.

I lean my head onto his shoulder and take a deep breath. The odd scent of his sweat-soaked, soil-stained shirt mixed with the bare freshness of his clean skin makes for a strangely comforting aroma.

I flip up my palm, my knuckles resting against my thigh, and offer my hand to him. He slips his palm across mine and our fingers curl at the same time—like every other time we've held hands, though it's not the same at all. This feels distinctly different. We crossed a boundary line when we kissed, and regardless of our urgent circumstances which pushed us so quickly across it, I can't go back to seeing him the way I did before.

I suddenly see him for the man he is and my skin itches for friction with his. My thumb moves across his skin, caressing him, calming him, testing sensation with him.

The sparking remnants of tension from our kiss hours ago builds through the light touch, sending a slow burning ripple up my arm. The warmth spreads to my chest and sparks tiny fires among the scattered ashes of my heart. I expect the warmth from his closeness, his tender touch, his care, but what I don't expect is the way the heat falls inside me, as if the sparking ashes float from my rib cage and light a new blaze through my belly, gathering low and deep.

I let out an unintentional whimper as the memory of his lips on mine makes my stomach clench in a pleasant way, in a strange way. His thumb slips with mine, rubbing my skin, adding more heat with his friction that rips through me again to cause that clench, that *need*.

What is this feeling?

I lift my head and look at him, finding his deep brown eyes have already fallen upon me. His lips are parted, his eyes narrowed, and curiosity flickers through his twitching jaw.

What's happening here?

What is this place?

What is this beautiful desire ripping through me?

My eyes dart down to his lips, and I think he knows…I think he knows I'm thinking about kissing him again. He leans closer and another clench takes me by surprise, forcing me to gasp with my lips only an inch away from his. His eyes flash with hunger and I feel every cell in my body come alive with anticipation.

Then, the rumble of an engine filters into the space, breaking Huxley from the moment in his hypervigilance. He snaps his head away to look toward the door.

Come back to me, Hux.

I shake my head.

Something's wrong with me.

I should be as aware as he is. We're trapped here, in danger here, and I should be focused on the doom we're facing. I pull my hand from his grip and rub my palms against my jeans.

With the moment broken, we silently wait as the engine cuts out, as the front door swings open, letting in a whoosh of howling winter wind. It slams shut and I hear the stomping of boots. After a long, anxious minute passes, he appears in the doorway…Ambrose Bishop.

He stops and stands there, watching us with his dark brown eyes—eyes that are jarringly similar to Huxley's.

After what seems like an unusually long moment of stillness and quietness, he speaks. "I know who you are."

Huxley clenches his fists and tension tears through us both. If Ambrose really does know who we are—who *I* am— he could hold me for ransom.

But maybe that's good.

I'm only worth something to him alive, then…right?

He steps forward and tosses something small into the cage. It lands on the hardwood floor with a metallic clang and when it settles, I can see that it's a small key.

"Take the cuff off her ankle and put it on yours," he says to Huxley.

Huxley gets on his knees and reaches across the floor to grab the key, then turns toward me and places his hand on my ankle above the cuff. He slides the key into the padlock, working to unlock it and remove the cuff entirely. I sigh in relief at having the heavy thing off my foot, reaching down to rub my ankle with both hands. But Huxley doesn't put it on his ankle. Instead, he stands and charges to the bars.

"I'm not putting it on," he says, his determination palpable.

Something shifts.

Something crackles.

Something slithers between the bars, coils around Huxley and Ambrose, and hisses.

I don't know what I'm sensing, but I can taste it, heady and thick in the air around us.

Ambrose steps away, disappearing into the front part of the house, but when he returns a moment later, the heady air erupts into sizzling, sparking chaos. The barrel of a shotgun swings into view as he marches into the room, stopping with the gun an inch away from the cage…aimed directly at *me*.

"Put it on your ankle or I kill her right now. I only need one of you to talk."

My eyes are wide, fixed on Ambrose over the barrel of his gun. His eyes narrow and shift from Huxley to me. He blinks and his head shakes slightly, almost as if he were confused by something.

I can *feel* his confusion.

I can feel Huxley's, too, as he turns his head to glance

back at me still sitting on the floor. I catch his eyes and give him a small nod.

"Put it on, Hux," I whisper. "It's okay."

Shouldn't I be shaking, trembling with fear?

Huxley turns to face me and crouches in front of me, putting his hands on my cheeks and sending that perplexing heat dripping down my insides.

He speaks so quietly that I could hardly hear him if I weren't so intently watching his lips move. "If you get a chance, you run, you leave me behind." I start to protest, but he stops me with a quick kiss that somehow steals my breath and leaves me speechless. "I mean it."

He slowly pushes to his feet. My eyes stay fixed on him, intently watching his form as he moves to grab the chain, sits down on the floor, and locks the cuff around his ankle. He slams the small metal key down on the floor and shoves it across the hardwood, pushing it between two of the cage bars.

Ambrose steps forward and the toe of his black combat boot comes down on top of the key. He drags his foot back, bringing the key with it, and out of our reach. He bends, shotgun still in hand, and picks up the key, placing it in his jeans pocket.

My eyes follow the motion and they get stuck on the curve of his hip, tracing across the line of his belt, and landing on the slight bulge at the front of his jeans. My eyebrows lift as I try to make sense of that, as I try to make sense of the fact that the sight stirs some sickness inside me.

My mind drifts, floating away and dissociating from what's happening. My eyes are fixed in place, and I can't think clearly. Moments or minutes later, I snap back into awareness at the touch of cool metal tapping the side of my arm.

My eyes dart down to see what touched me and widen in horror to see it's the barrel of his gun. I hadn't even been aware of the cage door opening. My head whips and I look up at Ambrose, his eyes locked on my face.

"Move, little bird," he commands, his tone harsh but forced. "Out."

I glance over at Huxley, brooding and seething and fighting so hard against himself to dampen his urge to fight for me, to save me. But even Huxley can't save me if this man is intent on pulling the trigger. That bullet will rip me apart if he fires, and the vision of it invades my mind. It's a vision of horror—the shotgun firing on me at point-blank range, my sinew and flesh exploding from my body, my blood washing over Huxley while painting the room in gore.

God, no.

Nausea rolls through my stomach and it prompts me to jump to my feet, both for self-preservation and to avoid my gory vision coming to life as that scene would haunt Huxley forever.

Ambrose takes a step back and I take a careful step forward. I expect it to be difficult to walk toward the stranger and his gun, but it's not. He moves back and I move forward, and our eyes remain locked.

God, his eyes are so dark and deep, like Huxley's. He could hide a million secrets behind those shadowed orbs, and I fearfully think that I could get lost searching for them. I know his secrets must be more sinister than any Huxley could ever hide. Part of me wants to look away, afraid to find the truth, but a more desperate part of me wants to plunge deep and find out this man's evil truth.

Evil?

Do I see evil in him?

I don't think I do...

Ambrose rushes to slam the door shut and lock it the moment I step foot outside the cage, trapping Huxley inside alone. I swallow hard, steeling myself against whatever is to come next, wanting to give Huxley a comforting glance but afraid to look back at him. If I see fear in his eyes, it might make me crumble.

It's easier to hold onto the darkness of Ambrose because every moment that passes staring into his eyes takes me deeper into a trance, further from reality. Yet I feel like I can handle the darkness in his stare. It's unsettling and it makes me feel uneasy, but it doesn't strike me with outright fear.

Perhaps that's what makes him dangerous to me.

Perhaps I'm naively unafraid.

Perhaps there's something deeply, darkly wrong with me.

Ambrose backs into the hallway and I step out after him. He points his gun toward the front of the cabin, guiding me to turn in that direction, but I pause just outside the doorway. "That way. Sit your ass down in that chair." He indicates a plain wooden chair that's pulled out from his plain wooden table beside his modest kitchen space.

The chair is facing outward toward the living room, facing the back of an old couch that floats in the small space on the other side of a long, narrow rug that I remember tripping over when I first came in. But there's something more obvious than couches and rugs and chairs that takes hold of my attention...it grabs me by the throat and squeezes me breathless.

The fear finally hits me.

Brown rope dangles from the rafters, two ends coming

to a stop just above the chair where he wants me to sit. I whirl around to face him as panic grips me.

What does he plan to do with that?

Hang me with it?

"No," I tell him. "No, please."

"Glory?" Huxley's voice comes from behind me, and I glance over my shoulder to see his face etched in worry as he wraps his hands around the cage bars.

Ambrose moves toward me so quickly that I can't back away fast enough to avoid the touch of the gun to the center of my chest. "*Move.*" He forces me to turn and walk backward down the hall.

He walks me backward until I feel the chair hit the back of my knees and my body falls to sit. The dangling ends of rope hit the back of my head and run over my hair before landing in front of my face. They sway menacingly from the movement before they settle.

I can't breathe.

I can't speak.

My fingers curl around the seat of the chair at my sides, gripping the wood so tightly that I imagine my knuckles are white.

Ambrose sets the gun down, letting it lean against a wooden armoire not even ten feet in front of me. I look at it, think about running to grab it and turn it on him, but in a flash, he's in front of me, standing so close it would be impossible.

So close.

I can smell him.

He smells like cigarette smoke and the sweet, earthy aroma of maple trees. It's faintly reminiscent of the scent of our family's maple candies, of the factory floor at Tolliver's Treats. It's an oddly comforting smell because it reminds me of my mother.

I only ever went to visit the factory with her—before she died, before my father remarried, before Huxley came into my life. I couldn't bring myself to visit again after she died because it just felt wrong. It felt sad without her, though the memories of visiting with her were so joyful. We would walk through, hand in hand, thanking the workers on the floor for doing good work, sampling treats, laughing, and being happy.

I haven't really known joy since she died.

Tears well at the reminder, a sudden sadness coming over me, so overwhelming that it washes away my fear entirely. My head falls forward and I start to cry, sobbing lightly in my seat. My grip on the chair loosens naturally as he bends over me, grabbing hold of both of my wrists and lifting them above my head.

I don't fight him. I feel the resignation of emotional detachment slither around my mind, threatening to protect me with my ultimate submission. The flow of my tears stop, and I submit to him to protect my sanity. I even hold my arms up as he wraps the coarse rope around my hands, binding my wrists together.

My eyes become unfocused, shifting away from reality. All I can see through the sheen of remaining tears is the black softness of his hoodie, just inches from my face. He finishes securing my wrists together and then reaches high above me. His hoodie lifts away from his jeans, exposing porcelain skin stretched tight across chiseled ab muscles.

Then he pulls and my hands jerk high above me, my shoulders stretching painfully as I'm pulled up from my seat.

I let out a shriek of surprise and I hear Huxley call my name.

I blink and when I open my eyes, they meet his dark ones.

Ambrose.

He sucks in a breath as he looks down at me, our four arms stretched above us, his working to do something above our heads as I breathe and stare. Then he moves, circling behind me, the sound of his heavy boots landing on the wooden chair. I can feel him move to step up on the seat and tower over me from behind.

I breathe in slowly and as I exhale, my chest sinks heavily—I feel as though my ribs crush the intensity of fear and sadness, crumbling it to pieces that fall like heavy rocks into my belly—and my stomach clenches.

Again…what is that pleasant ache?

Why did I feel it with Huxley?

Why do I feel it with Ambrose?

It's like need, but it's desperate and overwhelming.

I whimper as he gives a final tug on the ropes, effectively stringing me up so taut and high that my feet barely graze the hardwood beneath, not really touching, not really floating.

Wood screeches as he shoves the chair away and I feel the pulse of him as he circles me, like sonar waves that alert me to his presence as it passes every inch of my skin.

He comes to a stop in front of me and looms, towering above me with his height and lean muscle against my small, fragile frame. If he wants to hurt me, he can…he'll have no problem doing it.

My breaths quicken and I press my lips shut, swallowing the strange sensation he gives me and let it drop low inside me.

His voice is harsh, but deeply sinful. "Glory Tolliver.

There's just one thing I need to know before I kill you and your stepbrother."

My jaw tightens.

He really does know who we are.

One breath passes, then another, and finally he asks, "Where is your father?"

CHAPTER 10
Glory

"WHERE IS YOUR father?" Ambrose asks again.

I shake my head.

"You don't know? Or you won't tell me?"

I swallow, knowing I can't answer that question.

"This can be easy or hard, Glory. Are you going to tell me where your father is?"

I almost have an urge to shout it out, to tell him that my father is dead because I killed him and Huxley buried him in the woods. But I don't say a word.

Ambrose steps closer, his body pressing against mine. The rope sways as I struggle to keep my footing, my feet slipping across the hardwood floor as my shoulders twist and my body turns.

His hand snaps out, quickly darting between my shoulder and my ear, snaking around to grip the back of my neck. With a sharp jerk, he drags my body to his and holds me against him.

I gasp at the feeling of his hard muscles against my curves, my modest breasts flattened out by the way he pushes into me.

He opens his mouth to speak, but then his lips clamp shut again. Soft lips...so perfectly formed, with well-defined curves and plumpness in all the right spots. They're so different from Huxley's—his are wider and thinner.

Both mouths are beautiful.

I shut my eyes, trying to focus against the distraction of lips and thoughts of kissing them.

How could I ever think of kissing the lips in front of me?

I tug on my arms insincerely, trying to prove to myself that I want to fight, that I want them free, that I want to run far and fast. I should want all those things. The man in front of me is dangerous and sick—he kidnapped us when we were only seeking help and kept us in a cage in his home. A cage he must've built at some point. He's twisted with intention and there's no telling what he'll do to me, what he'll do to Huxley.

Scream.

Kick.

Fight.

My body remains motionless.

"Where is your father, little bird? This is the last time I'm asking."

"Why do you want to know?"

He cocks his head and a condescending smirk curls the corner of his lips. "She speaks."

I clear my throat and try to sound more confident, more intentional. "Why do you wanna know about my father?"

"That's not information you need to know."

"I'm not telling you where he is."

He nods a little and releases me, taking a step back, moving away so quickly that it makes me sway again. My feet scramble along the floor, seeking purchase to stop me from spinning on my wrists. I lift my head to look above me, to see how my skin turns pink beneath the coarse rope as it drags over my skin, my weight harshly pulling down.

The click and spark of a lighter catches my attention, and I level my chin to see him lift a cigarette to his lips, leaning forward with his head tilted over the small flame to spark it up. White smoke rolls from the end of it as he caps the lighter and shoves it back into his pocket. His eyes remain locked on mine as he takes in a long drag before blowing it out slowly, evenly.

I don't miss the way he looks at me, strung up like a piece of meat for him to do with as he pleases. I feel nauseous at the thought of it, but with the nausea is still that peculiarly pleasant tightening deep in my core. The tug of it shoots an aching need through me each time, a flurry of desire creeping through my veins and darkening my blood with lust.

It's lust.

I've been touched, licked, and fucked probably hundreds of times in my short life—both consensually and not. Even consensually with the boys from school, I never really cared for it. Choosing to be sexual with boys my father didn't approve of was an act of rebellion against everything he'd done to me—I never really desired it. I never felt that same explosive moment they had when they grunted, went rigid, and came inside me. I never felt pleasure.

I thought it wasn't possible for me.

I've never *needed* in this way before, never wanted, never felt anything physically...*good.* And I haven't stopped feeling it since I kissed Huxley.

It's because of Huxley, isn't it?
That desire?

It has to be because of our bond, how I feel so safe and protected in his arms.

Then why do I still feel it with this mysterious, twisted stranger as his eyes rake over my body?

Ambrose steps closer, holding up his cigarette between two fingers. "Do you smoke, little bird?"

"No." I swallow, hoping to shove down the gruff tone of desire that seems to be clawing up my throat. "It's bad for you…it will kill you."

He shrugs a shoulder, so carelessly cool that my eyes flutter at the sight. "So will I. But I still need to know where your father is. And since you've decided we should do this the hard way…" He reaches around me and grabs hold of my hair, fisting it at the base of my skull and tilting my head back with a sharp tug. I yelp as he moves in close again, our bodies kissing as he stares me down, his eyes narrowing on the tender flesh of my exposed throat.

I breathe deeply through my nose, feeling my nostrils flare at my rushed breaths. He shifts his cigarette in his grip, pinching the end of it, then he brings it down slowly, intently. The sparking end hits my skin at the sensitive spot just beneath the back of my jaw, near my ear. I hiss as he presses, then let out a yelp as he lifts it but immediately presses down again. It burns, searing heat shooting out from the spot, feeling like torn flesh. He does it again and again, burning a line down my jawline.

My skin burns, sizzling with each press, but after a few moments, I'm numb to the pain because it's second to the feeling of him against me, the feeling of his hard, masculine frame holding me in place and forcing me to take his torture.

This should hurt me far more than it does.

It should frighten me, but it doesn't.

I've been tortured enough in my life that I've grown accustomed to it.

But this…this is different.

I hear his heavy breathing, feel his pounding heart, see his jaw clenching with tension. It's different because he doesn't just burn me, he follows the hissing trail of burnt flesh with his lips, caressing my skin, softly peppering a line of kisses over the line of cigarette burns beneath my jaw.

His hand falls from my hair to my back, fingers splaying between my shoulder blades and pulling me closer.

What is he doing?

What am I doing?

Why am I feeling this sickness?

"This place, this fucking forest…" he whispers near my ear, "it plagues me." His lips trail down the side of my neck. "It makes me want you. I don't know you, and it makes me fucking want you."

His hips shift and I feel his erection against my stomach, hard and growing thick beneath the barrier of his jeans.

A vision snaps to mind—my hand wrapping around his thickness and tugging him to pleasure. It clouds my vision, pulling that pleasant thread of tension to my belly once again. I part my lips to let out a building breath and it comes out with a strangled moan that surprises the both of us.

I've never made a sound like that before.

It drags something urgent from me, something hot and desperate, something that takes my mind from the danger of my situation, the fear of this stranger, and burns it all to ash.

Slickness pools between my legs and I gasp at the feel

of it. I'm overwhelmed by it, light-headed from the way my breaths quicken, aching from the pull of my arms above my head, adrenaline flooding my veins for being at his mercy.

What's happening to me?

"Stop…" I half-heartedly breathe the word as he drops the cigarette to his hardwood floor and crushes it with a sharp turn of his boot.

He could've stepped away, put it out properly in an ashtray, but the way his hands come around to grip my waist with tight fingers and his tongue licks a line across my collarbone speaks to the frantic, confusing, disorienting energy between us.

"What are you doing?" I ask, my eyes fluttering shut at the sensation he creates.

"I don't know," he mutters into my skin.

"Am-Ambrose…" I stutter out his name.

He lifts his head and looks down at me, panting with perfect, parted lips. His dark eyes are hooded. His tousled, raven hair and the scruff of his black stubble make him appear almost feral—as if he's something more than human—and somehow, that makes me feel safer.

I must be broken.

How could I feel safer strung up in an isolated cabin with a feral creature than I could in my own home?

It's his eyes, I think. There's a softness to them, even though he tries to cloak it in shadows. I can see myself reflected there—a kindred spirit who's been battered and broken by those we were meant to trust.

"Who hurt you?" I whisper.

He blinks and jerks his head back.

I can feel his broken spirit tugging back, trying to pull him away, wanting to flee. Though I'm used to others pulling away from me, leaving me in my darkest hour, not truly caring about me as anything other than the heiress to the Tolliver fortune, somehow, I can't stand to think of this stranger disconnecting.

"Please," I say, though I don't know what I'm begging for.

Quiet falls between us and slowly, gradually, I feel his spirit come back. I feel it settling inside his bones. I feel it push against mine and his body is there, too. He molds to me, hands splaying across my back, arching me into him.

His lips crush mine, and it sets off an explosion within me. That stomach-clenching pleasure twists and coils, rushing good feelings down into my core. His tongue drives past my lips and it surprises me, but what surprises me more is that I don't recoil. Instead, I taste him.

God, I hate the smoky tobacco flavor from his cigarette. I hate it as much as I hate that he's my captor, someone who means to hurt me. Yet behind that awfulness is sweetness, like maple syrup on pancakes on a lazy Sunday morning.

Ambrose is like rotten fruit—still sweet to taste, though his sickness infects me.

The infection feels so good.

His hands are on me, moving roughly over my body, groping and gripping and touching. His fingers pull at the button of my jeans, tugging down the zipper. My hips jerk away on instinct to avoid unwanted touch there, but I swing them forward again the moment I realize that I *do* want his touch.

There's a painful ache between my legs, my pussy throbbing as more wetness than I've ever had before pools and drips. His body shifts along mine, moving beside me, his hard-on pressing into my side, just above my hip as he breaks our kiss. He shoves his hand inside my panties, and I cry out, my body swaying as I rock against the unexpected touch.

"What are you—"

His fingers curl, dipping low, stroking across my slick folds. "What is this?" he murmurs, his lips against the shell of my ear. "Why are you wet for me?"

For him?

Am I wet for him?

"I…" I breathe out as his tongue slips out and licks beneath my jaw.

I have no words.

His hand slips lower, the heel of his palm brushing across my clit, making me whimper as his fingers curve and press slowly inside me.

I sway in the binding, my hips rocking into his hand, my body driving me to seek this unknown pleasure he grants me. His other hand snakes around my waist, fingers gripping my side almost painfully to hold me in place, to keep my hip pressed to his cock. The way he pants against my cheek is unsettling in an utterly delicious way.

His desire for me is growing, thickening his cock, which he rubs against my hip as his large fingers stroke inside me.

Dark magic.

His lust is a potion he fed me on his tongue.

His fingers draw runes inside me, summoning a demon of pure, painful pleasure.

His heated breaths against my skin whisper an incantation to strengthen his spell on me.

Dark, dark magic.

It whispers within me, creeps beneath my skin, grows in strength and volume until I'm filled with it—so filled that it threatens to burst from me.

My head rolls against my arms, my weight heavy through my shoulders as my body slumps and trembles in his hold. The magic swirls low in my belly, sparkling like black diamonds that pile up and grow heavy.

"Come for me," he whispers. "Fucking come."

His words slash like a ceremonial knife, slicing across my insides and spilling that dark magic down, down, down. The black diamonds explode, shattering his sparkling magic into brilliant shining particles that shoot through my pussy and make my body convulse in raw, perfect pleasure.

I hear my scream as it rips through me, but my voice sounds so far away. The tingling pulsing perfection goes on and on…the way his fingers work inside me draws it out, pressing hard against a spot that feels like a magic button.

My body trembles and I go limp when the squeezing tension breaks its hold on me and lets go, as if the pleasure demon he summoned has been expelled from my body and released into the world.

I want it back.

I want to feel that again.

My eyes lock on his as the hand that stroked me leaves me, coming up to touch my chin and turn my face toward his. My scent on his fingers fills my nostrils and pours instant shame down my throat.

"No," I whisper, too little, too late.

His hand leaves my chin, and he brings his slick fingers beneath his nose. I watch him with hooded, sated eyes as he inhales my scent, gently brushing my wetness over his perfect lips.

"I want to taste you. I want to lick your dripping cunt until you're begging me to make you come like that again."

I whimper, the mere thought of it tightening through my core, though the shame of my vulnerability scatters the ashes of my heart.

"Wh-what do you want from us?"

He blinks, then again. He shakes his head and it's as if the spell is broken.

No…I want to remain spellbound in this twisted curse.

He steps back, ripping himself away from me, but I want his heat against my body again. I blink, the reality of him and what he's doing to us coming back into focus. And then I hear Huxley screaming for me, his voice troubled and aching and desperate.

He could hear us.

He could hear what was happening to me.

He doesn't know how good it felt and how much I want to feel it again. I've never felt anything like that before. I've never known pleasure before. I've never *come* before. God, I gave my first orgasm to my kidnapper, my captor, bound to the rafters and forced without him asking my consent.

But really, I did consent. I wanted it. I just never said the words out loud.

As if that matters. He didn't ask, and I didn't say.

Did Ambrose know how much I wanted it?

It's wrong, so wrong.

I should've given it to Huxley—he deserves my pleasure more than anyone—yet Ambrose took it.

No. Ambrose earned it.
He caused it.
He made it happen.
And I want more.

CHAPTER 11

I HEARD HER whimper.

I heard her moan.

I heard her cry out and scream.

I don't know what he's done to hurt her. I don't know why he's demanding to know where her father is. All I know is the pang in my chest because I'm helpless here inside this cage.

My knuckles are white as my fists curl around the metal bars. I shake and pull at them, hoping there's a weakness in their fusion that might miraculously give and let me escape.

Glory needs me, and I'm trapped.

I can't help her here.

I hear his heavy boots tromp across the floor and my jaw tightens. *Everything* tightens, my muscles straining painfully. I want to rip him apart with my bare hands for laying a finger on her.

He appears in the doorway, his chest rising and falling sharply with heavy breaths, fists clenched at his sides. He looks nearly manic, his thick black hair unkempt and his clothes rumpled.

I grit my teeth. "What did you do to her?"

"Nothing she didn't want," he says, fuming as if he's

angry at me. "Tell me where Beau Tolliver is."

I let out a harsh chuckle. "I'm not telling you shit."

"Do you want me to hurt her again?"

My grip tightens on the bars and I yank, unable to control my building rage. "Don't you fucking touch her again! What did you do to her?"

"Where is Beau Tolliver?"

I let go and raise the middle finger of both hands, reaching them out through the spaces between the bars. "I've got these two fucks to give about what information you want from us, and I'll shove them right up your ass."

He charges forward, reaching out and snatching hold of one of my wrists before I can pull it back. He squeezes as his other hand comes up, grips my middle finger, and starts to pull back. I shout as he bends it too far, as pain rolls in, barreling through my arm.

"That's a good way to get your finger broken," he says with a low grumble.

His sound vibrates through me, rippling through my chest, shocking my heart to a dead stop. I stare him down, giving him the full intensity of my rage for the fact that he dared to lay his hands on my Glory.

It's rage reflecting rage in the dark eyes we both share.

Anger reflecting anger.

Pain reflecting pain.

Fuck.

The pain in his eyes threatens to soften me, tugging at the savior string attached to the center of my heart. It weakens me, it slows me, it stills me. Gradually, he loosens his grip on my finger, though his grip on my wrist holds firm.

Then, he tugs, pulling my arm all the way through, wedging my shoulder in the space between the bars. I wince as he twists my arm, turning my shoulder, and I shout as his hand comes down at my elbow.

"I could break your arm. Take you down to the floor, stomp on your elbow, snap it in two. Is that what you want from me? You want to see the sickness inside me?"

He tugs again and my body crashes against the metal bars, my shoulder dragged through the opening. "Let go!" I demand.

He doesn't respond, though I can hear him breathing, ragged and heavy. I can only really see him from the corner of my eye. I brace myself as I feel him push forward from my elbow, adding pressure, making me think he's going to go through with it and break my goddamn arm.

He can fucking break it.

I'm not telling him shit.

I tense, my eyes pinching closed as I prepare for the snap…but then his fingers circle my bicep and squeeze, holding me firmly in place as his body moves, as he comes in closer.

I can feel his heat as he comes up to the bars, tight against my side, and my breath catches in my lungs. He reaches his free hand into the cage and grabs my cheek, his fingers slick as they slide across my jaw and his thumb squeezes my chin to grab hold of me.

Fuck.

I inhale and my knees go weak. I know the scent of sex as well as I know the scent of Glory, and there's a heady mixture of both all over his hand. I swallow hard as my lust for her swells. But more than that, I can smell him, too. His scent mingled with hers is overwhelming…intoxicating.

"Do you feel her wetness on my hand?" he asks quietly. "Do you smell her?" At first, I think he's trying to goad me, to upset me because he touched her. But there's a subtle waver in his tone, a flicker of desire that hints at sincerity. "I strung her up, bound her wrists, and fucked her with my fingers until she came on my hand."

Goddammit.

My balls tighten and my cock thickens beneath my jeans.

What the fuck is wrong with me?

His thumb brushes across my lip, tugging it down. "How does that make you feel, Huxley Hill?"

I should bite his hand, clamp down on his thumb and slice it clean through to the bone with my teeth. I should snatch his wrist with my free hand and tug his arm through the bars, break his arm like he threatened to break mine.

I should.

But I don't.

My tongue tingles with an ache to run across his thumb, to lick his fingers clean. The dark desire twists knots inside me that beg to be unraveled. Goddamn, I haven't wanted a man like this…not since Noah, and our brief fling ended over a year ago.

It's as if he can read my mind when he drags his hand back, letting his slick fingers pull across my cheek. His thumb pulls down harder on my lip and I part them, letting him push his fingers inside my mouth. I fucking groan at the taste of it…the taste of Glory and Ambrose on my tongue.

"Fuck," he groans as I suck on his fingers.

I'm lost.

I'm so fucking lost.

I don't know what's happening to me. How can I

desire him? How can I desire at all knowing she's out there, whimpering and alone, strung up as he said?

Bite off his fucking fingers.

My teeth come down, but they don't clamp, they playfully scrape across his knuckles, knowing how the burn and ache of them dragging over his skin must tease him into wanting.

I want him to want me.

I want her to want me.

I fucking want them both.

His fingers break free as he jerks his hand back. His body heat leaves me cold as he releases his grip on my bicep and steps back, releasing me.

His eyes are wide as he lifts his hands to his wavy black locks and combs his fingers through. I should be pleased at the way he shakes his head ever so subtly, happy to see him confused and clearly tumbling off his twisted game. I'm not pleased by it…I suffer for it.

I fucking suffer for the frustration on his face.

I always fucking suffer from the pain of others.

I want both our suffering to end…*all* our suffering.

I don't know what the fuck this is, but this shifting, pulsing energy between us is toxic, poisonous, and is eating me alive from the inside out.

He's sick and wanting him feels like an infection—throbbing and sore, spreading like wildfire.

In a flash, he's gone.

He disappears from the room, and I hear the front door open, then shut. I let out a long-held breath, and after a few moments of silence, I call out to Glory, "Are you okay? Are you alone?"

"He left…but I can see him outside."

"Can you see what he's doing?"

"Chopping wood," she replies, and her voice sounds strange.

"Can you get free?"

"I don't know. The ropes are tight."

"Try. You have to try."

"I *am* trying."

I hear her grunts and groans as she works. I take a step away and lean my back against the wall, slumping against it. I can't listen to her make those sounds. I'm fucking losing my mind.

Her sounds of exertion are punctuated by the *thud, thud, thud* of wood being chopped outside, and it's impossible for me not to think of Ambrose swinging an axe with power and grace.

"Can you see him, Glory?" The strangled words leave my mouth before I even think them.

There's stillness and quiet for a moment. Then, she says, "Yes," and the word draws out on a long exhale.

I rub my hand over my chest before my fingers curl into a fist that grips my T-shirt. This shouldn't be happening. None of this should be happening, but least of all, my cock shouldn't be hard.

It's hard for her…it's hard for him.

Does that make me sick?

I swallow down the sickness. "Glory?"

"Yeah?"

"Are you okay?"

"I'm…I don't know how to answer that."

"Yeah. Me, too."

"Why do you think he wants to know where my dad is?

Did he ask you?"

"I really don't know. But don't say a word to him, okay? If he gets the information he wants, then he won't need us anymore and we're as good as dead."

He won't need us anymore.

There's some disappointment in that thought.

"He's coming back," she says, her voice trailing off into a whisper.

I push off from the wall, moving to the bars again. "Just stay calm. If you can get away, you run, okay? Don't come back for me."

"I'll always come back for you, Hux. You would come back for me."

I open my mouth to speak, but I'm silenced by the sound of the opening and closing door, by the stomp of his boots at the entrance, and the tromping across the hardwood. I hold my breath and strain my ears, hoping somehow, Glory gets free.

CHAPTER 12

Ambrose

I NEEDED TO distance myself from the viral lust spreading through that house. I left Glory bound beside the kitchen table and came outside. I picked up my axe, and now, I'm taking out my aggressive desire on chunks of wood. Log after log, I place them on top of the tree stump in the center of the clearing just outside my front door.

Though the swing of my axe normally burns up my furious hostility, it fails to quell the brutality within me now. Except, this brutality isn't hostile…it's stained with lust.

I let out a primal roar of frustration, pain, and confusion with the final swing of my axe. The blade slices through the air with fury and wedges into the log with an echoing *thud*. The force of my blow is strong enough to split it down the middle. The splintered pieces fall, one half of the log tumbling off the stump into the snow.

My chest heaves as I bend to retrieve it, and when I stand, the movement from inside my home captures my attention. I can see Glory through the window, twisting and wriggling in her binds, and it twists and wriggles inside me, too.

The axe suddenly feels too heavy in my grip, and it slips through my fingers, dropping into the snow with a *thump* as it lands. Without conscious thought, my feet carry me back inside, move me across the floor, and bring me to a stop in front of Glory.

She's fucking stunning this way, strung up with her hands tied above her head. Her dyed blonde hair shows her natural dark brown color at the roots, tangled and messy, and her striking green eyes stare at me wildly. My cock twitches at the sight of her, but it had already been thickening for Huxley.

I need to kill them.

I need to find out where their father is and kill them all.

But when I look at her, I cannot fathom the thought. All I can think about is the way her cunt felt with my fingers jammed inside, the way she came so hard, shuddering and twitching as it took hold of her. And the way Huxley tasted her on my fingers…

Fuck, I want them.

I want them more than I've ever wanted anything or anyone. There's no logic to it, and it's dangerous because I have to focus. My job is to kill them, get the money from Maura, and then I can be free of this place and its infectious hold on me.

But…

If I'm going to turn to the darkness and murder seemingly innocent creatures such as these two, then I ought to enjoy them while I still have them. I still don't know where Beau Tolliver is, and I need to extract that information from them.

There's no reason I can't enjoy myself while I do it.

No reason…except for the little voice in the back of my mind.

I have to fight to ignore it, because it tells me to turn away from her, to stop looking down at her heaving chest, to stop thinking about her thick lips wrapped around my cock.

I reach out and twist my finger around a lock of her hair, twirling it, watching the way the fake blonde swirls against my knuckle. It's soft, though it's dirty.

That's how she is, soft but dirty.

I want to share my filth with her.

Her head falls, tilting to the side and leaning closer to where my hand twirls her hair. She leans into my touch, not away from it, and fuck, that makes my dick throb, begging to be inside her.

She wants it.

Take her.

I let out a haggard, heated breath and reach for her wrists, my fingers scrambling to undo the knots that hold her in place. I want her down on the floor. I want her on all fours. I want to fuck her from behind and make her scream. I want Huxley to shut her up with his cock inside her mouth.

It would be easier to take the ropes down from the rafters first and untie her that way, but my impatient mind is overrun by the insistent need to have her *now*. If I were a fool, I could almost think she wants me, too. Her breaths quicken, her eyelids hood over her dilating pupils, and I feel the heat of her gaze as my fingers dig between knots, frantically working to tug and pull her free.

I sigh in relief as the last knot unwinds and her arms drop heavily to her sides. I'm ready to grab her, kiss her, pretend I have her affection for a few blissful moments of fucking and coming undone together. But then her eyes dart from me to the door and back again.

She's going to run.

I lunge as she dives into a sprint, bolting for the front door that I stupidly didn't lock behind me in my cock-hungry state. She grabs the knob and pulls, but I'm fast, too. My palm lands on the wood above her head, slamming it shut before she can wrench it open more than an inch.

She whirls around as I step in close, my body pinning hers against the door. I reach over and turn the deadbolt, then secure the chain lock as she watches me.

"Come on," I goad, "hit me, little bird. Kick me. Fight me."

It's almost like she's not even trying with the way she stares at me, blinking up at me with eyes that look deceptively innocent, eyes that are somehow also dulled by the pain of experience. I know the look because I see it in my own eyes when I look in the mirror, and I wonder what kind of pain her experience has brought her.

I bring my other palm up to join the first, pressing against the door, locking her head between them as I bend over her. She doesn't look frightened, and I'm surprised by that. Given what I've done to her, fear is the only emotion she should feel.

My eyes are drawn to her throat as she swallows, and it makes me think about how fragile her slender neck is. It makes me want to wrap my hand around it and squeeze. It makes me want to lock her back up to keep her safe from anyone other than me who would try to harm her.

My fragile little bird.

I try once more to provoke her. "Come on, princess."

And something snaps.

Her eyes narrow, hooding from wide-eyed prey to predator, and something dark paints shadows across her rosy cheeks.

"Don't call me that. *No more.* Not ever again." Her voice

is twisted, gruff, and strained, filled with pain.

The pain resonates in my chest as familiar.

No more.

Not ever again.

The words themselves aren't familiar, but I'm aware of the emotion behind them. I know with the angry sneer spread across her cheeks and the violent glow behind the bright green of her eyes that she's been hurt like I've been hurt…and now she's about to fight me.

I realize I'm going to have to react a half a second before she snaps, which catches me entirely off-guard. Her tiny hands come up to meet my chest, and she shoves me powerfully—surprisingly strong for such a tiny thing—and I stumble backward. I rush forward to capture her against the door again, but she's gone before I can trap her. She darts around me and runs toward the kitchen, heading straight for…*the oven?* No, she's heading for the block of knives on the counter beside it.

"Shit."

I dart after her, reaching her quickly, and snake my arm around her hip, my forearm drawing a line across her pelvis as I roughly jerk her back.

"No!" she shouts as I lift her from the floor.

Her arms swing and her legs kick madly, and I wonder where this fight was before.

I triggered her. Something I said triggered her.

Princess.

I called her princess, and she snapped.

I can use that knowledge against her…though somehow, I know I won't.

Pulling her backward, I drag her kicking and screaming down the hall. I'm taking her to my bedroom where I'm going to fucking tame this wildcat. At least, that's my plan before she jams her heel into the crease of my thigh, barely missing my cock.

I flinch in surprise, groaning as my hold unintentionally loosens. She twists and flings, and with my grip momentarily slackened, she manages to break free, dropping from my arms. Her knees buckle as her feet hit the floor, and she falls forward, landing on all fours.

Fuck me.

"Glory!" I hear Huxley call as she crawls forward down the hall.

Her head turns as she moves in front of the cage room's doorway. She must make eye contact with him because it somehow seems to calm her. She freezes, going unnaturally still given the way she was just fighting me, and after a moment, she sits back on her heels. Her head is still turned toward him as she submissively presses her palms to her knees.

Interesting.

Assuming her calmness, I reach down, preparing to slip my hands beneath her arms and lift her to her feet. That's when she spins on one knee, planting her other foot on the floor, rising with swiftness and grace like a goddamn soldier, and comes after me to fight with fists and fury.

I catch one of her small fists in my palm as she swings for my gut. I twist her arm while our feet tangle together. She tumbles off-balance, tilting sideways before falling into the room where Huxley is caged. Her toes hook around my ankle on her way down and I stumble with her.

I brace myself, my palms slamming to the floor above her head as I land over her, my body making a bridge above her. Her foot lands on my thigh and shoves against it, forcing her body to slip backward along the floor. I slam my knees down to catch her hips between them, but she rolls onto her stomach and claws across the floor, moving toward the cage… toward Huxley.

Between the fight, the fury, and the sinful lust coursing through my veins, I devolve into a ravenous beast. Animal to animal, predator to prey, Glory's internal sickness calls to mine.

Digging my fingers in like claws, I grab her waist, jerk her back, and flip her over. I slam my hips down to hold her to the floor, my hard cock against her belly warning her of the poison inside me—poison that could turn her and make her vile like me.

My chest heaves as I look down upon her reddened cheeks and my exhale scrapes harshly through the back of my throat, coming out as a breathy growl. She gasps as I drive my hips down, and her eyelids fall, drooping to hood the wild green as they soften far too easily from all-out war to surrender.

We stare at each other, and she tells me of her weakness with a quick dart of her tongue and a flicker of her eyes to my lips.

"Fuck," the voice sounds gruff, lust-filled, like mine. But it's not my voice…it's Huxley.

My head turns naturally, something within me begging to see what his face looks like right now, but I hardly glimpse him. Glory's hands are on my cheeks, turning me back, pulling me down, and drawing me into an unexpectedly eager kiss.

I part her lips with mine, and the strangled moan she feeds me ripples a wave of pure need down my spine. It pricks through my hips and burns down deep in my gut. My balls tighten as she bucks up against me, as her small, soft tongue battles past my teeth to taste me fully.

I hear the metal bars of the cage groan beneath Huxley's grip, but all my other senses are with her. I taste her maple sweetness, smell her heady desire, see the darkness consume her before my eyes pinch shut, and I feel her…everywhere.

She's everywhere.

Looming and threatening my present, my future.

My future is far from this place—away from Sugar Wood Forest—but I need Maura to set me free from the secrets she holds against me, from all the dirty work I've done for her. And I have to do this one last job to be free. I have to kill them.

Stop.

Stop this now.

Throw her into the cage before you attach yourself to your prey.

My body trembles with need as I reach into my pocket with one hand, pulling out the key that opens the cage door. The ground shudders beneath us as I painfully drag my lips from hers, as I sit back on my heels and reach around behind her bewildered face to fist her fake blonde hair.

She shrieks in surprise as I drag her awkwardly along the floor, both of us twisting and scooting and fighting for control. I'm on one knee in front of the cage door as she kicks behind me. She reaches for my wrist, trying to knock it away from her hair, but she has no leverage with her ass on the floor.

She kicks her tiny feet, trying to find purchase, though

they only slip and strike over the hardwood. By the time she manages to get one foot planted, I have the cage door open wide. I shove to my feet with a grunt, and she screams out again as her hair comes with me as I yank her upright to her feet.

I toss her inside so violently that her shoulder slams into the back wall with a resounding *thud*, which makes her shout and wince. The sight of her face as it scrunches in pain makes my body tighten with guilty tension. I muster every ounce of strength inside me to slam that cage door shut, to turn the lock, to pull out the key.

Glory slumps to the floor and Huxley drops with her. They both snap their heads to look at me at the same time.

Don't look at them.

Focus on your freedom.

I swipe the back of my hand across my mouth, panting as I slowly back away while staring at a spot on the wall above their heads. "Don't fuck with me," I tell them. "I'll..." my voice shakes, and I fight to steady it, "I'll be back. And when I return, I want some goddamn answers about Beau Tolliver."

CHAPTER 13

Glory

HUXLEY'S HANDS ARE firm on my biceps, the only thing grounding me in reality as my senses swirl out of control.

I hurt.

I want.

I *need.*

I ache for relief, to feel that explosion I felt against Ambrose's fingers.

My sweaty palms rub against my knees, then my fingers curl, digging into my fleshy thighs. I draw my hands back, dragging aching lines up my legs as my head drops forward, intentionally avoiding Huxley's gaze.

"Are you okay?" he asks softly.

There's something odd in his tone, something exciting about the way his hands squeeze my biceps so intensely. My shoulder throbs with a pulsing pain from where it jammed against the wall when Ambrose threw me in. The pain mixes with the need running through me, making my skin crawl… but in a good way. It's like bubbles bursting beneath the surface, rippling pinpricks that tease and make me frantic to seek friction across my tickled flesh.

My head shakes from side to side and I can't bring

myself to speak, afraid of what will come out of my mouth. I press my eyes shut against the hum of need that vibrates through my core and pulses through my clit.

God, why do I feel like this?

How does Ambrose make me feel like this?

I want him so badly that I kissed him instead of fighting him harder to get free.

"Glory…" My name comes out gruffly, and Huxley shifts on his knees.

"Hux, I can't…I've never…There's something wrong with me."

"There's nothing wrong with you."

"I kissed him. I wanted him." It feels both good and bad to admit.

"Look at me."

Slowly, and with hesitancy, I lift my head. My eyes scrape over his body from his knees, up his muscular thighs, across the bulge in his jeans…

I gasp.

Does he need the way I do?

Is he infected by this house, by this man the same as me?

I pull my eyes away from his lap with great strain, lifting them to look at his face from beneath my eyelashes. My chest heaves. My tongue slips out to lick my bottom lip before my teeth catch hold of it. When I meet his brown eyes, the strange lust building inside me snaps together into a dense ball that drops heavy and hard, pulling that need down with desperation I can't fight.

I need to come.

I need to relieve this awful aching.

My hand slips between my legs as my knees slide apart and my fingers rush to press against my pussy. I touch myself over my jeans and the moment there's contact, my head snaps back and I moan in anticipation of the relief I'm so desperate to find.

I can't focus.

I can't think of anything else.

"Glory."

I rub harshly, though with no idea what to do to find the explosion. I should feel ashamed for what I'm doing here in front of Huxley, trapped in a cage in a crazy man's home in the woods.

I always felt ashamed of sex before—it was always something taken from me. It was taken by my father, but not only by him. It was taken by all the other boys I'd tried to find approval from, too. I'd let so many fuck me, hoping it would make them love me, but they never did. It never felt good; it never felt right. None of them ever cared if I enjoyed it.

I don't know if this feels right, but I know for certain that it's necessary. And Huxley has always taken care of me when I needed him.

I need him now.

I need this so much, I worry I might lose myself without it.

"He made me come," I whisper, feeling blood rush to my cheeks. "That was the first time I've ever felt that. Huxley, I need to. I need it now. I need to come again. I need it so much."

Warm tears prick at the backs of my eyes for the way this filthy need consumes me. I feel it through every cell in my body, each molecule screaming and begging to be touched. Moments of frantic rubbing against my jeans pass, and I'm whimpering, waiting for something to strike me and show me that I'm doing what I need to do to get that relief, but it only builds frustration and fear and deep-rooted shame.

I fear remaining pent-up like this, stuck in a painful desire that will never resolve itself like a chronic ache that will plague me until the day I die.

"Help me," I beg through a rasping breath, my eyes locking on his. "I don't know how to…"

He just watches me and breathes, his eyes burning through mine. I know he wants to, but he's holding back. He's holding back and each second that passes drives me further to insanity.

"Huxley, *please.*"

No movement.

I quickly undo the button of my jeans and tug down the zipper. I rise onto my knees, forcing his hands to fall away from my arms. I shove my hand beneath my panties and walk my fingers down between my legs, gasping out a ragged moan at the feel of my wet, swollen flesh.

I don't know what I'm doing. I've never touched myself before—I've never wanted pleasure and release, so I never sought out a way to get it. My mind is hectic with the whispers of my flesh as my body sends sparks of false starts and stops. My fingers are wild, rubbing and twisting, diving into my folds.

I need to come.

I need to come now.

"Huxley!" I shout at him.

I see him flinch, see his eyes lift to meet mine from where they stared down at my hand which disappears beneath the fabric. I watch his dark brown eyes as they swirl with intention, with thought, slowing to rest on mine as they still into determination.

Yes.

It's the look of determination he gets when he's coming to my rescue. The look that tells me he's here for me, that he loves me, that he's going to do whatever I need him to do.

And God, the way that look makes me feel…

I sigh as his fingers close around my wrist, as he pulls my hand out of my jeans and forces me to stop. I whimper at the absence of touch, but I trust him. I trust Huxley to help me, to make me better, to set me free from this odd desire.

His hands grip my waist and he spins me around in a flash, then snakes an arm around my waist to pull me backward against him. He shoves me down to sit between his wide spread legs, forces me to lean back against his strong chest, and the ashes of my heart spark to life, floating inside my ribcage like fiery flints drifting from a campfire.

He pulls my hair back over my shoulder and I feel his lips against my ear. "I've wanted to touch you forever. Are you sure you want this?"

I'm whimpering, gasping, *dying.*

I nod frantically. "Yes."

His hand comes around me as he leans back against the wall and I let my head drop back onto his shoulder. I jolt at the touch of his fingers across my belly, and I look down to watch as his hand gradually sinks beneath the soft barrier of my underwear. I can hardly breathe as he groans and shifts behind me, as his growing erection presses hard against the small of my back, as his fingers walk down, down, down between my legs.

"Ahh," I moan, my body tensing as he playfully wiggles

two fingers against my opening. I slam my hands down on his thighs and grip him tightly to brace myself. "Oh, my God."

"You can't just rub yourself raw," he whispers, his voice commanding with sinful instruction. "That won't get you anywhere and will just leave you frustrated. Touch with intention, Glory."

My back arches as his fingers curl and gently dip inside me. He nudges them a little deeper, and I can feel the pads of his fingers rubbing along my inner wall, moving precisely, as if he's searching for something. I know when he finds it because he presses against that spot. It makes my stomach clench, and heat rushes to my core. He holds his fingers still, putting pressure against that single spot before he starts to stroke, stroke, stroke.

"Tell me which feels better. Pay attention. More pressure," the pads of his fingers press upward harder as he strokes and my body convulses, wound up so tight that his touch has become a hair-trigger for pleasure, "or less." He continues to stroke, but softer, gentler…

That feels good too, but I need more.

"More."

He gives me what I've asked for, rubbing with perfect pressure until I'm writhing beneath him, until I'm whimpering and moaning, more desperate than ever for release.

"Fuck. You feel so good," he murmurs. His lips are on my neck, trailing a line of soft kisses down to the nape. "God, I want to make you come."

My eyes flutter shut. "Make me come." I'm not sure whether my words are audible.

I sink into pleasure, enjoying the way he drags intensity to my core, letting him fill every sense and take me to a purely blissful state.

Then his thumb lands on my clit and I scream at the pleasure that shoots through me. Huxley clamps his unoccupied hand over my mouth, and God, somehow that heightens the intensity of what I'm feeling.

"Shh," he whispers. "I don't want to risk him hearing you if he comes back. I want this for myself."

I moan, and I feel the way it vibrates against his palm. He must feel it too because his moan matches mine and he works his hand more intently, his focus and determination increasing. I can feel the way all his energy draws down to my pussy.

I want this for myself, he'd said.

God, the way he wants me…

"Fuck," he groans as he circles his thumb, as he strokes his fingers, weaving some kind of sick magic between my thighs. "My thumb…too much or not enough?" His hand drops from my mouth and lands on the side of my neck. It rests there lightly, though his touch feels heavy and significant.

"It's…" I pause to take a deep breath, "it's perfect."

"Close your eyes," he says. "Don't chase it. Just let it build. Let it pulse. Let it ache."

"It aches."

"Let it. Let it hurt. Let it make you desperate. Relief is coming, Glory. I'm giving it to you. Fuck, you make me need it, too." He shifts behind me. "Can you feel me? Can you feel how much I want you? How much I've always wanted you?"

I breathe the word, "Yes."

"You were always off-limits. My stepsister. This was forbidden, taboo, but *fuck*, the way I've wanted you. The way I've always wanted you."

"Hux."

His words are a rope wrapping tight around the swirling stars of pleasure in my belly, pulling them together, clustering them into one heavy star that collapses as he groans against my ear. It drops heavy and hard, then explodes, white light flashing behind my eyelids.

My eyes pop wide and my back arches as my whole body clenches, trembles, fights against onrushing climax… and my body fails to stop it. I scream, wild and uninhibited, as the most spectacular thing I've ever felt rips through my cunt, grips his fingers, pulses and throbs and fills me with moment after moment of pure, undeniable bliss.

And when the tension breaks, I fall limply in his hold, my body slumping against his, slipping along the floor. His fingers stop moving, but they're still lodged inside me, still curled against my front wall, as if he doesn't want to let go of me.

"What's happening here?" he asks.

What's happening here with us?

What's happening here in this place?

What's happening here with Ambrose?

"I don't know," I tell him honestly.

With care and reluctance, he pulls his fingers from my body, and I immediately miss them. His touch was different than Ambrose's. Huxley's touch was specific, precise, following a clear path to get me to climax. Ambrose's touch was rough, demanding, tumbling down a hill that inevitably took me to the same place.

Both were mind-numbing, and for a girl like me, who fell into dissociation at the faintest hint of sexual activity, it was bliss.

Mind-numbing bliss.

What is this magic house in the middle of Sugar Wood?

Is Ambrose some warlock who has us under his spell?

The sexual urgency has left me now that Huxley took care of me—like he always does—but there's a hint of it still floating in my belly, impossible to ignore because of him.

"You're hard."

"Yeah," he sighs, "it'll go away. I just need a few minutes."

I push myself up and slowly turn to face him, sitting on my knees between his legs. "Let me—"

"No," he grits, pinching his eyes shut. "I don't want you to touch me as a returned favor."

"It's not just that—"

"Glory, no." He reaches out, as if to touch my cheek, but stops short. His eyes fall upon his fingers, seeing the slickness from my arousal, and it stops him. For a moment, I worry it's upset him, but then he does something unexpected.

He licks his lips and pushes his wet fingers inside his mouth. His lips clamp down around his knuckles and he hums while he sucks them clean, his eyes falling shut as his head falls back against the wall.

Slowly, he drags them out and lets his hands fall to the floor on either side of his hips. He breathes deeply, though he doesn't open his eyes, as if savoring my lingering flavor on his tongue.

God, how that twists me up inside.

"On your sixteenth birthday, you wore a stunning red dress to the party your dad threw for you," he starts, still breathing slowly, eyes still shut.

"I remember," I tell him. "At The Plaza in New York."

He nods. "Yeah. You looked so beautiful that night, and

I don't think you were even aware of it. I couldn't stop looking at you. I always had trouble tearing my eyes away from you, but that night was when I really *saw* you and I knew…I knew I'd be comparing every person I ever met to you, and no one would ever be good enough." He opens his eyes and they lock on mine. "I wanted you then. I imagined dragging you away from the worthless boys who surrounded you, taking you upstairs, getting down on my knees for you."

My breath catches at the admission. "We shared a room that weekend…You and I stayed together in the same room."

"And I never struggled so much in my life." He sits up straighter, leans forward, and grabs my face in both of his strong hands. "That night I fantasized about you for hours while you slept in the bed beside mine. I thought about putting my hands on you, wondered how it would feel to touch your silky skin, fought against my urge to dive beneath the covers and wake you with my head between your legs and my tongue on your clit."

"Why…why didn't you?"

I'm confused. He could've done that, and I wouldn't have said a word. I would've let him. I always let boys do it when they tried because it was easier than saying no.

"There were so many reasons I couldn't. For one, I'd just turned eighteen and you were underage. For another, I was your stepbrother and it felt wrong. But that night, the most important reason was that you were vulnerable, and I would never take advantage of you in that state. You were upset that night."

I nearly flinch, the memory hitting me despite all my best efforts to suppress it. My father had promised he wouldn't touch me, that the night was mine, a celebration for me and only me. He swore he wouldn't, but he lied.

My hair had been coiled and twisted beautifully into a soft updo. It was exactly how I wanted it to look, and I was so happy that my sixteenth birthday party would be everything I wanted it to be. But my sick father took one look at me and broke his promise. He hurt me, used me, ruined my updo with his roughness, and made me cry, which ruined my make-up, too—all in the minutes before I was going to head down to the hotel ballroom for my party.

It ruined my night…of *course* it had.

He ruined me entirely every time he touched me.

I can't bring myself to tell Huxley any of those wretched details because I don't want to remember them myself.

"My father—" I start to say, but he quickly cuts me off, his thumb brushing across my lips.

"You don't have to say another word. I know now what he did to you, and you don't have to say another thing about it if you don't want to."

"I really don't want to."

He nods softly. "If he's the reason you were upset that night, then I'm glad I didn't touch you, that I didn't try. Any connection we would have made would have been tainted by that son of a bitch. I just…I just can't believe I never worked it out before. I would've killed him myself, and we never would've been in this mess."

"We still would've had to get rid of the body."

"I only buried him for you. I couldn't have you going to jail for killing him. You deserve to live your life and be happy. If I'd killed him myself, I would've turned myself in and happily lived the rest of my life behind bars knowing that you were safe."

I turn my head, glancing around at the bars. "I guess we both ended up in jail anyway."

He lets out a heavy sigh. "I'll find a way out of this, Glory. I promise, I'll get you out of this."

I've been told a lot of false promises in my life, but Huxley has never promised me anything he hasn't delivered on. And I have no doubt he'll try everything to keep this promise, too…though I don't know if he has any control over it.

CHAPTER 14

TOUCHING GLORY WAS more intoxicating than I'd ever dreamed it would be. I'd been trying to convince myself for the past six months or so that I was putting her on a pedestal, that I'd created a fantasy of what I thought she might be inside my mind. I'd tried to convince myself of that as a way to let her go, to push myself to find someone else to fill the void within me. But slipping my fingers inside her proved that all the fantasies I had of being with her were right. She was soft, warm, wet, responsive—more responsive than she knew.

It shocked me to find out that she's never come before, though I suppose it makes sense knowing what her father did to her during her formative years. If it were me, I probably would have cut myself off from pleasure, too.

Shit.

The thought of it makes me want to vomit.

Glory had laid her head on my lap to rest, falling unusually quickly into a peaceful, still slumber. I'm trying to remain humble, though a part of me insists that I somehow gave her that peace by making her come. She'd been so frantic for relief, oddly desperate, and I understood it. A strange, primal energy surrounds this place—an energy that grows stronger the nearer he is—and it's drawing out parts of me I've repressed for far too long.

Ambrose.

He returned sometime later, and the chain was moved from my ankle back to Glory's. He let me out of the cage, but not before shackling my feet together with two ankle cuffs, attached by a chain linked between them.

We move through the forest now. Some of the snow has melted from the storm, so it's not terribly difficult to tramp through as he leads me. The cold deepens as the sun sets, seeping into my bones. My muscles stiffen, especially my legs where I have to walk in short steps, my usual long strides hindered by the chain.

He leads me through the trees, creating a winding path as he weaves in and out and around the trunks. We trudge for fifteen, maybe twenty minutes, before a small clearing opens up near the base of a massive maple tree, and he comes to a stop in front of it. With his black boots, dark jeans, black hoodie, and overcoat, he creates a dark silhouette—a shadow—across the wide base. He shoves his hands into his pockets, and he looks up at the branches.

I draw my eyes along his outline. With his back turned to me and his hood pulled up, he's a faceless dark figure in a barren, cold forest. The image in front of me imprints itself in my mind—I instantly know that I'll never forget this disturbing vision.

Beyond his silhouette, the texture of rugged bark climbs high up the tree trunk, drawing my eyes to the bare branches stretching across the sky. The limbs are eerie in the way they sway overhead, bare in the dead of winter, twigs along the boughs scraping across the orange and yellow lines painted by the setting sun.

"My parents are buried here," he says.

I tear my eyes away from the branches to stare at his back. I don't know whether he wants a response, and I don't have one anyway, so I remain silent.

He turns to face me and leans back against the tree as he pulls a pack of cigarettes from his jacket pocket. His head tilts as he places the end between his lips, one hand coming up to block the tip from the chilly breeze as he sparks his lighter. He takes a slow drag before grasping his cigarette between two fingers and pulls it away, letting his hand fall to his side.

"How do you think they died?" he asks.

I shake my head, uninterested in playing this game, eager to get back to Glory.

"Any thoughts on why they're buried here in an unmarked location in the forest?"

I shrug. "Am I supposed to care?"

He glances at the forest floor where remnants of dead, crunchy brown leaves peek through the snow from the tracks he kicked with his feet. He takes another drag of his cigarette and looks off into the distance.

"I didn't build that cage you're in. I'm not some sadistic creep who kidnaps teenagers lost in the forest. That cage has been there since I was three years old, and it was never meant to capture anyone."

I feel a prick of interest in the way it tenses my muscles, and though I try to fight my words, they come out anyway. "Then what was it meant for?"

His dark eyes shift, though his head remains still, and

they lock onto mine, holding me because a flicker of pain flashes behind them—something I only recognize because I've seen it before.

I've seen it in Glory's eyes, too.

"It was meant for me."

I breathe in deep, my chest rising with unexpected indignation. "Who made it?"

He steps forward, away from the tree, and plants his feet wide, as if straddling a divide. "Our dearly departed Mr. and Mrs. Bishop, the pieces of shit beneath my feet. Does it make you curious to know what happened to them? How they died? Why they're buried here?"

Yes.

"Just say what you have to fucking say."

"That cage was my bedroom from the day I could crawl. I almost have to wonder how I survived the newborn stage with parents like mine, but by some miracle, I did," he scoffs and shakes his head. "Over the years, I got used to living in isolation, so much so that I avoid people as much as I can now." He pulls his legs together and paces across the graves, taking another drag from his cigarette. "You and your sister—"

"Stepsister," I feel the urgent need to clarify.

"Your *step*sister. The two of you found yourself in my company, somewhere you don't belong, and as far as I'm concerned, that's reason enough to end your miserable lives and bury you both with my fucking parents."

"Bullshit. If you had any urge to do that, you would've done it by now."

"Would I? Now I'm curious, Huxley…Do you think I'm an impulsive man?"

"A lost and frozen nineteen-year-old girl shows up on your doorstep in the middle of a snowstorm looking for shelter, and your gut reaction is to wrestle her down, chain her up, and lock her in a cage. Yeah, I'd say you're a little fucking impulsive in your decision making."

He stops, turns his head, showing me the twist of his sneer. "I think that makes me an *opportunist* more than it makes me impulsive."

"Cut the bullshit. There's no opportunity in this for you."

"You have no fucking clue how much opportunity is in this."

"Then tell me."

He turns to face me squarely and marches toward me, stopping so close that I flinch when he raises his cigarette to his lips, as the spark from the end flickers a breath away from my cheek. He exhales, blowing smoke out from the corner of his mouth, his dark eyes zeroed in on mine, brooding.

"Where is Glory's father?"

"Why the fuck do you want to know?"

"It doesn't matter. Just tell me where I can find him."

"Nah." I shake my head. "You're gonna have to be a little more convincing than that."

He drops his cigarette, and my gaze follows it to the ground, watching his boot sneak out to stomp and twist. Because my head is turned, I don't see it coming until it's too late. His hand thrusts forward and lodges around my throat. He shoves me back against a tree trunk and the force knocks the wind from me, causing me to gasp for breath as his fingers squeeze. "Is this convincing enough for you?"

Fuck me.

There's something sinister, yet undeniably sexual in the sizzle of his skin on mine…something I shouldn't feel from the touch of a madman who holds me hostage. Maybe it's the way he takes control that puts me out of my head, dampening the urgent rush of adrenaline that tells me to fight him, to come to my own rescue.

His touch starts a war inside my body, my need to be free—to rescue Glory—battling brutally with this odd, festering sensation that begs me to surrender. Ambrose is a threat—a clear and present danger—and my anxiety should be at peak levels with his palm latched around my throat… yet it's not.

I almost feel as though I could slip away in his firm hold, let go of worry, give up, give in—

Give in to what?

No, I need to be fucking angry.

I need to fight him.

I have to save Glory.

"You're not going to find her father," I spit out the words.

Ambrose tilts his head. "Oh?"

"No one is ever going to find him."

"Somehow I doubt that."

"If you know what's good for you, you'll let us go. You know who Glory is, don't you?"

"Yes, I fucking know."

"Her family has money, resources. They're probably hunting us down right now. It's only a matter of time until they find us, and then what will you do? You'll get arrested, charged with kidnapping, sexual assault—"

His eyebrows snap down into a harsh, straight line. "I

haven't sexually assaulted anyone."

"You had your fingers inside her. She told me you made her come. She didn't want that from you. You took something from her. She'll never get back the experience of her first orgasm."

"What?"

"You heard me."

"That's a fucking lie. She's nineteen. That couldn't have been her first—"

"Her father abused her for years! She's never known anything other than assault and violence from men, and you just took another piece of her goddamn soul."

His eyes widen gradually, his nearly black irises shifting as they take in every inch of my face, as if my expression holds a truth he doesn't quite understand. Then, whatever softness his eyes just exposed snaps back to hardness, and I swallow against his pressing hand.

"But you said I made her come."

I smirk. "And so did I. You only got it because you took it from her. Me? She gave it to me. She *begged* me for it."

"When?"

"After you wrestled her back into that fucking cage."

Now it's his turn to smirk. "You mean after she pulled me down on top of her to kiss her? Don't fool yourself. She wanted *me*. You were just the helping hand."

"Fuck you. What the fuck do you want with us? What the fuck do you want with her father?"

"I don't want anything to do with any of you," he says, though his gaze subtly shifts. "It's about what I *have* to do for myself."

Suddenly, I'm curious.

I'm curious about the way his jaw ticks with tension.

I'm curious about the way his dark eyes shift.

I'm curious about the way his fingers twitch against my throat.

I'm curious about *him*.

"Tell me where he is," he says.

I don't reply.

He steps closer, his leg moving in between mine as he presses in. My pulse quickens. I urge my anger to build, to wash through my veins and cleanse me of the fury-filled desire that threatens to creep through me. I focus on the fury, let it quicken my breaths and surge through the beat of my heart, but fuck, when his shoulders sag, I can feel it wash over him, too. I can feel the vibration of his angry lust because it matches mine.

Fuck. It matches mine.

His grip tightens, and when he shifts to crush my body with his, I lose myself. I lose who I am, what I stand for. I lose my will to fight, my need to escape this. I need to escape him, but more urgently, I need to *know* him.

I swallow against his grip, and with a smoky black flash across his eyes, he moves quickly and his lips land on mine.

The world changes when he kisses me. It turns darker, colder, but also, it's somehow filled with twisted magic—magic that makes me shudder and move, jerking my senses into awareness. He pinches my chin, holding my head firmly against the tree trunk as his tongue pushes past my teeth and begs to taste me.

I want to taste him, too, and I do…Fuck me, I do.

He tastes like sin, like a fucking curse. I'm so thrown off

by his warmth against me that I don't even care that he curses me, too.

We groan in unison, and the shared vibration sends a spike of frenetic energy whipping through the both of us. I know it's not just me who feels it, because his hips rock forward and his cock is hard against mine.

I want that.

I want his hard cock just as much as I want Glory's soaking wet pussy.

I let my hand float forward, slip between us, and grip him through his jeans.

Breaking our kiss, he mutters, "Fuck," though he doesn't move away.

The curse ignites aggression that sets my jaw and makes my teeth ache, aggression that makes me squeeze the heavy thickness between his legs with intention.

I should take advantage of him. I should snap his goddamn dick off for what he's done to us. I should snap it and run, go back to free Glory, steal his truck, and be free from this nightmare for good.

But the nightmare fuels me, feeds me, makes me hungry for roughness and sex and consumption. Darkness falls around us with the setting sun and the bare branches of the trees creak and moan in the blistering cold breeze, whispering their intent to hide all of our filthiest, darkest secrets, whimpering with the need for us to release and unleash this madness.

Without warning, he steps back, tearing his fingers through his wavy, raven hair.

"Fuck," he mutters. "I can't fucking…Just tell me where the fuck I can find her father."

"You won't find him because he's dead." I watch him as intensity makes my chest heave with heavy breaths, still filled with lust and anger. "He's buried in the goddamn woods."

He doesn't look shocked or confused. There's only a hint of curiosity in the slight tilt of his head. "What? How did he die? Who buried him?"

"Glory killed him, and I buried him." I've lost control of myself, of my filters, and words tumble stupidly from my mouth. But the more I speak, the more I feel the burden lift from my shoulders. "He was trying to fuck her, and she put an end to it. And I'm damn proud of her. I would've done it myself when I found out how he hurt her, but she beat me to it. So, I cleaned up her goddamn mess because that's what I do. I take care of her. I do whatever it takes to protect her because she's *mine*. She's always been mine."

A silent beat passes…silent except for the sounds of the creaking forest.

Then, quietly, he says, "She's not yours." His tone isn't commanding or harsh, it's not defiant or combative. It's matter-of-fact, so much so that he could almost make me believe him.

But I know he's wrong.

She *is* mine. I claimed her with my fingers in her cunt, holding her against me as she came.

But he made her come first.

"What the fuck do you want from us?" I shout.

"You would never have done it yourself."

"What?"

"If you'd found out what he was doing, you wouldn't have killed him yourself. It shows your arrogance to claim that now since she handled the job herself. There's no risk for you in saying that, and knowing you could never prove your claim, it's easy to say."

"You don't know what the hell you're talking about. I buried the damn body for her!"

"So what? You're a cleaner. You're not a mess maker. You'll always be cleaning up after her. She can never be yours if that's all that you are."

"Fuck off."

"Do you think that killers can ever really belong to someone?"

"She's not a killer. She did what she had to do."

He shakes his head at me, calm and cool as fuck. "I stabbed my mother in the heart while she was sleeping, but with my father…I took my time. I let him sit in the cage for three days before I ended his life with my axe. I split him like a fucking log. While you stand there and preach pride in your stepsister for murdering her abusive father, you'd condemn me in the same breath for doing the same to my own abusive parents, wouldn't you?"

"If you left him in a cage, you're talking pre-meditation—"

"You don't know what the fuck you're talking about," he scoffs. "You have no idea the hell I've lived. The hypocrisy of your soul tarnishes the pride you say you have in her, and for that reason alone, she's not *yours*. She can't be *yours*. She's a killer…just like I am."

Without another word, he turns and stalks off in the direction from which we came. I'm left stunned and speechless.

He's wrong.

It's not hypocrisy to judge him—what he did to his parents is entirely different.

But he says he was abused…like Glory.

It doesn't matter. Let him think I'm a hypocrite for seeing the vileness within him. There is no vileness in Glory, not a touch of it. She's perfect, angelic—

She's a murderer.

It doesn't matter!

I love her, and I'll do whatever it takes to protect her, to save her…to make her feel happiness again.

Silently, I turn and follow Ambrose, knowing that I can't run from him, can't escape him with the chains around my ankles. But even more importantly, I know I can't leave Glory behind.

I won't leave her alone with a cursed man.

I won't leave her alone with *him*.

CHAPTER 15

Ambrose

I WASN'T EXACTLY surprised when Huxley told me what Beau Tolliver had tried to do to his own daughter. I wasn't surprised because I'd already seen how broken she is, the way a single word could trigger her like the flip of a switch and change her into a brutal fighter…like me.

People don't just behave like that—they do that as a product of their genetics or as the result of trauma. Maybe it's a combination of both for her. The way the light behind her eyes had died when I called her *princess*—just before she snapped—made it obvious how she's suffered in her life.

And sick as it is, knowing this only draws me to her more…it draws me to *them*. Huxley is woefully ignorant of what she is, who she is, what she's capable of…Worse, he's ignorant of himself. But I don't doubt him when he says he loves her. I just don't know whether he loves *her* or the *idea* of her.

All of it makes me curious, interested…involved.

Involvement means connection, and connection is dangerous knowing what I have to do to these two beautiful creatures trapped in my childhood cage.

I turn the lock to secure the cage door behind me once

Huxley is inside, then I toss him the key to his ankle cuffs through the bars.

"That'll unlock her cuff, too," I tell him, nodding toward Glory's chained foot.

He bends to grab the key from the floor, and like a true gentleman, he moves to unchain her before unfastening his own locks. My eyes are fixed on his dexterous fingers as he works the key—nimble fingertips, long thick digits, popped veins drawing lines across the backs of his hands.

I wonder if he's ever wrapped his palm around someone's neck while he fucked them. I wonder if he'd do that to Glory. I think he would if she asked him to. I think he'd be glad if she asked him to. He's pent-up behind the gentleman game he plays.

I should turn and walk away; I should let them fester in worry for a few hours while I figure out my next steps with them, but my feet don't move.

"Did you really kill your father?" I ask Glory.

Her eyes narrow as her head turns toward me. I catch hold of her gaze for a beat before she turns to look down at Huxley as he pulls the metal cuff from around his ankle. She opens her mouth, but he cuts her off as he pushes to his feet.

"I'm sorry," he says to her, grabbing hold of her cheeks. "I told him everything. I was angry and I lost control of myself… it all just tumbled out."

She searches his face. Though her eyes are squinted in confusion for why he would tell me their biggest secret, there's something that looks like relief sagging through her shoulders as they fall in relaxation.

It was too much of a burden for her to carry.

"Is it true, then?" I ask.

Slowly, his hands fall from her cheeks and she looks over at me. Her throat bobs as she swallows, then slowly nods. "Yes, but I didn't mean to do it."

"That's a lie." I lift my eyebrows. "No one kills somebody by accident. There's always intention. Always."

"I had to defend myself." Her voice is quiet, meek, and she turns her gaze to the floor. "I had to."

"And there's the truth of it," I reply. "You *had* to. Just like I had to kill my parents. Just like I have to kill—"

Just like I have to kill you.

"Just like you have to kill *who*?" Glory asks, boldly stepping forward and wrapping her fragile fingers around the bars in front of her chest. "What were you going to say?"

I shake my head and lift my foot, prepared to back away. Before I can take a step, her hand shoots through the bars, and her fingers graze my forearm, catching me with a sharp prick, a bolt of lightning.

Static electricity.

That's all it is, that's all I feel when she touches me. But fuck, the sting of it lights a fire that could melt the ice around my heart. That electric current is sticky, latching onto me with a tacky grip, drawing me toward her. I step forward and wrap my palms over her fingers around the bars. She gasps at my touch and tries to pull back, but I hold firmly so she can't let go.

Maybe I can't let go, either.

"What I was going to say doesn't matter to you, little bird. What matters is that you and I are the same, aren't we? You and I are both killers."

"No," she shakes her head, "I'm not like you at all, I'm—"

"You're what? Different? Special? You get a free pass to

kill daddy because you're a tiny little girl who couldn't possibly pose a threat to anyone else?" I squeeze her hands, leaning closer, and I feel her knuckles bucking against my palms. "I see you, little bird. I see all of you, and I know exactly what you are."

She's quiet as she stares at me through several beats, her head tilting ever so subtly to the side. "You see me," she whispers, as if she's testing the words, testing how they sound, whether they're infected with sickness or twisted with dishonesty.

They're not.

I *do* see her.

"What am I then?" Her question is quiet, contemplative. She's truly asking me, not biting back with sarcasm.

Something shifts behind my ribs...a flutter, perhaps something resembling a heartbeat. And here I thought mine had shriveled up and stopped beating the night I murdered my parents.

My grip loosens, and my thumbs stroke her knuckles. I expect her to pull away from the bars, but she doesn't. She holds on. She keeps her eyes on mine. She stays with me.

I shuffle closer, as close as I can get with the barrier between us. Her nostrils flare as she lets out a silent, heavy breath, her tongue darts quickly across her lips, and her body sways closer.

"What am I, Ambrose?"

One of my hands breaks free, gently slipping down her wrist and across her forearm. "Something small and fragile. Something that should be free to fly, but you can't because your wings are clipped." She shudders at my touch. I look at her soft, porcelain skin beneath my fingertips as I stroke her arm. "My little bird…"

She breathes heavily, her green gaze fixed on mine in scrutiny. I can see that she understands me. I see her, I *know* her, and she knows me, too.

Can we see each other because we've both taken lives?

Because we both had the monstrous destiny of ending the people who brought us into this world?

"We can get you money if that's what you want," Huxley says, breaking the spell between us.

I let go of her and step back.

"Now that you know what Glory did to her father, you can hold that secret in exchange for letting us go. We'll never tell a soul you kept us here because you know what she did. You know I would never risk her getting in trouble for that."

I look squarely at Glory. "Do you really want to go, little bird?"

She swallows hard, then nods, but I don't believe her.

"He's right," she murmurs. "You know my secret. If you let us go, we won't tell anyone what you did to us, because if we do, we know you'll tell our secret, too."

Huxley reaches out to grab her hand and she instantly latches on, her fingers shifting between his and locking through his grip. It happens so smoothly, so easily, as if it were rehearsed—as if it's so natural for them to touch that the simple act of reaching out for each other is like watching a painter draw a perfect, smooth brushstroke across their canvas. It's like artwork in the making.

They're fucking beautiful together and it's burning me up inside.

I shake my head, moving back. "No. Fuck, no. I would never trust you." I run my fingers through my hair.

There's a part of me that's considering it—the naïve part that still believes in miracles and hopes for goodness and freedom. The only way I'll ever be free is to complete my task for Maura, hope she stays good on her word to set me free from the crimes of my past that she holds ransom against me, and get the fuck out of this place for good.

"Please?" Every molecule freezes at the sound of Glory's kind, pleading voice.

The way the word slips from her lips, gliding across the space as a hopeful question rather than a begging demand hurts.

I should kill them now and be done with this.

I should…

I can't.

I need to get the fuck out of here.

"You're fools to think I would ever trust either of you." I turn and leave before my little bird can call me back to her again.

MAURA SLAMS THE door shut behind her as I plop down in the chair across from her desk. "I want an update."

I reach inside my coat and lift my phone from the jacket pocket, subtly checking that the audio recording app I'd downloaded earlier is on and recording.

I've made a lot of stupid decisions with Maura over the years, but it occurred to me this morning that I might need some insurance of my own when it comes to this deal with her. I never thought I'd be able to leave my home, never once thought she'd give me the opportunity to be free from doing her evil deeds. And with Glory and Huxley on the line, it makes me want to be smarter about this. If I have to end those two beautiful things, I need insurance that she's gonna let me go. If she tries to take me down for my crimes, then I'm taking her down with me.

Satisfied that I'm capturing this conversation, I slip the phone back into my pocket while Maura settles in the chair behind her desk.

"Beau is dead," I tell her flatly. "Does that make you happy?"

A sick smile twists Maura's lips and tells me that it does. "He's dead? You're sure? How did you find him?"

"You asked me to handle it. I handled it. I'm not getting into specifics."

"How can I trust that you've handled it? What evidence do you have?"

"Why would I bring you evidence? Do you want us to get caught?"

"Us?" She slowly pushes her chair back and rises to her feet. Her heels click as she moves across the floor, circling her desk and leaning her ass back against the front edge while she looks down at me. "It's your word against mine if you get caught."

My jaw tenses. "If you want the job done, then you have to make sure I don't get caught so I can finish it. I want my money, Maura, and as soon as I have it, I'll be gone before anyone can find me."

She sighs. "You know I'll miss you if you go."

"What will you miss? The look of disgust on my face when you make me fuck you?"

She smiles and tilts her head. "Oh, it's the bad attitude I'll miss the most."

"Fuck you."

Unaffected, she pushes off the desk. The fucking sociopath. "I want his skull."

"What?"

"I want Glory's skull, too."

I chuckle without humor, glancing down and shaking my head. "You're fucking with me."

"No. I want their skulls."

My foot bounces where it's crossed over my knee, and I fold my arms over my chest. "And your son's skull? I suppose you want his, too?"

Her brow furrows, looking at me as if *that's* the most ridiculous thing that's been said during this entire conversation. "No, I don't want my son's skull. I wouldn't have asked you to kill him if it could be avoided, but sometimes you have to sacrifice to get what you really want…what you really *deserve.*"

I need a fucking cigarette.

Rage pulses through my veins, causing my legs to twitch. This whole thing should be easy. The universe delivered Glory and Huxley to me on a silver goddamn platter, as if it were my destiny to do this deed for Maura. They came to me before she even asked for their deaths, but fucking hell.

Their skulls?

The vision flashes through my mind—the two of them dead on the floor, blood spilling and splashing from Glory's corpse as I saw through her perfect, porcelain neck to detach her head; a vision of peeling her face from the bone to reveal the skull beneath and cleaning it to deliver to Maura.

A ripple of nausea rolls through my stomach and I shake my head to clear the visual. I want to destroy Glory in thousands of ways, but not like that…*never* like that.

I want her eyes on me.

I want her moans to meet my ears.

I want her hands on my flesh.

I want my name falling from her lips.

And Huxley…I want his tears and his agony as I fuck him harder than he can stand. When I've finished with him, I want him begging for more.

The thought of them dead fucks with my mind. I rake a shaking hand through my unkempt hair and push to my feet, anxious to get outside and light up a cigarette to calm my nerves.

"Two skulls, then. Is there anything else you want, Maura? I'd like to get the fuck away from you now."

She crosses her arms. "How long do you think it will take?"

"It'll take as long as it takes."

"I want it done by the end of the week or the deal is off."

"The deal's not *fucking* off. Beau is already dead. I'm a third of the way done and you're not backing out now."

She holds up a single finger from her crossed forearms. "One week, Ambrose. Find them, kill them, and bring me Beau and Glory's skulls. Otherwise, you can kiss your freedom goodbye."

CHAPTER 16
Glory

THE WOODEN CHAIR screeches across the hardwood floor as Ambrose drags it into our room. His presence is particularly dark at this moment. His presence is always dark, but before I could see a pinprick of light behind his eyes when he'd come close, when he'd touch me. I don't see any hint that the light is still there now, and it washes me in anxiety, rippling in waves beneath my skin.

He grips an axe in one hand, the handle seeming to pull him down as if a great weight were attached to the end of it. He stops and places the chair a couple of feet in front of the bars. He lifts a hand to rake through his wavy locks before lowering gently into the seat, his legs spread wide.

My throat feels dry, yet an odd sweat breaks out on my palms as I watch something I can only describe as despair push his shoulders down. He bends forward, resting his elbows on his knees and places both hands on the end of the axe handle, the heavy blade seated on the floor between his black boots.

There's a vague, twisted urge inside me that makes me wish I was sitting at his feet, close enough to touch the black leather of his boots, close enough to wrap my arms around his leg and rest my cheek against his thigh.

I suck in a shuddering breath at the thought of it, at the wicked vision of granting submission to my captor.

From the floor, I rise to my knees and grip the bars in front of me as Huxley shoves to his feet and stands wide, his feet planted shoulder-width apart and his fists clenched at his sides.

Ambrose takes in a deep breath and blows it out slowly. I'm rapt with attention, my ears straining to hear whatever he's about to say.

"When you showed up," he begins, "I had no idea who you were. I should've known. I should've recognized your face." He looks at me from beneath his eyelashes. "I didn't recognize it until Maura Tolliver called me into her office and asked me to do her a favor."

A strong breeze could blow me over.

He knows my stepmother?

He lifts his head and looks at Huxley, whose knuckles have gone white from the tension in his fists. "I deliver chopped wood once a week to the Tolliver's Treats' factory. It used to be my father's job, but I took over after I killed him to keep away any suspicion from his sudden disappearance. I've known Maura since I started making deliveries and sometimes, she asks me to do some…unsavory tasks for her. I'm not exactly proud of it." He pauses, looking down at his hands gripping the axe handle, but my gaze rises and fixates on Huxley at my side. "I've hurt people for your mother, Huxley. I've killed for her. The first time I did it, it was stupid. *I* was stupid. I was barely an adult when I let her hook me with the promise of sex in exchange for ending her stalker's life. I killed him for her because she had me convinced that she needed me to do it to keep her safe. I didn't know then what I know now. Your mother is a wonderful actress."

"What do you mean?" Huxley asks through gritted teeth.

"Your mother is soulless, heartless. That stalker she had me kill…He wasn't stalking her. He was an ex-lover who cheated once, and she simply wanted revenge. And because I was too dumb to see it, killing him cost me my life, my freedom. Because she knows what I did, and she holds me hostage for keeping that secret, for keeping all the other secrets that followed. But I've been given an opportunity. She's offered me my freedom in exchange for something… particularly gruesome."

A sick feeling of fear washes over me and goosebumps break out across my forearms when I look at Ambrose.

Ambrose meets my eyes. "Maura's not particularly fond of you. Or your father, as it turns out."

"Is she the reason why you wanted to know what happened to my father?" I ask. "Did she ask you to find out? Does…does she know what I did to him?"

"Nobody knows what you did to him except for the people in this room. Nobody knows what he did to you, either."

I turn my head, unable to look at him with the mention of what my father did to me.

"What's your point, then?" Huxley's agitation scrapes his voice with a harsh tone.

Ambrose chuckles darkly, tilting his head toward the floor before lifting it again, looking at Huxley through the wavy pieces of dark hair that fall in front of his dark eyes. "Your mom is a cunt. She's the reason we all need to have a very serious discussion right now."

"Right," Huxley scoffs, "as if a discussion during our captivity could be anything but serious."

"You two and Beau Tolliver were reported missing the day after you stumbled upon my home. Evidence at the scene pointed to foul play, and they found both of your vehicles at his house. When I made my delivery, Maura called me into her office to share her tragic news, though if you expect she was upset about it, then you're fucking wrong, because what she asked me to do next—"

"What? What the fuck did she ask you to do?" Huxley jerks forward, his palms opening, then quickly closing around the metal bars.

Ambrose pushes to his feet and the axe handle falls, crashing to the floor with a clatter. He paces away, shoving his hands inside the pockets of his black hoodie. He halts, turns to face us, and with a narrowing of his eyes that somehow looks remorseful, he lets his words tumble out. "She told me to make sure that the three of you were never found again."

"What?" I gasp at the same time that Huxley says, "You're a fucking liar."

"I'm not lying, Huxley."

Ambrose pulls a cell phone from his back pocket, the first time I've seen him with a phone since we stumbled onto his property. He taps the screen a few times and soon we hear recorded voices, and they belong to Ambrose and Maura.

She's talking about wanting our skulls.

Our skulls?

She wants me dead.

She wanted my father dead, too.

And she wants our skulls as a trophy.

But when she mentions Huxley, the ashes of my heart scatter, fluttering nausea through my stomach. My hands cover my mouth in disbelief at the realization that she wants Huxley dead, too.

She wants her own son dead.

The recording ends and silence surrounds us, wrapping around the room and closing us inside this shitstorm of a situation.

Then, moments later, Huxley breaks the silence, his voice venomous with contempt. "What's the axe for?"

My head snaps to look up at him and I stare, blinking.

It's only when Huxley asks the question that I know…I know what the axe is for. Ambrose is going to kill us. He's going to kill us because Maura demanded that he do it.

But why did she demand it?

Of course, I know the answer, and the realization of it strikes me hard in the gut. It's about the Tolliver fortune. It was always about the money for her; it was why she married my father to begin with. The fact that we went missing was simply a convenient opportunity to put out a hit on us.

Did she know we'd gotten lost in the forest?

She couldn't have known where we were or why we were there. And we'd only happened to stumble upon Ambrose's home seeking a way out of Sugar Wood. It was a coincidence that we'd found him, that he'd found us.

A coincidence brought us together.

Or was it fated?

Huxley's voice is softer when he repeats the question again, "What's the fucking axe for?"

Ambrose tilts his head to either side, stretching his

neck. He pulls a key from his pocket and bends to pick up the axe with his other hand, moving toward the cage door.

He turns the key in the lock. "I'll make it quick, painless."

As it clicks, so does my understanding.

The axe is to carry out the deed…to kill us both.

"No. *No*," I mutter, backing away and pressing my back to the far corner as Ambrose pulls the cage door open.

"No fucking way. I won't fucking let you touch her!" Huxley shouts and lunges for him.

Ambrose tosses the axe from his right hand to his left, then reaches out to snatch Huxley by the throat. It takes him off-guard as Huxley collides with Ambrose, who roughly tosses him away, causing him to slam shoulder-first against one of the metal cage bars, letting out a pained grunt as he hits.

Ambrose snatches me by the wrist and tugs me toward him, spinning us both and shoving me outside the cage before Huxley can reach for me. I stumble over my toe as it catches on a dent in the hardwood floor, but then Ambrose is ripped away from my back.

I right myself and whirl around to see Huxley attack him, landing a heavy punch to the side of his stomach, forcing him to double over with a groan. Ambrose brings his elbow back, hitting Huxley in the sternum and knocking the wind out of him.

As Huxley stumbles back, Ambrose rushes forward, fleeing from the cage.

I step backward.

I should turn.

I should run.

I should…but I don't.

I feel rooted to the spot—the same twisted energy that

makes me want him keeps me tethered to him. He's going to kill me, then he's going to kill Huxley, and somehow, I can't run.

What is wrong *with me?*

Ambrose slams the cage door shut and twists the key in the lock before Huxley can recover and escape. Then Ambrose turns, shifting as if he's ready to take off after me, but he freezes when he finds that I'm still standing there in the doorway, unmoving.

I stare ahead blankly, not even looking at Ambrose, just rooted inexplicably to the spot. I hear myself say, "No more," though my voice feels disconnected from my body. I can feel the dissociation happen. I try to fight it, but my mind is trying to protect itself from whatever Ambrose is about to do to me. "No more."

"Glory, run!" Huxley shouts.

"Please, no more of this." The words slip from my lips, but I feel like I'm saying it to no one.

My eyes are losing focus, though I fight. I fight losing myself in a moment where I need to be present, aware, fighting for my life.

I hear Ambrose drop the axe as it clatters against the hard floor. I sense him moving toward me, and I feel his callused palms against my cheeks. I don't flinch at his touch; I don't react to the energy he brings into my space—energy that's filled with pain and passion.

But as moments pass, I feel that energy pulse, seeping through my core, sparking like an electric current that shocks me back to life. My focus shifts from a distant point in space, gradually turning to meet Ambrose's dark eyes. My lips part to take in a gasping breath as our eyes connect.

I blink and my brow wrinkles in confusion. I gaze at him in awe because he brought me back. I came back to awareness for him...*because* of him.

"Ambrose," I whisper, my voice weak. "Don't do this to us."

"I have to. Maura has power, she'll—"

"Take me!" Huxley shouts, which startles us both.

Ambrose whips his head around to look at Huxley in the cage, gripping the bars with white knuckles, fierce determination on his face.

"Take me," he says again. "Take my fucking skull and let Glory go. Let her run or...or take her with you when you leave with your money. Maura will never know. Glory can show you where Beau is buried, and you can dig him up, take his skull. Give her mine and his, and let Glory go free. I swear to you, she won't fucking tell anyone. Glory kept the secret about her father for years. She can keep this secret, too. Can't you, Glory?"

I feel a single tear slip down my cheek. "Huxley—"

"Can't you, Glory?" Huxley repeats, his voice pleading, trembling.

No, I can't. I can't live without Huxley.

Beats pass in stagnant silence.

Ambrose lifts his hand and drags it down the side of my head, petting me, stroking me as if he's telling me everything will be okay. But nothing will be okay if Huxley dies, and I have to continue living without him.

I'd rather die than live without him.

"Please," Huxley begs. "She'll never know. You have to save Glory, Ambrose, you *have* to."

Ambrose's hand slips down my arm and latches around my wrist. He tugs me beside him as he pulls the key from his pocket, standing in front of the cage door.

"No," I protest, too stunned to fight.

"I'll do it. I'll take her with me," Ambrose says. "I'll take care of her."

"No!" I pull back on my arm, trying to wrench it from his grip, but he holds steady as he turns the lock and opens the cage door.

Huxley reaches for me as Ambrose drags me in front of him. I grab hold of a bar on my left, twisting my body, trying to grip it with both hands to avoid being put back in this cage. If I go back in this cage, Huxley will die.

"Stop!" I manage to hold the bar in my hands.

Huxley's arms wrap around my waist and pull me back. "Let go. Glory, stop."

Huxley pulls as Ambrose wraps his palms over my hands and pries my fingers free. I try to latch on again, but he works quickly, and when my hands fall away from the bars, Huxley drags me backward. He turns me and shoves me toward the back of the cage, causing me to stumble. I tilt forward but catch myself with my palms against the back wall. But as I spin to run after him, the cage door slams in my face.

The lock clicks.

I look at Huxley and Ambrose standing side-by-side, huffing as they watch me through the barrier.

Huxley should fight him. He should try to run, but he doesn't. He only looks at me with that expression of fierce determination.

My great savior coming to my rescue one last time.

And this time will be the last time because it's going to cost him his life.

CHAPTER 17

I START TO speak, to tell Glory that I love her, but I don't get a single word out before Ambrose has his hands on me. He grips my shirt at the center of my chest and twists, bunching the fabric in his grip before spinning me and shoving me backward into the hallway. He slams my back against the wall across from the cage room door, and I let out an *oomph* as air rushes from my lungs.

"Grab your axe," I snarl at him. "End this now."

"Fight me."

"What?"

"Fight me, Huxley. Fight for your life. Are you just giving up?"

"I'm not giving up. I'm giving in. I'm done with this bullshit. You were going to kill us both, anyway. At least this way, her life will be spared."

"I'm taking her with me when you're dead. When I have the money and my freedom from Maura, I'm taking Glory with me and I'm keeping her. I won't ever let her be free from me."

I have nothing to say in response to that. I have no control over what happens to her once I'm dead. I only have control over what happens right now, and right now I see him troubled and weak for her.

I knew if I could give him a solution that let him spare her life, he would spare it. At least, that's what I'm telling myself. We all see the sick chemistry that exists between them. If I can't stop him from finishing this deal with my mother, then at least I could save Glory's life by sacrificing myself. And it would serve my mother right if Ambrose brought her my skull. Maybe my soul will linger with it, and I can haunt her beyond the grave.

Nausea rolls through my gut at the thought of my mother ordering my death. I wouldn't have believed it if I hadn't heard it myself. Though I suppose it is believable—she was a cold and distant mother. She took care of my physical needs, but that was more for her own benefit. She liked to keep up appearances. But this…To want me dead so she can bypass our names in line for the family fortune…

It's disgusting.

It's vile.

And I can feel my soul splinter at the knowledge.

"Then keep her," I finally respond. "But don't kill her. Promise me you won't kill her. Let Glory live."

His head jerks back and his eyes soften. "Are you giving up this easily? *Fight me.*"

I pause, swallowing a dry lump in my throat. His grip on my shirt loosens and slips upward, latching around my neck instead.

Fuck.

"I don't see any other way."

"I could kill her," he says, dropping his voice. "I could kill her, take her and Beau's skulls to your mother, and take you with me instead." He comes closer, his cheek brushing mine as he moves in to whisper, "I could save *you* instead."

Those words crash into me and my strength spills like a waterfall, my body relaxing into his. I'm the one who saves, not the one who is saved. No one has ever been my savior, and here he is, offering to be just that. And I'm falling for it, hook, line, and sinker. He's toying with me and fucking with my feelings. He wouldn't save me over her, and I would *never* allow that to happen, anyway.

I will *always* be Glory's savior.

I put my hands against his chest and shove, causing him to release me in surprise and take a step back. "I don't need you to save me. Grab your fucking axe."

I turn and march for the front door so he'll be forced to follow.

"Fuck," he mutters behind me.

Then, I hear Glory scream, "No!" and I turn my head over my shoulder to look.

That's when I see him coming after me with his axe in one hand, a sneer on his handsome face, and dark determination in his narrowed eyes. The sight of Ambrose marching toward me, with his large hand wrapped around the handle and the axe dangling at his side, sparks outright fear.

What the fuck am I doing?

Why didn't I fight him?

The instinctive urge to save myself finally washes over me—I can't for the life of me figure out where the fuck it went when he had me up against the wall. I'm being stupid, so goddamn stupid with this opportunity where I'm out of the cage without shackles, and I need to fight for my life.

He stomps toward me as I turn to face him, and I let anger take hold of me. I run at full speed and when our bodies collide, I wrap my hand around his wrist. He lifts his arm, holding the axe, my grip squeezing his wrist. But strangely, there's no conviction in his movement, no strength as he tries to bring the axe up to swing at me…

It's almost as if he doesn't really want to.

I take a chance and let go of that arm, opting to throw a punch to his gut instead. He groans and stumbles back a step, the axe falling from his hand. It slams to the floor, barely missing my foot, but I ignore it.

I charge after him, bending, slamming my shoulder into his stomach, and shoving him backward at a run. His feet lift from the floor and he falls onto his back, causing me to tumble forward with him.

His hands clench into fists and swing at me as I fall on top of him. One connects painfully with the side of my face. The force of it knocks me hard and I fall sideways to the floor.

He rushes to flip over me as I blink against blackness that fades in around the edges of my eyes. His hips settle on mine, his knees squeeze in beside my waist, and his palms slam against the hardwood floor on either side of my head. My body goes still as I recover from that single, dizzying hit. Expecting another, my hands come up to protect my face, but another hit never comes.

The fury of fighting ebbs as moments of breathing pass. The black edges in my vision disappear and I come back to clarity…and all I can see is Ambrose above me.

His chest heaves and his elbows stay locked as he holds himself over me, as if he's struggling to keep himself there. His dark hair falls in pieces to frame his eyes and I'm locked in on them as rage turns…

It slowly turns.

It devolves.

And in comes the desperation.

His head dips, as if he's going to bend and kiss me, and I want him to.

I want him to kiss me.

I want him.

After a moment of hesitation, his lips land on mine with bruising force, and I eagerly part them. This fury, this fight, this twisted thing between us exists to supercharge our desire, and that's exactly what it does. It changes me, makes me stupid, makes me want to get fucked by a man who was going to kill me only moments ago.

Was he really going to kill me?

As strong and powerful as he is with his lean, chiseled muscle, the way he tried to raise the axe to swing at me was weak—pathetic, really—uncommitted. And there's nothing in this fevered kiss that tells me he wants me dead.

Captivity must have made me delusional. I know this, but it doesn't change the lust. It doesn't make me want him less. I'm already growing hard pinned beneath his strong body as his tongue fights mine for control.

I groan, lifting my hands to grip the sides of his face, to pull him down harder, to encourage him to sink fully into this depravity with me. And he almost does.

Too quickly, he snaps back, our mouths parting with a smack as he rears back, huffs out a heavy breath, then leaps to his feet. I sit up, prepared to fight for my life again, but he doesn't reach for the axe, he doesn't reach for me. He runs a trembling hand through his thick hair as he looks down at me, then shoves that same hand into his pocket.

He pulls out a key and tosses it to the floor beside me, the small piece of metal landing with a *clang*. "Go," he says softly. "Take her and go. Get the fuck out of this place before we all hurt each other. I won't hurt you anymore. I can't. This is killing me."

He spins away as I watch him with wide eyes, stunned from the turn of events. His hands dig into his hair, gripping and tugging as he paces, his agitation palpable.

Grab the key.

Free Glory.

Run.

The instructions rip through my mind, demanding me to act and act *now*. But my body hesitates to catch up, still watching him, still wanting him, still humming with need for him.

"*Go.* Get the fuck away from me, from this forest, this curse, this infection. This place is hell, and neither of you belong here."

With great reluctance that I don't quite understand, I reach for the key that landed beside my waist, push to my feet, and run back to the cage room to free Glory from this waking nightmare once and for all.

CHAPTER 18
Glory

I'M FRANTIC, LOSING my mind in a way I can hardly describe. I'm used to withdrawing, disconnecting from reality when bad things are happening around me, but this hysterical state that's washed over me is painful and overwhelming. Tears spill like waterfalls down my cheeks as I scream and cry, shouting for Huxley, screaming for his life.

Everything inside me hurts while everything around me swirls in chaos.

If he dies, I think I'll die, too.

I need him.

I've always needed him, and I always will.

I can't imagine a world without him.

When I hear quick footsteps pound across the floor, rushing toward me, I expect to see Ambrose appear in the doorway. My face drops in anger as a rage-filled roar bubbles in my chest, preparing to burst at the first sight of him.

But it's not Ambrose in the doorway, it's Huxley, and he's coming toward the cage at a full speed run. He has a key—the key to the cage—and his hands twitch as he fumbles to insert it in the lock.

"Huxley?" My rage turns off like the flip of a switch and

instantly becomes confusion.

"He told us to go. We have to run."

I release my death grip on the bars as he unlocks the door and it swings open, my eyes wide in shock from the turn of events. He grabs my wrist and pulls, turning to run back out the doorway, but I need him. I thought he was going to die, and I have a second chance with him in front of me right now.

I yank my arm back, stopping him, and when he turns back to face me, I reach up, grab hold of his face, and pull him against me. I kiss him harder than I've ever kissed anyone before. He starts to pull away, but he quickly lets up, grabbing hold of my wrists by his cheeks and kisses me back.

Only moments later, he drags his lips away and drops his forehead to mine. "We have to go. We have to run, okay? He's letting us go, and I don't know how long it will take for him to change his mind."

"He let you go?"

Huxley nods.

"He's letting both of us go?" Confusion washes over me. "I thought you were dead. I thought he was going to kill you. I thought I'd never see you again."

A flutter low in my stomach begs me to put my lips on his again, and so I do. I kiss him because I *need* to, because moments ago, I'd heard him fight for his life and I was already mourning the loss of him. I have to be close to him, I have to touch him.

I'm not feeling fearful of Ambrose, or an urgent need to flee…I just need Huxley. I arch my back and curve against him as I deepen our kiss. He sways backward and I sway with him until his back collides with the wall behind him.

He's hard against my stomach, and I'm surprised by it because he was just fighting for his life, but I don't care. I want him hard. I want him to need me as much as I need him—and I need him desperately. I need him within me, I need him all around me, everywhere.

His grip on my wrists tightens and he pulls my arms down with such force that it makes me gasp and breaks our kiss. His eyes sear into my soul as he stares down at me, his chest puffing with heavy breaths as his face strains. Several times, he looks as though he's about to speak, but words don't come out, only lust and need and fever.

When he finally speaks, it's a strained whisper. "We have to go. Now." His words express urgency to run, though his hips shift against mine.

I should be running. I should be taking his hand and dragging him along with me, bolting for the front door, running out into the forest if that's the only way to go.

Instead, my feet are rooted to the spot, my body molded to his, my lips swollen and aching to be kissed again.

"Let go of me," Huxley pleads. "Please, let go of me. We have to leave. We won't get another chance."

He's begging me to move, to lead, as if my touch holds him here more strongly than the threat of death urges us to leave.

"Glory, move." His voice shakes. "Move. Please, just fucking move."

"I don't know how to leave."

What am I saying?

All I've wanted was to be out of that horrid cage, to flee this place of insanity and try to find some fucked up version of normal with Huxley. Now that the opportunity is laid out in front of me, I can't seem to take it.

I don't know why.

I don't know how.

But the thought of leaving now—of leaving Ambrose behind—makes me feel sick.

"Huxley…" I say his name, begging for what, I don't know.

A crashing sound from the living room shakes us both and we jolt in surprise. Huxley blinks at me and shakes his head, somehow snapping out of whatever held him here with me.

But I don't feel it. I don't feel a snap, and I'm still here, still in front of him, needing him to stay here with me.

He sucks in a breath, then turns with my wrist still firmly in his grip and runs. In the blink of an eye, he's bolting down the hallway, towing me behind him, rushing me forward so quickly that I would stumble and fall if he loosened his grip even a fraction.

He drags me into the living space, across the divide between the living room and the kitchen, heading swiftly for the front door.

No.

I can't leave.

We can't leave.

I see Ambrose in the kitchen, his arms braced against the counter's edge and his head bowed above the sink. Broken dishes are scattered across the floor. He's not watching us, not chasing us, not trying to stop us. He's really letting us go. He really *wants* us to go.

No. I refuse to believe it.

I stop abruptly; so suddenly that it takes Huxley by surprise, and he lets go of me. I step back, then turn and creep forward an inch toward Ambrose.

"Are you really letting us go?" I ask with a tilt of my head.

"We're not waiting for him to answer that," Huxley says, grabbing my shoulders from behind and tugging.

I shrug him off, taking another step. "Ambrose?"

"Leave," he says through gritted teeth. "Leave before I change my mind."

This is when I feel it, when the knowing of something true—hated, though the truth is—washes over me. It rinses away logic and self-doubt until all that remains is desire and instinct.

I.

Can't.

Leave.

I don't know why, but I know I can't leave Ambrose. I feel for him, as much as I feel for Huxley, though in an entirely different way. I feel inexplicably connected to him, as if dead hearts belong together, as if the universe dragged us all here to this house in the middle of a winding forest.

I want my words to come out strong, with conviction, but as usual, they don't. "Change your mind."

His head snaps toward us as Huxley grips me by the elbow and tugs me back. I plant my feet and pull away with all my might, ripping my arm from his hold.

"Glory!" Huxley is shaking, but not with rage...with anxiety. I hate that I'm causing that anxiety, but I have to do this.

I'm so fucking stupid, but I have to do this.

I take a step in Ambrose's direction and clear my throat. He drops one hand from the counter and looks over at me, his dark eyebrows drawing a straight line across his forehead, eyes narrowed on me with confusion.

He takes a step forward and his movement startles me, the intensity of his energy so overwhelming that it makes me take a small step back.

"Go, little bird." His voice is thick and smooth. "Fly free. Leave and don't come back."

"Do you want me to leave? Do you want *us* to leave?"

His eyes lift, darting to glance at Huxley behind me. "What the fuck are you waiting for? Get her the fuck out of here."

Huxley grabs my biceps from behind and jerks me back, spinning me and shoving me toward the door. He walks me toward it, but I put up my hands, slap my palms against the wood, and push back.

"No!" I shout. "I'm not leaving. Not until he tells me that's what he really wants."

"He told us to *go*. Why isn't that enough for you?" Huxley raises his voice as I manage to whirl around to face him, my back leaning against the door as he crowds me against it.

"He told us to go, but it's not what he *wants*. He doesn't want to hurt us. He could've killed us, but he didn't."

"He held us hostage, Glory! What the fuck is wrong with you?"

I feel him before I realize he's coming, his aura pushing against us as he charges up to our side. "Go! Leave!" Ambrose grabs me and drags me away from Huxley so harshly that I stumble toward him. He catches me against his strong chest as he wrenches the door open with one hand.

"No!"

Huxley grips my arm once again, trying to wrench me from Ambrose's hold, drawing me into a tug-of-war between two men whose presence makes my body hum.

They both want me.

They both want me to leave.

But if I leave, this is over…this sick, festering infection will heal and the twisted perfection in my gut will stop.

It can't stop.

I can't let it.

I'm between them as they both push me toward the doorway. Beyond it, snow falls with slow, gentle flakes softly drifting to the ground. But I won't go. I refuse to go. And I can't think of any other way to stop them from pushing me than to take them both by surprise.

For one brief moment, I stop fighting. I let them push me, and their bodies come together, hips bumping as I stumble a step backward onto the landing. A spark ignites the moment they touch, an undeniable flash between them that could start a wildfire—and I know Huxley doesn't want to go, either. It's why he hesitated when I kissed him.

When they look at each other, I let go. I allow pure instinct to take over, knowing that in this house, my instinct drives me to sexual madness.

Anyone else may think this is crazy, but I know it's not. Crazy is the dissociation, the red filter that washed over me and disconnected my mind from the moments I became violent and murdered my father.

This—this fire, this heat, this sick and twisted thing between the three of us—is something I want. I leap forward, toss my arms around Ambrose's neck, and kiss him. Our lips touch and the soft warmth of his against mine is the catalyst to change everything we know.

I expect Huxley to pull me away, to push Ambrose back.

I expect to be shoved through the doorway again, to feel the frigid winter air on my cheeks and my breath stolen from me as I'm forced away from the only place I've ever really felt free.

"What's wrong, little bird? Does being locked in a cage frighten you? Or does it set you free? Does it give you permission to do things you've always wanted to do but never let yourself?"

Those words Ambrose spoke to me once before ring so true now, as if he knew me then…I think he must know me now.

I feel the air leave him as it rushes from his nostrils, heating my cheeks and spreading warmth down my body. Tension breaks away from him with a snap as his hands come up to grip my cheeks and pull me closer.

"Glory, stop," Huxley admonishes, though his voice is airy and lacks conviction.

Ambrose breaks away from me, still cradling my cheek in one hand while the other reaches out and grips Huxley by the shirt at the center of his chest. He jerks him against our sides and shuts him up with a kiss.

I gasp, shocked by the sight of it. My head jerks back in surprise, but Ambrose's large hand slips from my cheek, his fingers sliding into my hair, wrapping around the back of my head to hold me in place. Huxley's response shocks me because he doesn't fight…he gives in.

He gives in like I gave in because maybe he knows what I know. We were meant to find Ambrose and devolve together to the dark magic of the lust he conjures.

CHAPTER 19
Glory

THEIR KISS DEEPENS, twisting into hungry mouths and lashing tongues that battle the other for power. I hold my breath as I watch, held in place by Ambrose's firm hand at the base of my skull.

He could let go and I wouldn't move. Watching them devour each other has me rooted, as if their desire casts a spell on me to remain in place and witness their madness as my own coils through my stomach and sinks deep within me.

Huxley looks at peace, so unguarded, though the tension and rage that held him before still pulls tightly at his features. He looks needy, like I feel, and my belly clenches around the desperation within me.

As if he senses it, Ambrose breaks away from Huxley and looks down at me, his eyes casting deep shadows as they burrow into my soul. There are a thousand things I want to say right now.

I want to beg him to let us stay.

I want to beg Huxley not to make me go.

I want to plead with them both to share me, to want me, to love me…to make me come.

"I want you," he breathes the words. "Both of you. But

this isn't real. It's nothing. It's this godforsaken place that makes us feel this way."

With a snap, he releases his hold on both of us and steps back, turning and pacing away with his fingers raking through his black hair.

"I don't think it's the place," I call out, following him. "I think it's you. *You* make us feel this way."

Ambrose whips around to face me, tossing his hands to his sides. "And so what if it is? This can't become anything. You can't stay. You have to *leave.* Don't let me hurt you."

"You've had the chance to hurt me…to hurt both of us." I point behind me at Huxley. "You were going to *kill* him, but you stopped. You didn't do it. Instead, you gave him the key and told us to run. If you really wanted him dead, he'd be dead right now. And I heard you speak to him in the hallway before you decided to let us go. You warned him you would take me with you, that you'd never let me be free."

"And I *won't* let you be free, Glory. I can't. Not unless you leave right now. Get the fuck out before I come to my senses."

I lift my chin and straighten my spine. "If coming to your senses means you'll have me, if it means you'll have *us,* then—"

"Us?" He points over my shoulder. "He wants *nothing* to do with me. Don't you dare speak on his behalf."

Huxley moves to stand beside me, his body turned to face mine. "What are you trying to do here?"

I turn to face him and grab hold of his cheeks, bringing my lips close to his. "For once in my life," I whisper, feeling his body sway toward mine, "I'm trying to speak up for myself.

For once in my life, I know what I want, what I need, what will make me happy." My hips move freely without conscious thought, drifting toward his until our bodies touch. "I'm being stupid and greedy and selfish, possibly risking my life for a moment's satisfaction." My lips brush his and he sucks in a breath, his eyes hooding as he falls deeply into a spell I didn't know I was casting. "I want you. I want him. I want the odd, dark, intense feeling I have when you're both in the room with me."

A firm hand closes around my wrist, jerking me away from Huxley, swinging me around, and shoving me down onto a chair at the kitchen table. As soon as my ass hits the seat, Ambrose bends over me, his hands pressing down on my thighs as he comes in close.

"You're playing a dangerous game here, little bird. You're right that you're being stupid and selfish. As for risking your life…?" He pauses, gazing deeply into my eyes. "I don't want you dead. I never wanted you dead. Either of you. I…" He pushes off my legs, turning and pacing away. "I'm supposed to kill you both, but I can't. I *can't*, and I *won't*." Silence falls on us for a few tense moments. But then it breaks with a barely audible whisper from Ambrose, "My parents—" He turns to look at me, his eyes shifting from hopeless darkness to hopeful thought.

"Your parents?" I ask.

"If Maura wants two skulls, I have them." He turns his head toward Huxley. "My parents. We can dig them up. I can take her their skulls and say they belong to Glory and Beau. How would she ever know?"

I feel sudden and immense relief at this brilliant idea, knowing it effectively takes away any further risk to mine or

Huxley's life. It makes it safe for me to make this choice to stay, to ask Huxley to stay, for us both to find passion belonging to a warlock of desire.

"You would do that for us?" Huxley asks softly with an inclined head.

They stare quietly in anticipatory silence. Thousands of unspoken words drift between them, and I wait, watching them both, wondering what's being said.

"Only if you promise to stay with me."

Huxley audibly exhales and frustration comes out with it. "Well, we'd have to, wouldn't we? Where the fuck else would we go?" He throws up his hands, then lets his palms smack down against his sides as he turns and paces. "If Maura thinks we're dead, we'd have to hide. We'd have to go somewhere she'd never find us."

"And I could take you both away from here. I could hide you both, we could—"

"What?" Huxley interrupts. "We could what?"

"We could be free together," Ambrose says, and the words strike me hard in the chest. He slowly moves toward Huxley. "I'll give her my parents' skulls, and she'll assume you're dead. She'll probably ask me to plant evidence somewhere so your deaths will be assumed, and once your death certificates are signed, she'll get her fortune. She'll give me the money she promised and set me free, and *you* can be free with me." He stops in front of Huxley, barely a few inches away, and they watch each other with intense eyes and heavy breaths. Ambrose's voice turns painfully hopeful. "We could leave this life behind and find peace somewhere else…together."

I pinch my eyes shut, suddenly gripped with tension,

afraid to look at either of them. I'm afraid that if I watch this moment of indecision between them that the outcome will turn unfavorably—as if my watching eyes might curse any possibility of a future here.

I never imagined something so twisted and toxic could become my future, but I want it. I want every ounce of their poisonous passion.

It feels like years pass as I wait behind my closed eyes. But then, two gentle palms land on my knees and before I even open my eyes, I know they belong to Huxley. He's always so gentle with me, so concerned for how he makes me feel.

"Is this what you want?" he asks.

I start to say yes without hesitation, but he speaks again before I can.

"You want us to give up our lives, fake our deaths, and be with the man who held us captive?" He lowers to kneel in front of me. "Don't you dare say yes if you aren't sure, Glory, because there is no changing your mind in this. If we stay, then life as we know it is done. If we stay, we can never go back. If we stay…" he pauses, looks down, then back up at me, "I'm making you mine. I'll take you and ruin everything we were before. With him, I'll lose my mind. I'll let go and you'll see parts of me you didn't know existed. It will ruin what we are."

I swallow. "But what will we become?"

"Poison."

Air rushes out of me as his hands slip up my thighs, creeping over my hips, and beneath the hem of my shirt. I gasp and shift in my seat as his skin touches mine.

"We'll be ruined for anyone else because no one will be able to survive our poison. Only us. You and me…and Ambrose."

Fear mixes with sharp desire and it sends a shiver of adrenaline down my arms. I've never seen this darkest shade of brown in Huxley's eyes, never heard him speak this way. Huxley's hands slide, running up my sides, then back down again. He grips the hem of my shirt, ready to peel it up and take it off.

"Now tell me…" he waits, his chest heaving, "is this really what you want?"

"Yes."

God, yes.

He lifts my shirt and takes it off over my head in one swift motion, and then I bend, grabbing his cheeks, kissing him roughly. He knocks my hands away and grabs my face with his instead, rising on his knees to meet me as we get lost in this wicked need.

"Come with me," Ambrose says and it steals attention from both of us, breaking our kiss, and tugging our gazes along with his movement. He does nothing else, says nothing else… he simply strides past and moves into the hallway, quickly disappearing into the bedroom at the end of the hall.

Huxley shoves to his feet, as if possessed by Ambrose's command. He bends over me, grabbing my wrists and pulling them around his neck before letting go to slip his hands beneath my ass.

"Hold onto me," he says.

I grip his neck, hugging him close as he lifts me from the chair with ease, encouraging me to fold around him entirely—my arms around his neck, my legs around his waist, my soul around his heart.

"Hux," I whimper, and he kisses me again as he moves.

Is this really happening?

He carries me down the hallway, past the room where we've been caged for so long, just wanting to be free. I can't believe how free I feel right now going to the bedroom of the man who held us hostage. The sickness of it all twists inside my stomach, clenching through my belly, and sending a dark rush through my veins. The pleasure of it is painful. It's poison running through me—just like Huxley said—and I'll never be the same after this.

I don't want to be the same after this.

I'm lost to the slip of Huxley's tongue across mine, the eager yet controlled way he tastes me. It's restrained and unhinged all at once, and it makes me sink in his hold, my body growing heavy with desire. Then suddenly, my back touches the mattress and my eyes pop open.

Ambrose.

Where is he?

As if he can hear my silent question, he appears above me, reaching for my wrists and stretching my arms above my head to rest on the mattress. My eyes flutter shut again at his touch. There's something about them both being here together—equally involved in this depravity—that helps me relax, helps me sink into it and open myself to them.

Huxley covers me, kissing me deeply while his hands find my stomach and creep higher. My fingers flex and stretch above my head, grasping for something to hold on to. I feel relief wash through me as Ambrose takes hold of my hands, gripping them tightly in his palms as I feel his energy shift toward Huxley.

"Stop kissing her and look at me."

Defiantly, Huxley deepens the kiss, and *God,* I love that. I love the way he falls into me, the way he completely devours me with his open lips and urgent tongue.

Ambrose releases one of my hands and then Huxley is jerked away. My eyes snap open to see Ambrose's hand in Huxley's hair, gripping the golden blond strands to lift him away from me. I watch from beneath them as Ambrose bends close, his nose nearly touching Huxley's.

"Have you ever been fucked by a man before?" Ambrose asks.

"Yes," Huxley replies.

Oh, my God.

"Good," Ambrose breathes. "Because I want to fuck you both."

I gasp as Ambrose removes the distance between their lips and kisses him roughly. Huxley responds with equal roughness, kissing him back as desperately as he kissed me.

Shouldn't that make me jealous?

It only makes me want them more.

My hips move and my pussy grinds against Huxley's cock, which is quickly hardening through his jeans. He groans as Ambrose tastes him.

I want to taste them both.

Ambrose pulls back from the kiss to whisper against his mouth, "I want to watch you drive her to insanity. I want her writhing in madness and begging for release. I want you to come inside her while I come inside you."

I watch Huxley's face as Ambrose speaks, and the way his expression morphs—so lost to his lust—is honestly the most beautiful thing I've ever seen. His face is tense, yet relaxed, as if Ambrose's words, his commands, provide him some relief. I'm sure it's a relief because Huxley always takes the lead. It's a burden I can't lift from his shoulders, but Ambrose can… and he does.

"Strip her," Ambrose says, his hand releasing Huxley's hair to come down and grip my palm again.

Then Huxley's hands are at the button of my jeans. He strips me bare all at once, taking my underwear down with my pants as he tugs them past my hips and peels them down my legs.

Once they're off, I hesitate, snapping my thighs together, suddenly aware of how exposed and vulnerable I am. Instinctively, I tug my arms, but they hardly budge with Ambrose holding my hands.

How I love the feel of his palms on mine, but being held down so rigidly as he presses my arms into the mattress is nearly triggering. Darkness tugs at my mind, trying to pull it away from awareness, but I fight it. I fight it with everything within me because I want to be aware.

Ambrose must sense my panic because he lets go of my hands. I instantly mourn the loss of his touch, but I don't mourn for long. He comes to kneel on the bed, shuffling closer until his knees are practically straddling my head.

I raise my hands as I gaze up at him, the need to touch him too strong to ignore. I grab hold of his hips as he bends over me, his eyes on mine, his dark hair falling around his face to frame it sinfully. He takes hold of the cups of my bra and pushes the fabric down, exposing my breasts to the cold air inside the cabin. I gasp, then moan as my nipples immediately harden.

His palms come down to cup my breasts and the warm contrast is divine. Wetness gathers between my legs as he kneads the mounds, the heels of his hands digging in against my nipples.

"Put your mouth on her," he tells Huxley, who drops to his knees in front of me. "Taste her."

His lips touch my skin in a hurry, pressing to my knee as he spreads my legs with his hands and settles between them. His tongue touches the inside of my thigh, and he licks all the way up, sending a shiver down my spine.

"Hux."

His gaze is fixated between my legs, dark eyes inspecting me with intent, curiosity, and desire. His tongue runs across his lips and he inhales deeply. "Is that all for us, Glory?" His thumb teases, coming up to brush lightly across the line of my slit. "Have you ever been wet like this with another man?"

"Never," I breathe the truth.

Ambrose draws his hands back to pinch and roll my nipples with his fingers. My hips buck off the bed with a jolt of electricity through my core. Huxley lays his palm on my stomach and presses me back down. That gentle control he exhibits makes me crazy as every inch of my skin tingles with need.

"Do you want me to taste you?" Huxley shuffles closer and I can feel his heated breath across my flesh. "Will you like it if I slip my tongue inside you? Suck on your clit? Edge you to the brink of insanity, like Ambrose wants?"

My stomach twitches as my muscles clench. "Y-yes…"

"Stop teasing and taste her." Ambrose reaches for him, grabbing the back of his head with one palm and shoves him forward.

Huxley doesn't fight him; instead, he buries his face between my legs and attacks me with his mouth and tongue, kissing me as urgently as he kissed my lips before. My thighs twitch as pleasure instantly swells between my legs and ripples up my insides, overwhelming me in a way that makes me feel sick, but in the best way possible.

Huxley licks and laps and sucks while Ambrose holds him down, their heat blanketing me from above. The air is thick with moaning heat and passion. The sounds, the breaths, the moans and whimpers shared between us are like venom in my veins—poison taking hold of me like Huxley told me it would.

I'm changing.

They're changing me.

My legs close around Huxley's ears as tension builds in my center, as my body floats with theirs on an invisible cloud of lust.

God, this feels so good.

Ambrose is thick, his erection growing behind his jeans—I can see the bulge where his hips hover above my face.

I want it.

I lift my hands, scrambling to unbutton his jeans, but he moves my hands away with a gentle push.

"No, little bird, no. You don't lift a finger right now."

"Why?" I whimper. "I want to."

He releases Huxley, who continues his frantic consumption without direction. His touch changes from hard to soft as he caresses my skin, rubbing his hands down my chest, over my breasts, down my stomach, and back up again. "We're all here because of you. Because you chose to stay when I let you go. Because you *wanted* me. I've never been wanted like this, and all I want to do is drive you mad with pleasure. I don't want to make you disappear by shoving my cock down your throat."

"I won't disappear…" I say, though I know he's right.

"You've been hurt that way enough."

His hands continue to move along my curves as Huxley swipes his tongue heavily over my clit. He clamps his lips around it and sucks, and the jolt of pleasure makes my hips rise from the bed. All four hands are on me—Huxley's on my hips, Ambrose's at my belly—and they're all pushing me down, holding me still with a gentleness I've never experienced before. They can hold me down if they do it this way, by granting me such pleasure that my mind can't leave the moment.

"Please," I beg, "I can't…"

I can't take this much of a good feeling.

The broken parts inside me want them to hurt me, use me, abuse me. I want that because it's all I've ever known. Their gentle, determined control is baffling my senses, overwhelming me, and making me pant. I feel like I can't catch my breath, and though my lungs ache, I'd happily stop breathing here and now, my last dying moment on the edge of perfect bliss with the two men who own the remaining particles of my ashen heart.

I want to speak; I want to tell them what I'm feeling, but all that comes out are gasps and moans and strangled sounds that get caught in my throat. I'd be thrashing and squirming if I could, but Huxley has wrapped his arms around my legs, gripping my thighs and squeezing my legs together around his head so I can't move.

His face is buried in my cunt and I'm half-afraid he'll suffocate down there…but the way he eats me out makes me think he'd happily die that way.

I don't understand the way he wants me, the way either of them want me. But I love it.

I *love* this.

Ambrose pulls back and slips his hands beneath my shoulders. He lifts me, scooting closer before sitting back on his heels. He leans me back against his lap, perfectly angling me to look down at Huxley's face between my legs.

"Look at him," he whispers through my tangled hair. "Look how much he wants you, how much he needs to taste you. Watch him while he makes you come. Come apart for us, little bird."

The way he whispers brings about that dark magic that wraps me up in lust, and I succumb to it entirely. My body tenses around my center. Huxley's eyes snap open and hit me with darkness—the brown hue of his irises looks like shadowed blackness in his spellbound consumption.

The look captivates me entirely, holds me still, draws every molecule of pleasure to my wet, pulsing core. I didn't know sex could be like this. I didn't know it could feel safe and freeing. I didn't know it could grip my senses and free my mind. It's never been freeing before—not until Huxley and Ambrose.

Ambrose nudges my hair away from my neck with his nose before kissing me there, sucking lightly at my skin as he presses his face into the curve of my neck. They both lick and suck and it makes my head feel light. My skin tingles as fire burns low in my belly. My body curves around the pleasure as something twists inside me.

I grip the comforter with both hands as every muscle tenses, warning of the explosion that's building and building and building…and then it erupts. Tickling, tingling pleasure fires through my clit and sets off a chain reaction, a drawn-out series of eruptions that pulse through my pussy and shock me into bliss.

I gasp and whimper.

Huxley sucks and groans.

Ambrose licks and hums across my skin.

My thighs twitch as Huxley loosens his hold. He pulls away and stands with a sinful smirk playing across his cheeks—and it makes me want more of him. He places a knee on the bed beside my hip, coming in close as he leans forward, his body hovering above mine. I want to kiss him. I want to taste myself on his lips.

Ambrose has the same idea. "Let me taste her," he says.

Huxley groans, a deep rumble from his chest, as his eyes flash with hunger. He bends as Ambrose leans, and their mouths meet with fury. They kiss each other so intensely that I feel as though I'm a part of it.

I *am* part of it.

I'm the taste on their tongues.

I'm the flavor their erotic hunger craves.

I can hardly tear my eyes away, but I do for a moment, long enough to glance down and see the bulge in Huxley's jeans.

My fingers urgently work on his buckle, his button, his zipper. He snaps away from the kiss before I can reach inside to touch the part of him I never knew I could need this way.

He grabs my hands and shoves them aside, reaches to wrap his palm gently around my throat, and dips down to press his forehead to mine as he meets my eyes. "I wanna fuck you senseless. I wanna see you lost in passion. I wanna drive you to the edge of insanity and pull you back just before you fall."

"Please," I breathe out.

Ambrose suddenly disappears, and I fall back onto the bed with Huxley landing on top of me before he moves on his knees to straddle my hips. I scoot backward along the bed so I can pull my legs up from where they dangle over the side, and Huxley moves with me.

His lips touch mine and my tongue slips out to taste him eagerly. He kisses me as voraciously as he did between my legs, nudging at the inside of my thighs with his knees to spread me wide for him. He releases my throat to finish what I started, reaching down between our wriggling bodies to free his cock from his jeans.

The kiss breaks when I reach down for him, my hands scrambling between us to find his warm flesh. We both moan when I wrap one of my hands around him, and I find myself breathless again, panting for more.

As quickly as Ambrose left me before, he returns, his face appearing over Huxley's shoulder as he dips to kiss his neck. Huxley's eyes flutter shut, and I feel a jab of pleasure shoot through me at the sight of him.

I need to see him come.

"Take off your clothes," Ambrose commands, pulling him off the bed, leaving me cold and bare.

I press up onto my elbows to look at them. Ambrose is nude and spectacular—someone too beautiful to be so broken. I glance at his moving hands and see he's preparing to tear open a condom.

Warmth spreads through my chest at that simple act. I'm sure he's only trying to protect himself, but I could fool myself into thinking he's trying to protect *me*…to protect all of us. Regardless, I don't want the barrier. I want them both raw. I need to feel them come inside me.

"No." I shake my head at him. "Don't put it on. I have

an IUD."

I expect some hesitation, some doubt, a demand for proof. But all I get is eager trust, and fuck, that feels as good as coming. A low growl rumbles in his chest and he tosses the packet aside. He steps closer to Huxley, leaning in toward him. Ambrose lifts the hem of his shirt, peeling it up and tugging it off him. Then his hand wraps around Huxley's cock, sprung free above the elastic of his boxer briefs and jeans.

And magically, *spiritually*, all three of us release a collective sigh of relief, because somehow, pleasure for one of us means pleasure for all of us.

Huxley sways, leaning into his grip, and soon they're kissing again, hungry mouths consuming one another. My hand drifts of its own will, slipping down my stomach, seeking the warmth between my legs as it begs for another release.

Except my touch alone isn't enough.

It could never be enough with the way I need these men.

"I need you," I whisper, and they both turn to look at me.

Huxley finishes undressing as Ambrose climbs over me. My breaths stutters in my lungs as his energy pulses through me, kicking up adrenaline for the fear that still lingers. I don't fear what Ambrose will do to me anymore. Instead, I fear how hard I might fall for him—I can feel it happening already. It makes no sense, but I don't care. I *want* to fall for him.

I want to fall for them both.

I have already fallen for Huxley.

Ambrose grips the inside of my thighs, spreads my legs, and presses them down onto the mattress. Without warning, he thrusts inside me. I'm so wet from the orgasm with Huxley that Ambrose slips in with ease, though his thick cock stretches me as he pushes in deep. I gasp, savoring the fullness of his intrusion, and I drop my elbows, falling back onto the mattress to revel in the feeling, inviting him to fuck me however he wants.

He fucks me slowly as Huxley climbs onto the bed and kneels beside me, showing me his cock that's high and proud, begging to be touched. I turn my head toward him, licking my lips and signaling my desire to taste him the way he tasted me.

"You want it?"

I nod, twisting and lifting my upper body toward him as Ambrose continues to slowly thrust into me. Huxley shuffles closer, bringing his thick cock toward my lips, and I sigh when he's close enough for me to lick. I run my tongue across the tip, watching his stomach muscles clench at the first contact.

I want all of him clenching and twitching.

I want him writhing and shouting as he comes.

I wrap my lips around him and take him into my mouth.

"Fuck," he hisses. "Glory."

His hand lands on my head, stroking down until he reaches the base of my skull. He combs his fingers into my hair and holds me there, gently pulsing his cock inside my mouth.

He doesn't force me to choke on him, and I don't really know what to do with that. He's gentle, careful with me, thrusting shallow strokes with appreciation and gratitude for my desire to please him.

He's grateful.

He cares.

He makes me feel human.

They make me feel *worthy*.

It makes my eyes fill with tears and I blink, trying to hide them because I don't want him to stop this. I don't want either of them to stop this. Both of them are touching me, caressing me, worshipping me with easy strokes of their hard cocks.

They aren't taking from me…they're *giving*.

And I know right now that I'll never leave them. I'll never leave either of them.

Huxley's thumb brushes beneath my eye, grabbing hold of a tear and swiping it away as I blink up at him. He pulls his cock away, but I lean for it, open my mouth wider for it, begging for him to come back.

"Tell me you're okay," he says softly, and suddenly, Ambrose stops, too.

They both stop and look at me, waiting for my response as if they would stop this right now if I told them to. My chest tightens and aches. It feels as though my ribs are fusing together, forming a barrier around the ashes of my heart, crushing the smoky particles back together, and trying to spark the embers of the shattered organ back to life.

It hurts, but it feels good, too.

It feels like strength is building within me.

It feels like my weak voice could become strong again, like my words have meaning here.

"Do you want to stop?" Huxley asks.

"*No*," I say firmly. "No, don't stop. Please don't stop. Not for anything. I want this. I want you both. *Please.*"

Warmth descends. Ambrose covers me, bending to kiss my neck as he starts to move inside me again. Huxley caresses my cheek, brushing his thumb across my bottom lip and tugging gently. I open for him again and he lets me take him, he lets me lick him, he lets me run my tongue along the underside of his cock before I wrap my lips around him and suck.

The three of us move in perfect harmony, pleasing each other as if it were as natural and necessary as breathing... *because it is.*

We twist and twitch and beg and breathe, beautiful tension building and pulsing between us as a single heartbeat, a single need that could only ever be fulfilled between the three of us.

At some point, Ambrose takes control, shoving Huxley onto his back and lifting me on top of him. He holds my hips from behind and guides me onto Huxley's cock, pushing me down slowly to take him deep inside me. I gasp, tossing my head back as I sit down on him and he fills me more completely than I ever thought I could be filled.

I feel Ambrose's hardness press into my lower back as he holds me there, as his fingers dig into my flesh to hold me still and keep me from moving.

I want to lie on Huxley, spread my cheeks for Ambrose, and have him thrust inside my back entrance. I want him to claim me entirely. But he won't let me move.

"Please," I beg. "I need to come."

"Don't move," he says against my ear.

I feel him spread Huxley's legs beneath me, shifting me forward, and I have to spread my knees a little wider to keep straddling him. I feel Ambrose move behind me, his hand stroking down my spine, all the way down between my cheeks, and lower still...until his touch disappears.

I know where his hand went.

I see it on Huxley's face as he gasps and his eyes roll back in pleasure.

He wants to be filled as much as I do, and God, how I want that for him. I want his pleasure more than I want my own, though I know that his pleasure is linked with mine. I can already feel it cresting and swelling.

I feel Ambrose against my back again, his cock down low beneath me. I know the moment he starts to push inside Huxley because he gasps and his eyes snap open wide, his head tilting back as the most erotic groan I've ever heard rumbles through him.

"Fuck him, Glory," Ambrose commands, one hand landing on my hip. "Use him to make you come, and we'll come with you."

"Fuck. Glory, fuck me," Huxley begs.

A new rush of wetness flows between my legs, my pussy already pulsing and my stomach clenching with need. My cunt begs for friction and pressure, but I'm not used to being on top. I'm used to being fucked, not taking pleasure for myself.

I start to move, lifting and lowering onto his cock, and I can see how much Huxley likes that, but it's not quite right for me.

"Stop. You'll exhaust yourself that way." Ambrose grabs hold of my hips with both hands, stopping me, holding me down on Huxley's lap. He guides me, pressing my hips forward and back. "Like this, little bird. Rock your hips. Keep him deep inside you and rub your clit on his stomach."

How do these men know my body better than I know myself?

A wave of pure bliss ripples through me at the way they know me, at the way they guide me, at the way they want to make me feel good. I love the way they both can take control of me without scaring me.

I love all of this.

I love them.

I do what Ambrose tells me and in moments, my whole body tightens. A shudder tears through me as I moan, as I drop my body forward and press my palms to the mattress on either side of Huxley's head. I rock faster, pressing my hips down hard and rubbing my clit against the base of his cock and his lower stomach. My eyelids flutter, but I try to keep them open as I feel Ambrose behind me, matching my rhythm, thrusting inside Huxley from beneath me.

Huxley holds my gaze as our lips part, as we both moan and whimper in desperation.

"I'm gonna come," I whisper as I feel Huxley's cock swell inside me, thickening and pulsing as he nears his own release.

"Fuck," Ambrose groans behind me, leaning into me and pressing his lips to my spine. He peppers kisses all over my back and I'm overwhelmed by the sensation. "Come for us, little bird. Scream for us. Let us know how good it feels. Make us come with you."

"Fucking do it, Glory," Huxley demands with hooded eyes. "Fucking come on my cock. Take me with you."

I feel the tightening, the tensing, the building climax as my rocking thrusts become frantic. "God," I breathe out. "God, I'm coming. I'm…I—"

My jaw drops open and my eyes squeeze shut as something more powerful than dark magic rips through my soul. A sound breaks free from my chest—some strange combination of a gasp, a moan, a strangled scream. My body goes rigid, trembling as the climax consumes me, swirls around Huxley's cock inside me, and tugs at his release.

I feel warm liquid punch inside me as the waves of pleasure hit me again and again, as Huxley lifts his hips from the mattress and fucks into me as he shouts out his release.

And Ambrose, the man who's dark magic twisted us all together in this toxic lust, groans and fucks into Huxley harder, faster, plunging into him until he comes undone with a rough groan that echoes throughout the room.

We come together.

We collapse together.

We find bliss in the madness together.

CHAPTER 20

HUXLEY

AMBROSE IS DEEP inside Glory as he holds her from behind, spooning her. They each have a hand on my cock where I lay in front of her, kissing her with passion as we build her up again toward a third orgasm. Ambrose's hand tightens around the base of my cock as his jaw tenses, as his muscles grow rigid, as he fucks her with jerking, panting thrusts.

Glory moans into my mouth and the vibration of her sound is incredible. It shakes straight through me, making my cock twitch in their hands.

"Fuck," I mutter against her lips. "Fuck, I need inside you."

They let go of me while Ambrose nudges her forward against my chest, shifting behind her, then rising to one knee. I grab her leg and lift it over mine as he fucks her from behind, hard and fast. Glory wraps her arms around me, hugging me close, and I feel the warmth spread from her heart to mine as they beat together, pounding out a pulsing rhythm of need.

"Come inside me," she whispers. "I want you both to come inside me."

I let my hand slip down her side, roam over her hip, and slip over her ass. I grip her cheek and pull, spreading her wide for him. "Can you take him here? Take us both at the same time?"

She shudders, kissing my neck. "Yes. Please, *yes.*"

Ambrose pulls out suddenly and tears her away from me. She gasps but doesn't fight as he twists her around to face him, switching our positions. "I'll hurt her if I fuck her there," Ambrose says to me. "She's too fucking tight. I'll lose control."

"And you don't think I will?" I rub my finger down the crease between her cheeks as she hitches her leg over Ambrose. I feel around until I find the puckered hole and circle it with my finger, making Glory jolt and squeeze her leg tighter around Ambrose. "Do you like that?"

She doesn't respond with words, only a fervent nod as she turns her head back to look at me over her shoulder. I kiss her cheek, trailing down her neck and over her shoulder as Ambrose reaches between their bodies. He grabs his cock, lines it up, and enters her pussy again. Her eyes flutter shut and her lips part—so pink and perfect and sensual.

I reach down to gather wetness from her cunt, to soak my fingers and spread it around her back entrance. I ease into her with my finger, pushing slowly inside her and circling, preparing her to take me. It's not long before she's panting and twitching, her body begging for more. I gradually pull my finger out, and line up my cock to enter her as Ambrose holds steady, waiting for me to join him inside her.

I push in slowly as he grabs her cheek, turning her head toward his. He kisses her deeply, drawing her in like she's his last gulp of air before sinking beneath water. Watching him kiss her like that, and seeing the way she responds, causes a pleasant yet painful tightening in my stomach. There's a twinge of jealousy in my gut, but it's slight—slight enough for me to ignore.

Her body resists as I push into her, the hole tightening as I wedge myself just a little deeper. She gasps, breaking her kiss with Ambrose, and turns her head back again to look at me.

"Tell me to stop if it hurts."

Her gorgeous green eyes grab hold of mine. "It doesn't hurt…I like it."

Fuck me.

It feels like a privilege to touch her, to kiss her, to fuck her. It *is* a privilege—one I don't ever want to sully. Though I want to shove inside her and fuck her until she begs me to make her come again, I ease my way in with care, giving her time to adjust because Ambrose and I are stretching her in a way she's probably never been stretched before.

Past a certain point, her inner muscles grab hold of me, grip me, and tug me in to the hilt. The three of us groan because we all feel it…we all feel the way she grips us both.

"God," she breathes out, turning toward Ambrose and burying her face in his chest. "God, this is so good. So, so good."

I give Ambrose a quick nod and he starts to move again, gently pushing in and out of her. Glory moans as her back arches, as her head rolls on the pillow and her eyes flutter in the pleasure of it all. If I could put that look on her face every fucking day, I would. The way I want her is desperate and forever.

I slowly start to move with Ambrose, thrusting in unison to give her the ultimate thrill. But as our eyes lock on each other, I know the thrill isn't just for her—and it isn't just *because* of her. All of this, the three of us together, it's because of *him*. It's because we stumbled across him out here in the middle of nowhere.

Would anything have happened between me and Glory if we hadn't found our way here? If we hadn't found Ambrose? Is he the reason Glory is in my arms right now?

I feel a sense of gratitude wash over me as he stares at me over Glory. Like glue, she's the substance between us, the thing that draws us together and keeps us here in this place. I was ready to leave when he let us go, but she begged to stay.

She *fought* to stay.

And I stayed because of her.

Maybe I'll come to regret it later, but in this perfect moment where I feel complete acceptance and adoration, I'm happy she fought for this.

Ambrose reaches for me over Glory, his hand landing on my cheek, his fingers combing through my hair, tugging me closer. We both lift our heads and our lips meet above Glory's twitching body, kissing above her whimpers and moans as we use her to connect. My tongue dives inside his mouth as our pace quickens, as our thrusts meet inside her body and drive the three of us up a steep cliff.

Our kiss ends as we pant, as we both feel Glory tighten and twist around us.

"I don't want this to end," I whisper to them both.

"It doesn't have to," Ambrose says, and I see sincerity in the dark depths of his tormented soul.

I want to save him.

Like everyone else I've ever cared for in my life, I want to save him.

But saving him means reaching into my own darkness and ripping it to the surface. If that darkness comes out, it may never be put back again.

"I love you," Glory says so quietly, I think I mishear her. Ambrose and I both look down at her, her eyes squeezed shut. "I love you both. Come with me, please." Her mouth drops open as her body twists back, as her hips rock and encourage us to fuck her into oblivion.

I take Ambrose's lead as he picks up a furious pace. We throttle her from both ends until she's shaking and screaming, and finally, breaks apart around our cocks. Her orgasm is the catalyst for our mutual explosion. We moan and shout and loudly fuck through our climaxes until each of us are beyond spent. Then we collapse in perfect exhaustion.

I wrap my arm around Glory as she burrows into Ambrose's chest, and he grabs hold of my hand. He grips me tight, as if he needs me just as much as he needs her.

And I know he does.

We rest for a while before we take a shower together and fuck again. Before long, Glory's complaining about hunger and thirst, so we take to nourishing her.

She sits beside me at the kitchen table, wearing only her underwear and a flannel shirt she borrowed from Ambrose, which is far too big on her. She leans her head on my shoulder as we hold hands and I graze her knuckles with my thumb. Ambrose stands at the stove, making pancakes for us at midnight.

I watch as he flips the food in the frying pan, noting the subtle smile that touches his cheeks. He's looked nothing but surly and angry from the moment we showed up here, but now he looks happy...*almost* happy.

There's still a looming darkness there, but it no longer feels like *his* darkness. It feels like a darkness that haunts him—the same darkness that seems to haunt this house, this forest. It's not some enchantment, though everything about him feels like black magic.

My face falls as I realize what truly plagues him.

My mother.

She has a hold on him.

She ordered him to kill us—not just her stepdaughter, but me, her *son*, her own damn flesh and blood.

Rage bubbles in my veins, heating my skin, and I squeeze Glory's hand too tightly.

"Hey." She lifts her head from my shoulder to look at me. "What's wrong?"

Ambrose turns back to look at us.

I shake my head. "My mother. I just can't believe she wants me dead."

"It's horrible," Glory agrees. "But after we give her what she wants, we can all leave together. We'll never have to think about her again."

"You mean after we dig up his parents." I jerk my chin toward Ambrose. "He gives her their skulls, thinking they belong to you and your father, and takes all your money."

"I don't care about the money," she says. "I don't need it anymore. Not if the three of us are together."

"It's not about the money, Glory. It's the fact that she wants me dead so she can have it all to herself. Money that doesn't even belong to her. Money that belonged to *you* when your father died."

"Fuck her and fuck the money," Ambrose says, bringing plates to the table and serving us. He places a bottle of Tolliver's famous maple syrup on the center of the table—I fucking love that stuff, but suddenly, it makes me sick to look at it. "She'll get her skulls, she'll give me my cut, and the three of us will disappear. She'll think you're dead, and she'll never bother us again."

I let go of Glory and lean forward, resting my forearms on the table. "See, that's where I think you're wrong."

"What do you mean?" he asks.

"You said you know her, so you must know how she is. You can't trust a word that comes out of her mouth. I wouldn't trust what she does after you hand over the skulls. And what the fuck is she going to do with the skulls, anyway?" I toss my hands in the air before letting them fall to the table.

Ambrose looks away with a sigh. "I know. I know we can't trust her completely. But it's the only chance she's ever given me to leave with the promise of a clean slate. And the cut of the inheritance she's promised me will help me start over again in a new place—"

"That money will be tied up in legal for months. And that's only after they decide to call off the search for us and declare us dead. How long do you think that will take?"

Glory looks at me and Ambrose narrows his eyes as understanding comes over him. "Fuck. *Fuck*, I didn't even think about that."

"I'm sure she was banking on that. She's a manipulator, an *abuser*…She can't fucking get away with this."

"We don't need money to run," Glory adds. "We could just leave, disappear, go off-grid."

"It's nearly impossible to live off-grid these days," I tell her.

"But we could try—"

"No." I lean back, folding my arms over my chest. "No.

There's only one option here and I…" I hesitate. "There's only one good option."

Ambrose meets my eyes and I see my thoughts reflected back at me. He understands. "Do you really think you could live with yourself?" he asks quietly.

"What?" Glory asks.

I stare at Ambrose. "Can *you* live with yourself? After what you did to your parents?"

"Yes. They hurt me. They deserved it."

"She wants us dead," I say. "She wants to take my Glory's money…money that she *deserves* for all the bullshit she's been through. The abuse she's suffered from her father, the bullshit of being in the public eye, criticized for every decision and mistake she's ever made." I pause and take a breath. "Yes, I could live with myself."

"What are you talking about?" Glory's forehead is wrinkled in confusion.

I turn to look at her, meeting her gaze squarely. "I'm talking about ending my mother's life."

"You're…*what?*"

"If we end her, that's it. She won't have a hold over Ambrose. We won't ever have to worry about her hunting us down. That will be it. She'll be gone. We can leave and be free."

"But you understand what being free means, don't you?" Ambrose asks, pushing from his chair and pacing away. "You both will still have to live like you're dead, unless you want to put Glory back in the spotlight for her father's death. She'll have to go to court, testify, fight for a self-defense claim. And what do you think will happen then? She might lose and go to jail. She might win and be free. But either way, it will open the door to more investigation. They'll start digging into Maura's disappearance, my connection with her, my connection with the two of *you*. We'll go up in flames for killing her. The only way for you to be free of that would be to live like you're dead, hide away from the world with me forever. I don't know that either of you are ready for that kind of commitment."

Glory looks at me, then back at Ambrose. "I am. I was only home the night my father died to get money for college, but I'd thought about it…I'd thought about taking that money and running away, hiding somewhere so he could never find me again. I don't want to be found again."

Walking toward the table again, Ambrose gives her a small smile, then turns to look at me. "And what about you? Are you prepared to give up your life for this?"

Glory turns sideways in her seat to face me, reaching to take my hands in hers. "I would never ask you to give up your life, Hux. You always wanted to go to law school. It was your dream."

"It was never really my dream…it was *hers*." I reach out to touch her cheek with my hand. "And you're not asking me to give up my life. I'm willing to do it because I want you." I glance at Ambrose. "Fuck, I want both of you. And as much as I want that…I want her dead."

CHAPTER 21

Ambrose

"ARE YOU SURE you want to do this?" I ask.

Huxley takes in a deep breath, determination wrinkling his brow, though his knees bounce anxiously. "Yes," he finally says.

I crouch between the chairs at the table where Huxley and Glory sit and place my palm on his knee. He stops the anxious bouncing and snaps his head to look at me.

The darkness dancing in his brown eyes catches me and refuses to let go. It was never darkness that drew me to him. If anything, there's more darkness in Glory than there could ever be in Huxley, though he doesn't recognize that the way I do. Yet, I see what's there, the depth of it that exists within him and the way it's clawing to be released upon the one person who could destroy all of our futures.

But it's his *mother* we're talking about murdering, and that's never an easy decision to make, especially for a child of privilege like him. I'd had a lifetime of hatred and abuse at the hands of my parents to fuel me. I'd had their cruelty brutally handed to me, day in and day out for most of my life. And still, it was hard to end them.

Not *them*.

My *mother*.

Part of me wants to think that her cruelty was the result of my father's…that perhaps she may not have been as cruel if I'd had a different father. Perhaps that was only wishful thinking. Regardless, a connection unlike any other exists between mother and child, and Huxley found privilege from his mother's decisions.

Though Maura's soul is as ugly as my father's was, I think she did well hiding that from her son…until now.

"I'm sure about this," he says slowly. "It has to be done. For Glory, if for no one else."

No one else.

The words strike my chest and it burns.

Of course, it's for Glory. I want it done for Glory, too.

But the *no one else* he's referring to includes me, and though I'm happy to be in this at all, it hurts to know I'm second to them both. It makes me wish, for just a moment, that they'd left when I gave them the chance—if they had, I'd be alone now.

Could I ever be happy alone now that they've brought me back to life?

I shove to my feet and turn my back on them, pacing away a few steps before I stop, shoving my hands into my pockets to search for a cigarette and a lighter. "I'll talk to her tomorrow. I'll invite her over for the night. I'll pick her up and bring her back here." I hold the cigarette to my lips and spark it, taking a good drag before blowing it out. "We'll take care of her and bury her in the forest." I turn back around. "Maybe a final sacrifice is just what this place needs to let us go."

Glory's head dips as she hides a secret smile, but we've come to a point where there can be no secrets between the three of us. Everything has to be laid out on the table or we'll never be able to trust one another.

"What are you smiling about?" I ask her.

She whips her head up to look at me, the tiny smile falling away quickly. "It's nothing…"

"It's not nothing. You have to be honest with us about how you're feeling about this. If you don't think you can—"

She raises her palm to cut me off with some newfound overt confidence that makes me want to tie her hands and cut *her* off with a kiss. "It's not what you're thinking. It was just a passing morbid thought."

"What thought?" Huxley asks. "Tell us."

She looks at him as her face hardens, as she shuts down and pulls back. I slowly walk toward them as Huxley reaches out to caress her cheek.

"You can tell me anything," he assures.

My eyes narrow on her features as she darts furtive glances between us—darkened glances. Her green eyes—which are usually bright and vivid—have grown dark with shadows.

"Just say what you were thinking," I urge, closing the distance and standing beside them.

She swallows and looks down. "I was just thinking how twisted it would be if you put us back in the cage before you brought her here. Let her think you found us and locked us up to kill us like she wanted." Glory lifts her head, locking eyes with Huxley. "I was thinking about how good it would feel to wipe the smug look from her face just when she thinks she's won."

A pregnant pause hangs in the air, and after a beat or two, Glory tries to turn away. Huxley grabs her face to tug her back, leaning closer to her and looking deeply into her eyes.

Carefully, I ask, "And who would be wiping the smug

look from her face?"

"You. Me. Huxley. The three of us…together." Her features twitch with shame. "Sorry, it's fucked up, I know."

She says it as if *fucked up* weren't normal here.

The three of us are fucked up in every imaginable definition of the term.

"Yeah, that's fucked up," Huxley says, and I want to backhand him for being so careless with his words, "but it's fucking brilliant. *You're* fucking brilliant, Glory." He presses a quick kiss to her nose and lets his hands fall away before he looks up at me. "It would give her one last chance, wouldn't it? One last chance to see us, to look me in the eye and tell you she wants me dead. It would wipe my conscience clean to know she had one more chance to save me."

I blow out a ball of smoke over his head. "And what if she takes that chance? What do we all do then?"

"She won't take it," Glory says. "I know she won't."

I know that, too, but I need Huxley to really think this through.

"If she chooses to save my life, then we'll frame her for Beau's death. It would be our word against hers, wouldn't it? Three to one…I'll take those odds."

"I don't think it's that simple."

He shakes his head. "I don't think it is, either. But a chance to fully clear my conscience of what we're talking about doing is worth the risk for me."

Glory makes a small sound, something like a hum of agreement, though there's the breathiness of a moan mingled with it—a desire-fueled moan I'm becoming familiar with.

I drop to my haunches between them, hooking my elbow

over the back of her chair and grinning up at her. "What exactly is it about this conversation that's turning you on, little bird?"

"I didn't say—"

"You don't have to say a word. I can feel the pulse of your lust a mile away."

She leans her shoulder against the back of the chair and rests her head against my arm. My chest swells with warmth at the simplest touch from her.

"I want you to fuck me again," she purrs.

My cock twitches. "I know that, but why?"

"I don't know what you're asking."

"You know exactly what I'm asking. What part of this conversation turned you on? Is it the thought that Maura will soon be dead? The power you'll have over her? The control? Is it the idea of being locked in that cage again? Or…is it the violence?"

Her breath catches and she hiccups out a gasp.

"It's the violence." I look at Huxley. "How do you feel about that? Knowing the thought of hurting someone who deserves it gets her off?"

His eyes flicker and narrow. "I don't know."

She looks at me, seeking my gaze to comfort her because the thought of any type of rejection from Huxley is too much for her to bear—it's written all over her face. I reach out to touch her cheek, wrap my hand around her chin, and rub my thumb across her bottom lip.

"It's okay, Glory. I like the violence, too. There's nothing wrong with admitting that. It's human."

"Is it?" Huxley's voice cuts between us, slicing our connection like a knife.

I direct my irritation toward him. "If you're not man enough to admit that the thought of ending someone who wronged you gets you excited, it's fine. But don't direct your judgment at her."

"I'm not judging her, but I'm not going to admit something that isn't true just for her benefit. I don't get off on violence. I don't—"

"Did the sight of Beau Tolliver's bloodied body make you sick? Did you run from the room to vomit because the sight of it disgusted you so much?" I stand and turn my attention to him, slowly straightening to my full height and hovering over him. He lifts his chin to look up at me. "Did it make you feel anything at all? Did the sight of blood on her hands make you weep with regret that you weren't there to take the life for her? You've said it yourself…you would've killed him when you found out what he'd been doing to her if Glory hadn't done it herself."

His jaw is tense. "What's your point?"

I reach down and slip two fingers beneath his chin, tilting his head back all the way. "You're more concerned with clearing your conscience than you are about the fact that we're going to murder your mother. It's the only reason you want to give her one last chance to change her mind—not because you'll be forgiving if she does. But because she raised you to take care of her and everyone else around you. She raised you to be a savior, not a reaper…and I know how that eats you alive inside."

His chest heaves as his breaths deepen, as his fingers twitch. I hear Glory breathing behind me, heavy and heated. The way they want me is exciting, intoxicating, deafening.

"You know you're still her savior." I jerk my head back to indicate Glory. "Regardless of what happens with your mother, in her eyes…" I bend over him, bringing my lips close to watch his part with a sharp exhale, "you're God." I reach over and put my cigarette out in the ashtray on the table. I release him as I take a quick step back, reveling in the fact that both of their beautiful blond heads turn to follow me. "Glory would get down on her knees and worship you if you asked her. She'd beg at your feet for forgiveness of her sins, even when you and I both know she doesn't need to."

Glory takes it upon herself to slip from her seat and lower to her knees before him. He shifts back, as if trying to lean away, though his knees stay spread apart and he reaches for her.

"She doesn't need to beg forgiveness for her sickness, because this demented thing between us doesn't bare a passing resemblance to the true depravity of humans, does it? Maura Tolliver deserves to die, and so she will. There's nothing wrong with looking forward to the violence that will end a deserving creature. She's not innocent, and she doesn't deserve your conscience."

"Huxley?" Glory sits back on her heels, looking up at him with worried eyes. "Are you mad at me for wanting her blood on my hands?"

Oh, how my little bird wants to fly.

He snaps forward, gripping her face, bending to press his forehead against hers. The way they love each other is haunting and beautiful. They could never be together out there in the real world. The press would have a field day with the heiress dating her wannabe lawyer stepbrother who she grew up with. But here, with me, they can be exactly who they are.

And I can be myself with them because they saw the worst in me and chose to stay.

They chose to stay with me.

I pull my shoulders back when a feeling I'm not familiar with runs through me—*pride.* I'm proud that they chose me, that they chose to stay. I'm proud of them for the way they keep breaking down walls and how they sink into their deepest, truest selves through the chaos that swirls around us.

"I'm not mad at you," Huxley tells her. "I'm not mad at all. If anything, I'm…scared."

"What are you afraid of?"

He shuts his eyes. "I'm afraid of myself…of what I might be beneath the surface. I'm afraid of finding out that I'm not the same as you." He says it to her, but then he turns his forehead against hers and opens his eyes to look at me. "Either of you." He holds me with his stare, speaking directly to me. "I'm afraid I'm not real enough for you. That the two of you will sink into depravity without me, that I could walk away and you two would find comfort in each other without me. That you'd be fine without me."

"Don't you understand how much we need you? How you balance this thing between us?" I step closer, reach out, and stroke the back of his head. "We draw you into the darkness with us, and if you left us there, we'd never come back from it. You're our tether to reality…You bring us back after we lose ourselves."

With sudden agitation, he pulls away from Glory, shoves his chair back with a screech, and lets it topple to the floor as he marches away and paces. "Do you have any fucking idea how much pressure that puts on me? The responsibility of bringing you both back *from the darkness?* What the fuck is even happening here?" He rakes his hands through his hair, confusion etched in his face.

I know what he needs…what he's not willing to admit. He needs permission. Permission to let go and stop thinking responsibly. Permission to unleash. Permission to give in to his urges and needs.

I charge after him, my outstretched hand reaching for him as he takes a step back. But he doesn't move away fast enough, and I latch my palm around his throat, jerk him wildly, and slam his back against the wall. His hands come up, as if he means to claw at mine, but his fingers merely rest there. His brown eyes are wide and waiting as he huffs through his nose.

"There is no pressure." I mold my body to his, my dick throbbing as it aligns with his. "You don't have to *do* anything to bring us back. Your presence is enough. *You* are enough."

His gaze shifts and narrows, studying the lines of my face, and though we've already fucked like animals, I feel more naked and exposed than ever before. It makes my stomach clench with nausea, but I don't hate the feeling because it's mixed with raw emotion and primal lust—feelings I've never know before Huxley and Glory came barging into my pathetic life.

I tilt his chin, pressing in harder, squeezing his jaw between my outstretched thumb and index finger. Just as I bend to kiss him, I feel her presence at my back—her gentle touch along my spine contrasts with my roughness. She softly kisses between my shoulder blades and nuzzles her cheek against my back. Though she makes me want to melt for her, I don't let her take away my heat.

I kiss Huxley with the harshness he needs, spreading his lips with mine and shoving my tongue between his teeth.

I keep him still with my body as I rub my thickening cock against his.

Our kiss breaks naturally as we both groan at the friction between us. I lean against him, bringing my lips to his ear. "Stop trying to control yourself. Let me tell you what to do."

"What," he pauses to hiss in a shuddering breath through his teeth as I bite his earlobe and tug, "makes you think I trust you enough to do that?"

I slip my hand between our bodies, wrap my palm around his cock, and squeeze. "Because your body already does. Let your mind follow its lead."

I take a quick sidestep, release him, grab Glory, and shove her forward to take my place. I press along her backside, sandwiching her between us as I lift her hair over her shoulders. "What would you let him do to you, Glory? Do you trust him with your life? With your light? Do you feel safe enough in his presence to descend into darkness knowing his heart will always bring you back to the light?"

"I'll let you do anything you want, Hux," she says, her chin lifted to look up at him as she grips his sides. "Let me go. Let me be dark. Then bring me back with your light. I just want to feel this…You can hurt me, fuck me, tie me up."

"Christ, Glory," he exhales, and I know he's been waiting far too long to let go of that breath.

"Please, Hux—"

She barely gets out his name before he snaps. He grabs her shoulders roughly, whipping her around with such force that it causes me to stumble back. He slams her backward so her ass hits the edge of the stove. She puts her hands back to catch herself and her fingers accidentally brush the burner where

I'd made the pancakes, which is still hot. She hisses and flinches, jerking her hand away, but Huxley shuts her up with a kiss.

He consumes her so intensely that she melts, her face softening as she falls into him and forgets about any lingering burn. His lips move frantically across her cheek, along her jaw, down the side of her neck as he pushes against her and holds her in place with his body.

His hands work between them, gripping her panties and shoving them down her bare legs. She kicks them away and he raises the hem of her shirt—my shirt—as he grips her hips and whips her around to face the stove. He reaches down as she arches her back and grabs behind her knee, forcing her knee up and onto the stove, only inches away from the hot burner.

She doesn't flinch, doesn't tell him to stop, doesn't try to move away. She trusts him so implicitly that she'd let him risk burning her for the promise of pleasure—because we both know he'll deliver.

I see the way he strains, the way he fights getting down on his knees to worship her cunt.

"Take from her," I tell him. "She asked you to take from her, so do it."

His shoulders relax with the reminder of the permission that's been granted to him. He grips her hips and jerks her ass back, forcing her to bend over the stove. He pulls down the gray sweatpants I loaned him, along with his boxer briefs, and in seconds, he's fucking naked in my kitchen.

My eyes linger on his sculpted ass as he fists his cock, lining up behind her. He's a work of art, such a perfectly chiseled specimen of a man that he looks unreal, too perfect for this world. But if he can embrace the darkness within, he'll be perfect enough for my world…for Glory's world.

Huxley's hand slips between her cheeks, reaching beneath her to shove his fingers inside her pussy without warning or ease. She cries out as her hips buck forward against the stove edge.

I have to fucking see it.

I rush to move beside them, dropping to my knees next to Glory's lifted knee so I have a perfect view of her glistening pussy. I groan as I watch Huxley add a third finger and he fucks her roughly with his hand. She squirms, bucking her hips away, but he slams his hips forward, wedging his hard cock between her cheeks, holding her there as her palms come down to grip the edge of the stove.

"Ow!" she shrieks and pulls her hand back—she touched the burner again. "Hux…" There's a small hint of warning in her tone and I see his jaw tense.

"Don't let up," I tell him. "Add another finger. Stretch her wide. Let's make it hurt before we let her come."

With a low, chest rumbling growl, he turns his hand, twisting it to wedge his pinky finger inside her with the other three. She gasps and whimpers and pulls away, but she doesn't stop it.

"Does it hurt, little bird?" I whisper.

She nods ferociously as her body jerks and Huxley suddenly stops. As soon as he does, she's reaching behind her with one hand, waving aimlessly for his arm. "Don't stop. Hurt me like I've been hurt before…then make it all better like you always do. I want this from you."

He grabs hold of her, pulls her from the stove, turns her, and shoves her to the floor on all fours. He slams to his knees behind her and pulls her back against him as she struggles to right herself and push up onto her palms. He lifts her ass into the air as he pulls his hips back, then slams into her, his cock slipping into her soaked pussy.

Giving up the fight to rise, Glory cries out and lets her upper body drop to the floor instead, her cheek pressed to the hardwood. Her head turns toward me, her eyes seeking mine. I smile at her as Huxley pulls out and slams back inside with a groan, as her eyes roll and her lashes flutter.

I want to lay beside her, stroke her hair, grip her neck, shove her face down hard into the floor, caress her cheek. I want to give her endless pleasure and at the same time, take everything from her that she has to give. Her beautiful face scrunches, her pink lips parting as she pants, her cheek scraping the floor with each of his rough thrusts.

"Fuck," she gasps, "fuck, that's so good. Come…come inside me, Hux. Please."

I slip my hand beneath her, grip her throat, and lift her from the floor. They both whimper and moan as I bring her upright with one hand with Huxley still inside her from behind. Her back arches as she comes up on her knees. He lassos an arm around her waist to hold her as I force her to crane her neck back against his shoulder. On my knees, I move in front of her, our bodies touching as I move in close.

I lean over her, pressing a quick kiss to her throat before skating my lips across her skin to whisper against her ear. "You come with him, or he doesn't come at all."

She huffs out a breath as her head flops back heavier on Huxley's shoulder. "I'm not there yet…"

My thumb brushes beneath her chin. "Then fucking get there."

Huxley and I move as one, as though our instincts and needs have fully aligned with Glory's fragile beautiful body between us. I drop my hand from her throat and shove it between her legs. He grips her waist tighter with his arm while slipping his other hand inside the unbuttoned V at the collar of her shirt.

Her back arches impossibly more at our synchronized assault of her senses. She presses her breast into his hand while thrusting her cunt forward against my fingers.

He grips and claws and toys with her nipple as my fingers play down below. I can feel how hard his cock is as my fingertips graze the length pressing inside her. The three of us easily find our twisted rhythm. Though I'm still fully clothed in a hoodie and sweatpants, I feel as bare as being naked before them.

Huxley's eyes hold mine with a look of pure possession—a look that battles with my own because I feel the primal truth rumbling through my chest, awakening my cold, dead heart.

These two are *mine*.

They have been mine from the moment I laid eyes on them in the forest.

I will never, *ever* let them go.

Something resembling a growl rumbles through both of us as we push against her, destroying her pussy with his cock and my fingers. She lifts her head, though her expression shows how lost she is to the passion; her eyes half-hooded and perfect lips parted to let out audible, moaning breaths. Our gaze turns all at once to look at her, as she turns her eyes to look back and forth between the two of us.

Her eyelids flutter closed as a shiver runs through her, a

vibration so strong that it shakes all of us. "Kiss me," she begs.

She could be talking to either of us, but Huxley and I both know the truth—she wants it from both of us. We both lean for her at the same time, press our mouths to hers at the same time, part our lips for her at the same time.

She opens for us and lets both of our tongues battle for space inside her mouth. Her hands come up to grip the backs of our heads as she twists her upper body, fighting to kiss us both at the same time. Three tongues taste and lick and battle and sin.

Huxley's tongue is thick and forceful, tasting with precision and skill. Glory's is soft and sensuous, licking languidly and lapping up every ounce of pleasure we feed her. And mine is eager and grateful, quick and sharp, delivering sensation to them both with force.

Our hips rock and thrust, grind and roll, moving aimlessly through beats that won't serve the release of an orgasm, but instead, build the intense desire for more, more, always fucking more.

I've never wanted anyone this way, no one, but now, I want them both in equal measure and I'll do anything to keep them...

Fucking anything.

This thing between us isn't sick. It isn't depraved. It isn't twisted—not in the way I thought it would be.

They are the antidote to the poisonous energy that plagues me.

They are the vaccine against my future suffering.

They are the cure I didn't know I needed.

Six hands grow frantic—gripping, scratching, holding, touching—each of us falling into obsessive madness to please one another. Something has to give, something has to flex and bend, or we're all going to snap with need.

And just as I expect it, Glory bends for us. "Fuck each other," she says with heat in her eyes. "Let me watch you fuck each other before you both come inside me."

"Glory—" Huxley starts, but she interrupts him with her teeth nipping at his bottom lip.

"Shut up and do it for me, Hux."

His hand slips so quickly from her chest to her throat that it surprises me to see it rise. He grips her, shoves her sideways, and takes her down to the floor, slamming her on her back and settling over her.

"Is that what you want?" He runs the flat of his tongue up the side of her neck, and I pull my hoodie off over my head.

She shivers in his hold and manages a sharp nod against his grip. "Yes."

"Then I'm gonna come inside your mouth after he fucks me."

"Yes," she repeats.

I wrap my arms around his waist and tug him off her, flipping him over me and slamming him face-first against the floor. He rewards me with a groan as I settle my weight on top of him, grabbing his wrists and forcing his arms above his head. He clenches his fists, but he doesn't fight me because he wants this. He loves being in control, but he loves giving it up to me even more.

His ass lifts from the floor, pushing against my hips like he's begging for it. He *is* begging for it, and fuck, I want to give it. I let go of one of his wrists to reach between us, tugging my sweatpants and boxer briefs down just enough to free my cock.

I lift my hand and wave my finger at Glory in a come-hither motion. "Come here."

She rolls and gets on her hands and knees to crawl to me—a fucking goddess crawling to *me*.

I sit up on my knees behind Huxley and bring both my hands to his ass, giving a good squeeze as I hold Glory's attention. I tug at his cheeks, eliciting a strangled groan from him as Glory's eyes widen with desire.

"Spit," I tell her, tracing my thumb along his crack. "Make him wet for me."

She nods eagerly as Huxley presses up onto his forearms, turning his head to look back over his shoulder. "Fuck," he hisses.

Glory bends over him and I watch her lips twist as she pushes saliva to the front of her mouth. She spits soundlessly, dripping liquid down his crack. I'm about to tell her to spread it for me, but I don't have to. She reaches out and traces the saliva down the seam, circling around the hole I'm aching to fuck.

With gritted teeth, Huxley begs, "Christ, *fuck me*."

I let Glory play for a minute, watching the curiosity in her expression as she circles the spot. Then she bends over and spits again, happily preparing him to take me. I have to grip her wrist and pull her hand away just to get her attention, and she gives it to me with a snap of her eyes to mine.

"You wanted to watch," I tell her. "So watch, little bird. Go. Sit. Watch." I jerk my head toward the table just behind us.

I give her a crooked smile as I let go of her, one that makes an absolutely filthy smile spread across her rosy cheeks. She tugs her bottom lip between her teeth as she climbs to her feet, turning and stepping backward toward the table as I fist my dick to line it up with Huxley's entrance.

I start to push inside and his body jerks. "Fuck, yes."

Wood table legs screech across the floor behind us, followed by a crash, a thud, and a surprised, "Oh, shit," from Glory.

Huxley and I both turn our heads to look back at her, her palms gripping for purchase on the edge of the table as she bumps into it with her backside, the maple syrup topples off the table to the floor.

"Sorry," she mutters as she bends to pick it up. "Don't stop."

I keep my eyes on her as I continue to press into Huxley, waiting until she sets the bottle on the table and gives me a small, sweet smile while bringing the side of her hand to her lips, licking off some of the spilled syrup.

I hear her hum as I turn my attention back to Huxley, as he tightens around me while I inch my way inside of him. He's up on all fours and I grip his hips, holding him steady until his muscles relax, until he pulls me deep inside him, inch by steady inch.

Fuck, he feels good.

My eyes fall shut as I savor the feel of him squeezing around me, as he groans and reaches down with one hand to fist himself when I start to move. I fuck him slow and deep, and it only takes moments for me to fall into a trance, to get lost in the rhythm and the warmth of him around me.

And then I feel her beside me, her sensual energy sliding into my space as she drops to her knees and comes in close. I open my eyes to look at her and find her gaze filled with heat and hunger.

Slowly, she licks her bottom lip. Then, she brings up one finger and draws a line across that very lip, drawing a sticky substance across it. She leans in and kisses me softly, gradually opening for me in her raw sensuality.

My tongue seeks to mingle with hers and that's when I taste the maple syrup on her lips—the maple syrup they make at her dead father's factory in addition to their maple candies.

But fuck if it doesn't taste just like her, sickeningly sweet. I grab the back of her head and hold her against me as the kiss deepens, as I lick every last drop from her lip and make sure there isn't any lingering on her thick tongue.

"I could never make a treat more delicious than you, Glory." I drop my forehead to hers as she looks up at me from beneath her lashes. "I want to consume every part of you, taste every sweet morsel of madness you feed me."

"I want you," she pants. "I need you both…always."

As easily as breathing, I promise her, "Always."

Huxley reaches back with one arm, swatting her hip. "Have you watched enough yet? I need your mouth on me, sugar."

Sugar.

A very appropriate nickname for the sweetest thing in my life. She tastes like heaven, but if you take too much from her, she'll turn on you and make you wish you'd never taken a single bite.

A vicious vixen.

She turned on her disgusting father when he took too much, and she's going to do the same to Maura.

And I can't fucking wait to see it.

The thought of it throbs through my cock and forces me to move my hips, to fuck and thrust as Huxley rises, lifting himself upright while I fuck him. Glory quickly bends over his lap to give him what he needs, because she would give him anything.

I think she might give me anything, too.

I hold on to him as I find a rhythm, as Glory wraps her soft, sweet lips around Huxley's cock and takes him inside her mouth. His head falls back as his hand lands on the back of her head, not pushing her down but stroking her fake blonde hair.

I wish I could strip the dye from it and see the dark color of her roots all the way down the strands. She's stunning exactly as she is, but I selfishly want to see the darkness take her entirely, stripping what's left of her mask to leave her raw and bare and entirely real.

I watch as her head bobs in his lap, as one of her hands disappears to reach for her pussy. As much as I love seeing her consume Huxley the way I want to, I can't bear the thought of her making herself come when we can do it for her.

I slip my hand over Huxley's hard chest and up his throat, pinching at his jaw to tilt his chin back. I whisper against his ear, "I want your cock inside her cunt so I can fuck her through you."

His body shudders and sinks in my hold as I loosen my grip, letting my hand drift across his chest before falling away so he can move freely. He slips his fingers into her hair, grips her harshly, and tugs her head up from his lap. Her lips leave his cock with a smack, and she pants, looking at him with hooded eyes, the skin around her mouth flushed pink.

"Lay down in front of me," he tells her, and she does.

I feel an awakening deep in my soul, a reverberation of perfect harmony I've never felt before. The perfection of the three of us together is something I cannot describe with any level of accuracy. And I know they feel it, too.

It's Glory's way of needing us both to command and

care for her, the way she needs to trust us so she can let go and let us give her everything she needs.

It's Huxley's perfect balance between control and submission—the way he lets me command him so he can feel free while dominating her senses.

It's my ownership, my claiming of the both of them that leads us all and drives us into blissful insanity.

It's healing for all of us.

We all feel that perfect alignment as Glory spreads her legs and Huxley tugs her closer, slipping deeply inside her. We feel it together, all at once, letting out a single moan in unison as he buries inside her to the hilt while I'm buried inside him. He lays over her, letting me control us, letting me fuck him, which moves him inside her.

We let go inside our peaceful madness.

As heat grows, tension builds and pleasure looms. When Glory convulses in her release, it sets all of us off at once and we fall together.

We fall deeply.

We fall madly.

We fall forever.

CHAPTER 22
Glory

I'M IN LOVE.

Profoundly and strangely in love with two men I never should have fallen for—my stepbrother and my former captor.

Even stranger, I've allowed my former captor to place me back inside my cage for a sick test of my stepmother's morality.

And it was my idea.

My mind isn't right…I don't think it ever has been. Yet somehow, that doesn't bother me anymore. I've found passion and pleasure and devotion in this sickness, and I never want to be well again.

But Huxley still struggles and keeps me soft, keeps me gentle and loving because I never want him to feel hurt or fear. He paces the small space as we wait for Ambrose to return with Maura. He sent her a vague text, letting her know he had something to show her, and she agreed to let him pick her up and bring her to his home.

I don't know if she's stupid, careless, or fearless because it's well past four in the morning and she's letting a man drive her to an unknown place deep in the woods.

Ambrose says she's never been to his home before—that no one ever has—and I believe him. I saw how the path his truck would travel disappears into the tree line, narrow and hidden. He said it would take him thirty minutes to drive through the forest and get to the paved road. We've been here for over an hour, waiting for his return, and Huxley's anxiety grows with each passing minute.

"What if he doesn't come back?"

"He'll come back, Hux. Why wouldn't he?"

"What if all of this is just some…some game to him? What if he's not coming back?"

"How can you even think that now? After everything that's happened between us. You know he's coming back."

He spins to face me. "I think I have good reason to question it at this point, don't you?"

I shake my head. "No. Not at all."

This is odd, this flip between us where I'm calm and sure and he's anxious and suspicious. I go to him, slip my arms around his waist, and hug him close as I press my cheek against his chest. He sighs, wrapping his arms around me and cradling the back of my head in his hand.

"I know you're right," he whispers after a beat passes. "I know. I'm just afraid."

"What are you afraid of?"

"Afraid I've found something I can't let go of. Afraid for our future. Afraid that I'm ruining my life over some fleeting passion."

My eyebrows twitch as anger seeps in. But somehow, I'm able to push it away, shove it back, keep it from gripping me and shutting me down. That alone is enough to make me know how real this is, how important, how special this bond is between the three of us. It keeps me present. It's the only thing in the world that could keep me grounded in reality because it's the only real thing I've ever really wanted.

I lift my chin to look up at him. "Do you really think this is just fleeting passion? Do you really think we could ever part ways and be okay? If that's what you think, then you should never have gotten back in this cage with me. You should've left me behind and found your own way home. Go back to school, become a lawyer, and forget we ever happened to you."

He swallows hard, a pained expression tugging at his features. "But then I'd be without you…without him…"

"And what does the thought of that make you feel?"

He squeezes my head, pushing my face against his chest again as he pulls me closer. "Like falling from grace."

I sigh, squeezing him tight. "You could never fall from grace. Not with me. I love you. I'm in love with you both, and the thought of being without either of you just—"

"You don't have to think about that." He strokes my hair. "You don't ever have to think about that."

The low rumble of an engine interrupts the silence that surrounds us, and I feel Huxley blow out a long breath. "Help me, Glory. Give me strength to do this." The way he whispers his words sound like a prayer, like a dark prayer to a goddess of vengeance—to *me*.

I'm quickly overcome with rage and determination, as if his faith in me spins my soul, turning away my meekness and revealing the blood-red screen of justice that took hold of me when I murdered my father.

He had it coming.

And so does Maura.

We let go of each other as we hear the front door open

and voices—specifically Maura's grating tone—fill the house. I back away from the bars, pressing my back to the wall behind me, but Huxley steps forward and grips the bars in his fists.

"You really need to quit smoking," I hear Maura tell Ambrose. "Your house reeks."

"Thanks for the tip," he replies coolly.

Her voice shifts, her tone dropping into something heady and expectant, and it makes me want to gag. "So, what did you want to show me? Your bedroom? God, I hope your sheets are clean. How can you stand living out here like this?"

"I didn't bring you here to fuck, Maura."

Huxley's knuckles go white as he grips the bars tighter.

"Then what the fuck did you bring me here for? I'd rather not stay any longer in this fucking wilderness retreat than I have to. Christ, who lives like this?"

"I want my money."

She laughs. "You haven't finished the job yet."

"It's almost finished. That's what I brought you here to show you. But I'm not finishing it until I have money in my account."

A brief whisper of doubt ripples through me, a quick shiver that makes me wonder if Ambrose would betray us. If he would, in fact, kill us now to get the money from Maura. But I quickly push the thought away because I know the entirety of his soul, just as I know Huxley's, and he would never, *could* never, do that to us.

"What do you have to show me then?"

"Follow me."

Their footsteps approach and I hold my breath, waiting for them to appear in the doorway. Anxiety over her reaction, over Huxley's reaction, makes me sick to my stomach.

Ambrose appears first, giving us both a moment's eye contact—a quick flash of his dark eyes to acknowledge that nothing has changed, that he still loves us and wants us, that he would never betray us for her.

Though he still holds the key to the cage that keeps us bound to him.

He moves inside the room, stepping off toward the side and crossing his arms over his chest. Then Maura appears in the doorway, stopping dead in her tracks the moment her eyes land on the metal bars.

She's dressed sleekly, as always, in a black pencil skirt, tucked in white blouse, and pointed high heels. She would be dressed to the nines this early in the morning—always so damn concerned with her appearance. She's always looked younger than her thirty-seven years, though that's mostly because she's used my father's money to pay for injections and treatments to keep herself looking fresh. I suppose she had to pay to look younger to keep my father's attention.

Sick, fucking bastard.

Her mouth drops open in surprise and she turns her head slowly toward Ambrose, though her eyes stay fixed on us.

"Mom?" Huxley says in mock surprise.

He needs to test her to clear his conscience, and I understand it, I do. I just hate that he feels like he has to put himself through this show to prove that she deserves this.

"I told you to kill them, not keep them alive in a *cage*," she says and red begins to consume me.

I push off the wall and move to stand beside Huxley, wrapping my hands around the bars like he does.

Ambrose turns and leans his back against the side wall, kicking one foot up against it. "I thought you might like one last chance to save your son."

What kind of mother doesn't want to protect her child?

She doesn't even look at Huxley, doesn't attempt any comfort or encouragement or reassurance that she loves him. She just stomps toward Ambrose. "I don't want to see him," she grits through her teeth. "I just want the job done. Can you handle it? If you can't, there will be no money for you, Ambrose. Only jail time."

"Jail time?" Ambrose pushes himself upright, forcing her to take a step back as he moves into her space. "Oh, I don't think so."

She pushes right back, jabbing a finger into his chest. The moment she touches him, the red filter descends. I feel myself fade away, feel myself losing to violent rage and an urgent need to wrap my hands around her throat. I reach out for Huxley, grasping for something to hold on to, anything to keep me present and awake and aware.

He sweeps his arm across the small of my back, wraps his fingers around my waist, and drags me close, holding me tightly against his side. It grounds me, though the rage is heating inside me, boiling me from the inside out.

"Do your job," Maura tells Ambrose. "End it now and then we'll talk about your money."

"And my freedom," he adds, twisting his lips into a cocky smile. "You promised me freedom from you. Freedom from all the dirt you have on me."

She waves her hand dismissively. "Yes, you'll fucking have it, but this," she swings her arm, pointing her finger at us instead, "needs to be done now."

Huxley's fingers curl, digging into my side, helping me stay present. "What needs to be done, Mom?"

Her eyes snap to his and she looks him up and down… but she doesn't see him. She couldn't possibly see him with the way she looks at him so dismissively, so uncaring and cruel.

I hate her.

I fucking hate her.

Hot tears well and burn behind my eyes as she easily tugs her gaze from him, as she turns away from her own goddamn *son* and looks at Ambrose without ever answering Huxley.

"Kill them. Do it now. I'll fucking wait." She turns and leaves, her high heels clicking over the hardwood floor.

Pain washes over me, so much pain when she turns her back on my Huxley, that somehow, it washes away the rage. It overcomes me, filling me with the worst kind of sorrow I've ever known—it breaks me because she's hurt my love, and that hurts more than anything anyone could ever do to me personally.

Unable to stop the tears, I cry, and Huxley grabs me, turns me, pulls me into him to wrap me in his warmth. Ambrose slams the door to the hallway shut and comes to us quickly, slipping his key into the lock and opening the door.

I feel a strange sort of relief ripple through Huxley as the cage opens, as Ambrose pushes inside and circles behind me and they both cover me with warmth in their joint embrace.

"I'm sorry, Hux," I whisper. "I'm so sorry for what she's done."

I feel the twitch in his chest against my cheek, the catch of his breath as he tries to halt his emotions to comfort mine, and I feel selfish.

I have to stop.

I have to make this better for him.

I look up at him, wiggling my arms to free them so I can grab hold of his cheeks, force his face to angle down to meet my eyes, and hold him there.

"I love you," I tell him with raw honesty. "I love you so much, and I won't ever let anyone hurt you like this again."

He nods slightly, but I see the sheen forming over his eyes and it hurts me so much. My mother was everything to me before she died, and I can't imagine her rejection, her hate, her willingness to let me die.

"You still want to do this?" Ambrose asks from behind me. "I can do this for you if you need me to. Your hands can stay clean."

Huxley shakes his head slowly, anger forcing a sneer across his cheeks as his eyebrows dip inward. "I don't want clean hands in this. Not after that."

"I want to hurt her..." I tell him.

His gaze darkens, narrowing in on me as he lowers his forehead to mine. "I won't stop you."

The relief I feel in that permission is overwhelming, painful, blissful, as all-consuming as my violent rage, but so, so much better.

I'm not a bad person...I know I'm not.

But the thought of hurting her, killing her, destroying her for the way she's hurt him makes me shudder with need.

"Then let me go after her." I lower my hands to his chest, pushing softly, not to push him away but to encourage him to let me go and hurt the one who hurt him.

He visibly swallows, then presses a kiss to the top of my

head. "Go," he says, then releases me and steps back.

I'm frozen on the precipice of this dark moment—a dark moment that will define the rest of our lives together. If we go through with this, if we kill Maura, our fates are sealed together forever. We'll have to leave everything we know behind and flee, find our own place together, somewhere we can hide from the world. And though a part of me hesitates to leave behind the comfort of a wealthy lifestyle, the rest of me begs to run from it, from the life that burnt my heart to ashes and broke my soul into pieces.

I want my future with Huxley and Ambrose, even if all we have is each other.

Ambrose presses his palm to the small of my back as he steps away, encouraging me forward. "We're right behind you," he says. "Go."

I turn my head, looking back and forth at both of them before I nod, before I step from the cage, open the door, and step out into the hallway.

I turn, take a step forward and there, standing in the kitchen where I fucked her son, stands Maura, holding up her cell phone, trying to find a signal. She won't get one, and it wouldn't matter if she did.

No one can save her now.

"How do you live like this?" she says as she lowers her head to look across the room at me, thinking I'm Ambrose coming out to tell her the job is done.

Her eyes lock on mine and her face falls. Her head cocks to the side, and I see the confusion shadow her expression. She pushes off the counter where she leaned and takes a step forward.

"What are you—"

But I never let her finish the sentence.

The angry red tries to take hold of me, but my pain is stronger, crossing my vision as a dark black shadow…and it's so much better. It doesn't take me away. It doesn't disconnect me or hide me from reality. It wraps around me and strengthens me, emboldens me, gives me the fury I need without hiding me away, trapped in my own mind.

With the darkness surrounding me, I run for her.

CHAPTER 23
Glory

MAURA RUNS FOR the door as I come after her, tripping over her heels as she reaches for the knob. But I'm quicker, and I reach her first. My left hand wraps around her wrist, tugging her back as I reach with my right and squeeze my palm around her throat.

Her hand comes up to shove my forearm, but I'm stronger in my fury, shoving her back and slamming her against the door. Air rushes from her lungs with a satisfying *oomph* as she slams into the wood, the back of her head bumping against it.

The fear that lights a blaze behind her eyes fuels me, tears through me, strengthens my primal rage that calls me to tighten my grip around her throat. She fights me, throwing her hands and hitting my arms, my shoulders, even my head. But there's no pain when I'm so focused, so intent on choking the life out of her for all the pain she caused Huxley, for all the nights I'd made myself forget that she'd been a witness to the horror I had experienced.

She was there…

She saw what my father did…she *knew* what he was doing to me. I guess I've repressed the memories, but suddenly, it all comes rushing back. She'd seen it happen. She'd witnessed my torment. She'd called me a whore, watched my father shut and lock the door, and she did nothing.

Nothing.

She turned a blind eye to my abuse and blamed me for it, but she's not getting away with it anymore.

No more.

No more.

No. Fucking. More.

I feel something hit the side of my head, like a sharp point slamming into my skull. I hear Huxley and Ambrose shout, anger sinking through their voices as one of them drags me back. I blink and look at her hand as Ambrose grabs Maura by the shoulders, spins her, and tosses her to the floor. She's holding her stiletto in one hand.

Is that what she hit me with?

Huxley's hands are on my shoulders as he twists me to face him. I lift my hand and press my palm against the spot where I was struck, just above my ear. It throbs and aches, but it's nothing more than a headache.

"You okay?" Huxley asks, bending to level his eyes with mine.

I nod. "I'm fine." I look around him to see Ambrose straddling Maura's waist on the ground, struggling to grab hold of her flailing wrists as she fights him.

I give Huxley a quick glance—another reassuring look that I'm okay—before I move around him, marching past Ambrose and Maura's struggle on the ground beside the kitchen table. I head for the stove and the knife block beside it, but the red, violent filter falls in front of my eyes, dragging me back to a memory that stops me in my tracks only a step away.

Bent over the kitchen island.
Cell phone ringing.
Reaching for a knife.
My father's bloodied, lifeless body on the floor.
Landing on my knees in the snow.
Hands red, covered in his blood.
Huxley appearing before me to come to my rescue.

I snap from the red filter of memory and twist back into black reality, taking the last step, reaching out and pulling a long blade from the block. I turn and take a step, ready to drop to my knees beside Ambrose and drive the tip of my weapon through her sick heart, but Huxley's calm, determined voice stops me.

"Wait." He looks down at Ambrose. "Tie her hands so she can't hurt Glory again."

Maura's eyes widen as fear grips her, as understanding hits that her son is with *us* and not with *her.* "Huxley! What are you…*Do* something!"

He pulls a chair from the table and spins it to face her, his eyes cold and hard as he watches Ambrose pull her up from the floor. "I am doing something, Mom. I'm taking my life back."

"Your—" she stammers, her fight slowing with her quickening confusion as Ambrose twists her around and shoves her down onto the seat. Her blouse is half untucked and her pinned up hair falls in tangled pieces around her head. "What are you saying, Huxley? What are you *doing?*" She adds a pained inflection to her voice, and it's so fake that it makes my blood boil.

I stomp forward, brandishing the knife and waving it in her direction. "We're doing to you what you wanted done to us. Don't act like you're surprised."

She shakes her head. "I don't know what you're talking about."

"You can't lie to us, Maura!" I point the tip of the knife down the hallway. "We were right there when you told Ambrose to finish the fucking job! He recorded you in your office and we heard it all…We know everything you asked him to do. We heard every goddamn word you said!"

She turns her head, looking up and over her shoulder at Ambrose as he pulls rope in tight knots around her wrists, her arms held behind her back. "Ambrose?"

"You were fooling yourself to ever think you could trust me," he says. "I never even liked you. You were an okay fuck when I didn't have someone better, but now you're just a waste of space standing in my way." He gives a final tug, eliciting a sharp moan with the tightening of the rope as Maura straightens and purses her lips. He moves around to her side and bends to give her striking eye contact. "And your son gives me far better orgasms than you ever did."

"You fucking liar," she spits as Ambrose straightens and moves to stand beside Huxley. "My son isn't gay."

Huxley's voice is flat, monotone, and darkly perfect for the situation at hand. "I wouldn't say I have a preference, Mom." He looks her up and down. "But I would say I have a far greater capacity to love than you do."

"It's not that I don't *love* you…" Maura starts, scooting forward on the seat, trying to play the part of contrition.

"It's *exactly* that you don't love me. You never did, did you? You played it off as sick, sarcastic humor all those times you said I ruined your life, but it was true, wasn't it? Did you hate me from the moment I was born?"

"How dare you even ask me that? I gave you *everything*, the whole fucking world, and you see where it got me? I sacrificed and sacrificed for you. Do you know how many dicks I had to suck before I found a man who would take care of us both? I didn't want you when I was sixteen, but I—"

"And you don't want me now," Huxley charges forward. Through his outstretched arm, he points his finger back in Ambrose's direction. "You told him to find us and kill us."

"I wouldn't have asked him to kill you if you hadn't already been missing. You were probably as good as dead anyway, weren't you? Where did he find you, anyway?"

"As if you care. As if it matters. You told him to *kill* us."

"The opportunity presented itself—"

Huxley snaps. Reaching over her shoulders, he grabs hold of the top of the chair with both hands, bending to look her squarely in the eye. "The *opportunity?* Do you even hear yourself? I ought to let Glory gut you like a fish and let you bleed out."

Maura's face shifts, all the fakeness melting away and giving way to her cold, heartless reality. "What do you want, then? Money? Freedom? Take your pitiful allowance from my checking account and go. I couldn't care less if you disappear from my life."

Huxley's head twists to the side. "But that's the problem, isn't it? You're lying right to my face. The only reason we're all here together is because you want Glory and me dead... because we stand in the way of you gaining complete control over the Tolliver fortune. Almost as if Beau knew you were a gold-digging bitch and made sure you were the last in line to get his money. But the damn bastard didn't bank on just how heartless you are, did he? He didn't bank on Glory fighting back and ending his life for all the pain he caused her. And you didn't bank on the fact that Glory is stronger than all of us; she loves deeper than any of us are capable of, and her loyalty to me is thicker than blood. When you hurt me, you hurt *her*. And do you know what she does when she's hurt?"

Maura has the gall to turn her head, to look at me with a sneer, and speaks to me with a mocking tone. "Cry and bend over for daddy?"

I grip the handle of my blade tighter. Ambrose shoves Huxley aside before backhanding the bitch, his knuckles landing with a reverberating *smack* that echoes through the room. She slips sideways from the chair, falling to the floor on her hip, unable to keep herself up with her hands tied behind her back.

Ambrose drops to one knee beside her, bending down and gripping her cheeks so tightly that I can see her skin turn white beneath his fingers.

"Do you have any idea what happened to Beau?" Ambrose asks. "Are you the biggest moron on the planet? *I* didn't kill Beau. He was dead before you even knew he was missing. Glory murdered him after he raped her, and your son helped her bury the body. And we're going to let her end your life the same way she ended his."

Maura thrashes, tugging against her binding as Ambrose grabs her elbow and pulls her from the floor to her feet. He lets go of her and she wobbles, trying to catch her balance with one shoe off and the other still on.

"Fine," Maura says. "So kill me. End all of our chances at getting any of that money. They'll find out Glory killed Beau and she'll go to prison." She looks at her son. "And you will, too, because you helped her. What were you thinking?"

"I love her. That's all I was thinking about," Huxley says through gritted teeth.

"So much that you would go to prison for her? Huxley, please. You've lost your fucking mind."

"Maybe I have." He shrugs. "But I've found something I need more than my mind."

She fake pouts, tilting her head. "Oh, and what have you found, my clueless child? *Love?* You think that will last?"

I see the shift in him, the way Huxley's eyes flash as something inside him snaps and sets him free. He stands taller, stronger, somehow brighter and darker all at once. It's like watching him take ownership of every deep and dark part of himself, and it sends a rush through my veins. My heart beats faster.

"It's not just love, Mom. It's sacrifice. I've done nothing but give my whole life. I've sacrificed and saved, but no one was there to save me when I needed it. No one until them. Glory and Ambrose want me enough to sacrifice everything for me, to help me do this, to get through this—"

"Get through what? Killing your mother?! That's your goddamn choice, Huxley!"

"Oh, shut the fuck up, Maura," Ambrose says coolly, drawing my eyes to where he stands beside the kitchen table.

I watch as he sifts through Maura's black leather purse, finding and pulling out a couple of candies which are individually wrapped in brown plastic—our famous maple candies from Tolliver's Treats.

"I think we've heard enough," Ambrose starts, taking the candies with him as he circles Maura to lean his ass against the back of the couch. He looks over at Huxley. "Have you said what you needed to say?" He holds out his palm full of candy, beckoning him over. "Let Glory finish this. She's fuming."

I only realize it when he says it that I'm breathing heavily, huffing through my nose with my nostrils flaring. Both of my fists are curled tightly, the knife strongly in my grip at my side. I'm barely controlling myself, but I hadn't even realized it until Ambrose said something.

Huxley stares at Ambrose, a strange, dark calm softening his features into complacency. Darkness and hatred shadow his eyes. He deserves to hold that darkness if he wants to, but I hate seeing him this way, in so much pain. I go to them before I can think about going to her, even though anger builds and builds inside me.

Stopping in front of Huxley, I reach up to caress his cheek with my free hand. He leans into my touch, his expression softening just a bit as he lets his eyes fall shut. "I'm going to make this right," I tell him. "Just let me end her and then we can be happy again. All of us."

His eyes open gently, and he turns his head to kiss my palm. "She's left us no choice. It has to be done."

"It has to be done," I repeat.

I let my hand fall away as I take a step back and flash my eyes at Ambrose, silently begging him to comfort Huxley or shield him or something, *anything*. Because I know Huxley is too good for this, too pure, too loving, too kind. Though he's raging and hurting in this moment, I know he will feel guilt for this later.

I take another step back as Ambrose turns to him, cradles his cheek softly in his strong and dominant hand, and leans forward to press a gentle kiss to his lips. My breath catches as it deepens, as Ambrose feeds him comfort in these violent moments.

I turn to Maura, ready to drive my knife inside her, to stab her, slice her, rip her to shreds, but I'm frozen when I see her smile at me.

"Wipe that grin from your face." I try to sound strong, but I feel my meekness creep back in the longer she looks at me that way, with an evil grin spread across her cheeks that sets off warning bells in my mind. "You haven't won. You've lost everything."

"Maybe," she says, then tilts her head. "Maybe not."

I hear the crinkling of plastic wrappers and she and I both turn to look. Ambrose pops one of the maple candies into his mouth and Huxley does the same a moment later.

"I like a little treat with my entertainment," Ambrose says in response to our attention. "Don't let us interrupt."

I give him a nod and he smiles at me. It gives me strength, though I'm suddenly feeling anxious. I try to shake it off, turning my attention back to Maura. I take a step toward her, and she steps back, but the damn smile is still on her face and it's unsettling.

"Glory," Ambrose says abruptly, and it stops me. His voice is suddenly strange. When I turn to look at him, he steps toward me, his eyes wide, smile gone.

"They say you shouldn't take candy from strangers," Maura purrs. "But perhaps you shouldn't take it from heartless women, either."

Ambrose slumps, his knees hitting the floor.

"Fuck...*fuck*..." Huxley says. He snaps his head to look at me as his fingers touch his lips, coming to the same conclusion I'm drawing at the same moment.

The candy…

What did she do to it?

"I wouldn't worry too much," Maura says. "He'll be all right. Both of them will." Ambrose tumbles sideways to the ground, and I rush to his side, but he's already unconscious. "He was never going to get away with any of this, you know. I was going to make sure he'd done what I asked him to do, make sure he had a sample of our newest flavor treat, and leave him to sleep peacefully while I drove his truck back to get the police." Huxley's eyelids droop as he stumbles to his knees, and I drop the knife, turning to grip his shoulders as he sways. "It all makes sense, really. Ambrose was my slighted lover, who murdered my entire family thinking it would allow us to be together. You'd all be gone then, and nothing would stand in my way. The fortune would be mine, and I wouldn't have to give a dime to Ambrose."

"Do it," Huxley whispers as he blinks, as his eyelids drift shut, and he falls sideways, too heavy for me to hold up. I manage to guide his fall, and he lands with his head near Ambrose's knees.

I watch them both, my eyes on their chests, making sure they're breathing and okay. When I'm certain that they are, I let it take me.

I let the shadow wrap around me, wring out whatever goodness might have been left in my soul, and let it take me entirely. I wrap my palm around the handle of the blade and slowly rise to my feet.

"You weak, pathetic, little girl," Maura mocks. "Do you think you scare me? Do you think I'm afraid that you'll hurt me?" Her face shifts from mocking to loathing. "I *know* you won't. You're not capable of fighting back. You let Beau hurt you for years, bending for dear old dad just because he wanted it. Your father was sick, and you probably are, too."

I feel a calm wash over me. "I'm not sick. I'm strong. Stronger than you."

"Stronger than *me*? You don't know what strong is. Strong is having a baby at sixteen, getting thrown out of your house, and learning to fend for yourself. You're an entitled, privileged little bitch who never had to work a day in her life."

"Maybe I am. But you know what you are?"

"What?" She cocks her head to the side in challenge.

"Entertainment."

I circle around behind her and grab hold of the rope that binds her wrists in my free hand. I shove her forward, marching her to the door. I let go of her to grip the knob, twist, and pull the door open wide.

I shove her into the entryway, seeing the snow fall slowly, but heavily behind her...slowly and heavily, like how the darkness falls over my soul. She turns to face me, looking at me with wide eyes.

I turn the blade in my hand, widen my stance, and let the darkness take control of me. "Run."

CHAPTER 24

I'M STUCK IN a strange sort of slumber. I can feel something behind my head, a bony knee slamming into the back of it, jarring me awake. But opening my eyes is hard, and unconsciousness pushes blackness around the edges of my vision.

I hear a groan and it's familiar.

Am I in bed with Ambrose?

That can't be right…

When did I fall asleep?

Where? How?

"Huxley?" I hear my name faintly, and I'm sure the voice belongs to Ambrose. "Huxley," he says more urgently, and I feel him move around me.

I blink, trying to open my eyes, but the lids are fucking heavy. Everything in my body tells me to relax, to let go, to fall back into sleep. But my mind is awake inside my shell of a body, and it's insistent that something's wrong, that I need to snap out of this and wake the fuck up.

I feel his palms on my cheeks and a prickle of electricity from his touch ripples through me. His hands fall to my shoulders, and he shakes me. I try to blink again, fighting against this sleep that wants to win. I feel him tug me over onto his lap and his warmth sinks through me.

His heat is harsh against the chill I feel in my bones—it's so fucking cold in here. There's a wintry breeze blowing across my face, which contrasts the heat of his legs beneath my shoulders.

"Huxley!" He shakes me again. "Wake the fuck up! Glory and Maura are gone."

Fuck.

I fight to open my eyes, blinking until they stay open for longer than a half a second. "What?" I manage to mumble.

He tugs at me, lifting me upright, and the movement sends energy rushing through me. He wraps his arms around me, hugging me close. My arms slowly prickle back to life and wrap around him, though my grip is weak.

His fingers dig into my hair at the back of my head, cradling me against his strong chest, and I hear the rapid beating of his heart. "Fuck, Huxley. You're okay. You're okay." The tremor in his tone hints at his relief—as if he really didn't know whether I was okay before.

My grip around him tightens, my muscles twitching to life at once with urgent need to comfort him. But then I recall our circumstances and what led to me passing out on the floor.

Glory.

I pull back with a jerk, gripping his shoulders and looking squarely into his dark eyes. "Where's Glory?"

"I don't fucking know, but she and Maura are gone."

He glances over my shoulder behind me, and I turn my head to follow his gaze. The front door of the cabin is wide open, and a heavy snowfall dots white falling speckles against the dark backdrop of the forest.

"Shit." I shove to my feet as my heartbeat quickens, but immediately, I sway and stumble, dropping back down to my knees. "What happened to us?" I ask, bringing the heel of my palm to press against my throbbing forehead.

"Maura. Maura fucking happened to us. I think it was the candy."

"What?"

"I think she put something in it."

"Why the fuck would she—" I start, but I cut myself off. At this point, everything is believable. "It doesn't matter." I plant one foot on the ground and wait for the swirl in my head to steady before slowly pushing to my feet again. "We have to find Glory."

I pause when I'm on my feet, breathing carefully through the whirling nausea that threatens to bring me to my knees again. I glance over to see Ambrose standing, but bent forward over the back of the couch, gripping it to steady himself.

My soul feels ripped in two. One half pulls me toward him, urges me to help him to bed and force him to rest while I take care of him. The other more insistently begs me to get control and run as fast as I can out into that forest until I find Glory. Both parts of me need to save both of them, but I'm so fucking sick I can hardly keep myself upright.

"We have to go," Ambrose says, then takes an audibly deep breath before shoving himself upright. I watch him out of the corner of my eye as he half walks, half stumbles across the room. He unlocks a standing cabinet nestled in the back corner of the kitchen and pulls out two things.

A shotgun and an axe.

Holding them shakily, one in each hand, he makes his

way toward me, holding out the axe. I glance down at it and feel a rumble of rage vibrate through my chest.

My mother wants me dead.

She drugged me and Ambrose with her fucking maple candy. And now she's out there in the forest with Glory, and I don't know whether she's okay—but I know my mother wants her dead, too, and that woman is a fighter.

I wrap my palm around the handle of the axe and give him a nod. It falls heavily in my grip when he releases it, but the weight is grounding, affirming, steadying me through the remnants of nausea and dizziness.

He looks at me with painful intensity as his free hand reaches out for me, slipping along my cheek, fingers digging into my hair at the side of my head. He tugs me forward and leans his forehead against mine. My heart jumps at his touch, at his closeness, at the indignant vengeance that pulses from his soul and shakes through mine.

"No more games. We find Maura and we fucking end her."

I nod against his head. "We end her and bring Glory home safe."

His eyes flutter shut and at first, I think it's because of the poison still running through his veins. But then he tilts his chin and presses a soft yet demanding kiss to my lips that makes my entire being ripple with his intensity.

"We all come home," he whispers against my lips.

Reluctantly, we tear ourselves from each other and make our way through the front door. Our feet sink into the snow as more continues to fall fast and furious from the sky. It's nearly blinding how it falls, painting bright white streaks down the dark tree trunks at the edge of the clearing. The cabin light from within allows us to see that far.

I'm relieved to see Ambrose's truck still parked here—at least neither of them drove away. But that means they're out in the forest somewhere, and there's no telling how long they've been out there or how far they've gotten.

"This way," Ambrose says, and I turn my head to follow his hand as he points down to some quickly fading footprints in the building snow.

If I could take off running, I would, but I still feel the sway as I move, the world around me constantly tilting and shifting with each step I take. I can see how it effects Ambrose in the way his upper body tilts with every other step. But we both fight through it because we have to. Neither of us will stop until we know Glory is safe and the woman who calls herself my mother is dead.

We follow the tracks to the tree line and Ambrose darts into the forest with familiarity. As soon as I step past the tree line to follow him, the world is shrouded in darkness. I can barely see a foot in front of me, and I blink, hoping my eyes will adjust quickly.

"Stay with me," Ambrose says as he picks up his pace.

Though the dizzying sway is gradually wearing off, I feel even more disoriented by the dark, how I strain my eyes trying to see but can hardly make out a branch before it smacks me in the face. But Ambrose…he moves with ease and grace, as if nature is the antidote for the drug swirling within him, as if the trees speak to him and guide him on his path.

We rush through the forest for maybe ten minutes before we hear something snap—a loud crack echoing through the night as if someone stepped on a twig. We full stop and fall into the silence that follows.

For a few moments, the world is still and quiet. I can nearly hear the *whoosh* of the falling snow as flakes rush to the ground, hurrying to fill the spaces between the trees.

"Don't move. Don't breathe. Don't make a sound, Maura." Glory's voice whispers and echoes all around us. I turn my head, seeking the source, but I can't find it. "I'm closing in on you now."

Someone breaks off into a run—we can hear the footfalls padding heavily through the snow.

Ambrose grips my shirt at the center of my chest, tugging me close to him as he says, "That way." He then shoves me to the right.

I don't think, I just move, taking off on a run in that direction, chasing after my mother or Glory, I don't really know. The footfalls I heard grow louder and more distinct as I run, dodging black tree trunks and clawing branches. I'm catching up to someone and I'm wary, not knowing if it's my mother or Glory. I have to be careful not to hurt Glory by mistake.

But then I stop dead in my tracks when I hear my mother cry out, a pained and fearful scream echoing through the dark forest. It makes me pause, triggering my need to save, though I know now she wouldn't extend the same courtesy to me. She had the chance, and she didn't choose to save me.

The scream turns into echoing sobs as an eerie glow begins to peek up from the ground in the distance. Sunrise is nearing, and soon there will be light in the forest.

"Stop, please!" my mother shouts and I run toward the sound.

Soon I can see a silhouette moving across the trees, hobbling and struggling to get away, and I immediately know it's my mother.

"Run, Maura. You can't hide anymore…" Glory's voice sounds far away and near all at once. "Run. Run. *Run.*"

Fuck.

Glory is gone. She's lost to that bloody, violent rage again, and that makes me more fearful for her safety than if she were calm and acting like her usual self. She's lost control, and without control, mistakes are made. She could hurt herself and keep going because the anger pushes her onward.

Light continues to grow, lifting from that line in the distance, and slowly reveals our scene. My mother comes into full view as she backs her way around the trunk of a wide tree in a small clearing.

The tree is familiar.

It's a tree Ambrose brought me to once before.

Hugging the trunk, she peeks her head around it, looking for Glory with no idea that I'm standing right behind her.

Her hands are untied, though the rope still clings to one of her wrists, as though she was cut free. She's still wearing that impractical pencil skirt and her feet are bare in the snow. There's blood coating her left leg and all her weight is shifted onto her right.

She looks like shit.

Glory's been toying with her.

I take a step forward and a branch snaps beneath my shoe.

I stop.

Maura stills.

Then, slowly, she turns. Standing at the base of the large

maple tree—just above the graves of Ambrose's parents—she looks at me with fearful eyes, a tremor running through her body.

"Hu-Huxley…" she stammers through blue-tinged, trembling lips.

And fuck, it tugs at my heart, at the string that activates my endless empathy and my fucking need to save people from themselves.

She wanted me dead.

The axe weighs me down, pulling through my arm and shoulder, reminding me that it's there in my grip. I take another step forward as the light grows, as the sun continues to rise.

My heart races as my mother cries, black eyeliner streaking down her cheeks, her hair a tangled mess, as her bare feet walk forward, stepping on the graves of Ambrose's parents.

Does she deserve to die like they did?

My conscience demands a re-evaluation and I'm forced to allow it. As her steps quicken toward me, my heart sinks, forcing unease to flow through me at the look of my mother. I step back, afraid we've made a mistake, afraid I'll regret this forever.

And then her face switches from sadness to outright rage, and she screams at me across the small clearing atop their graves. "I wish you'd never been born!"

A single gunshot rings out and I jump, startled by the sound of it. I watch with wide eyes as a dark stain slowly spreads from my mother's stomach, flowing out gradually, soaking through the fabric of her blouse.

She glances down at it with shock, then looks back up at me. And though she whispers the words, a breeze kicks up around them as they tumble from her lips, sweeping them through the bare branches and swirling them to echo all around me.

"I never loved you."

I.

See.

Red.

A primal roar forms in my gut, gathers strength in my lungs, and bursts forth from me uncontrollably. My feet move without thought, charging after her at a run as the axe shifts in my grip, moving to be held by both hands, raising high above my head.

Maura falls to her knees as her hand comes up to touch her side, pulling it away to look at the blood that pools. As I close in on her, my mind kicks up a rhythmic chant, telling me to *strike, strike, strike.*

Just steps away, a blur rushes in from my side, a running blur with fake blonde hair and rage in her eyes. She's quicker than me, fiercer than me, more determined than me.

Glory barrels into Maura, slamming her body to the ground before settling on top of her, straddling her waist, bringing her knife up high above her head in both of her tiny hands.

I stop and watch as Glory does what I wanted to do.

She brings down her knife, stabbing it into Maura's chest. Her body jerks and her head falls to the side as she coughs blood, spilling crimson liquid over the bright white snow.

Glory pulls out her blade and strikes again.

Strike, strike, strike.

I'm stunned.

I'm frozen.

I watch as Glory stabs my mother repeatedly, grunting with each plunge of her blade as blood spatters her face.

Ambrose appears from the trees, walking slowly from the direction Glory came, sauntering toward her casually and without care, carrying the shotgun he used to incapacitate my mother in his hands.

Ambrose stops behind Glory and slowly turns his head in my direction. "Do you want me to stop her?" he asks as Glory unapologetically continues to stab her.

"*No more. No more. No more,*" she chants with each drive of her blade.

Before long, Maura stops coughing, stops rolling her head, stops moving entirely. Yet Glory continues her assault as angry tears stream down her face, glistening on her cheeks as they reflect the rising sunlight.

"*No more...*" It becomes a whisper as her speed and vigor slow, as the time between each stab extends.

With a final jab into her chest, Glory stops, her hands still wrapped around the handle, her head bowing as she begins to sob. The axe drops from my grip and lands heavily in the snow. Ambrose sets down his shotgun and we both move for her at the same time.

I reach down for Glory, and she lifts her chin to look up at me. "I lost control again," she whispers, pain wrinkling the features of her face.

She lifts her hands, reaching up for me like a lost child who needs comfort. I will always give her comfort. I grab beneath her arms and lift her off Maura, unconcerned with the blood that soaks Glory from head to toe as I draw her into my arms and drag her away from the body.

She wraps her arms around my neck and holds me close, crying into my shoulder. Ambrose joins us a second later, wrapping his arms around us both, offering me comfort in his embrace as I give everything I have to Glory. I can give endlessly to her now because he strengthens me; he replenishes me when I've given her all that I have to give. And more than anything in the world, that makes me feel whole. It makes me feel aligned with the universe. It makes me feel peaceful.

Despite the vileness of our lives and the bloodshed that brought us here, we're together now. Our three broken souls stitched together forever as one with this final act of violence to end the person who meant to destroy us.

Except…my hands are still clean.

And that feels wrong.

It feels out of balance.

They've both bloodied their hands in this, and mine are clean. I don't think I can move forward with that weighing on me.

I pull back from Glory, gripping her shoulders, dipping down to level my eyes with hers. I give her a small smile, the encouragement she so desperately needs. I tuck a strand of bloody hair behind her ear, then lift my eyes to meet Ambrose's as I push her back against him. I step back and release her. Then, he grips her by the shoulders and spins her to face him, quickly enclosing her in his warm embrace.

I bend and pick up the axe, and it feels like I'm holding the weight of the world as I drag it along with me to my mother's gory corpse. It should hurt me to see her like this, and though it does pull at my humanity, I'm reminded that this is what she wanted to have done to me. She wanted this to be *me,* sliced and lifeless. She wanted this to be *Glory.*

I draw in a deep breath of indignation, letting the righteousness fill my lungs as I move the axe to be held between both of my hands. I lift it above my head, drawing the monumental weight higher. My gaze falls to her blood-streaked neck and I hear her words from Ambrose's recording echo in my mind.

"I want their skulls."

She wanted my Glory dead.

She wanted my Glory's *skull.*

And that reminder is enough to make the true image of her come to life before me. A monster lies here on the forest floor, dead atop the graves of the monsters who drove Ambrose to murder. And Glory's monster is buried in this forest, too.

Ambrose and Glory were brave enough to slay their monsters, and though she's already dead, I'll do the same to mine just to be worthy of them.

The dark magic feeling of Sugar Wood Forest ripples through the branches, clawing at the frigid air, infecting it with sin that sinks inside me. It crawls up my arms, blackens my veins, and bursts through my fingertips with insistence to deliver the final blow.

With a whisper of encouragement from the tainted trees, from the forest that gave life to Tolliver's Treats and the monsters who ran it, I let my arms fall.

Swinging down with a swift and heavy blow, I strike, slicing the axe blade cleanly through her neck.

"I want their skulls."

She'll never have Glory's skull, but the forest can have hers.

I feel Ambrose wrap his hand around my wrist, tugging and encouraging me to let go of the axe. I loosen my grip, let go, and take a step back.

And Glory's right there to take me away from the violence and into the peace of her arms, pulling me away and hugging me close.

I squeeze her, bringing my hand up to cradle the back of her head and hold her tightly in place. I rest my chin on the top of her head as the bright sun rises behind Ambrose. The sight of his darkness shadowed by light is the first moment I realize that the snowfall stopped, and I wonder how long ago it had. The falling snow lifted from the forest like the plague has lifted from our souls.

"It's done," Glory says, pressing a kiss to my chest. "It's all done now. It's over."

The captor who changed everything smiles at us with the sunlight framing him like a fallen angel. "And the rest has only just begun."

CHAPTER 25
Glory

FIVE YEARS LATER

I BRUSH MY palms over my thighs, wiping the soil from my hands onto my jeans as I look out from the vegetable garden where I kneel. I think I spy a fawn on the other side of the wooden fence Huxley built around the garden.

I push to my feet and walk between the rows of freshly sprouting tomatoes, carrots, and basil. We have a greenhouse for year-round self-sustenance, but Huxley knows how I love being outside in the sunshine during the spring and summer.

After the long, dreary winters here in the Pacific Northwest, it's healing for me to be out of the cabin. Really, it's healing for me to have my hands in the soil, to connect with the Earth and show my gratitude for the life she gives—for the happiness we've been blessed to find here.

Sugar Wood was stained by evil and ruined forever by my family. The Tollivers took from that forest, bleeding the trees of their maple, and profiting from it—and never giving back to it everything they took from it.

But here we've found precious, uninhabited land, tucked away in the depths of forest that stretch for miles along the West Coast. We came upon this spot seeking shelter, a place to hide away from the world as if we were dead walking, because that's how we have to live—as if we're dead.

We came upon this place with gratitude, mindful of the way human energy lingers and twists and influences the mind. Sugar Wood held all the negative energy of the monsters we buried there, but we won't be monsters upon this perfect piece of the world we've found.

We've had to take some from nature in this stretch of woods, but we've given back to it in equal measure. Gardening keeps me grounded, reminds me where life comes from and where it ends. Planting new vegetables and flowers outdoors each season allows me to give life back to the Earth, something new for it to nurture and grow, and my soul has felt lighter since I began doing it.

I'm determined to keep as much good energy as possible in this perfect piece of the planet that we've found.

At the end of the row, I place my elbows atop the wooden fence, resting my chin on my forearms to peek over the top. The small fawn on the other side bows her head, sniffing along the fence. Her tan fur is speckled with white dots that remind me of snowfall.

Part of me dislikes that we've had to put up the fence to keep the critters out of the garden, but it's become necessary as I seem to have attracted the lot of them to our cozy hideout in the forest. Deer, rabbits, birds, chipmunks—all manner of creature find me here, and it always puts a smile on my face.

I never cared much for animals or nature in my life before, but as the years pass, I've grown more and more fond of it, happier than I ever thought I could be in a life outside of privilege and wealth.

Everything that belongs to us, we built together. We had no money when we left Sugar Wood. It wasn't worth the risk trying to pull funds from bank accounts when we needed the world to think we were dead. We had a truck and each other and nothing more.

But it was enough.

Peace is the most valuable thing to me now.

The fawn lifts her head and looks up at me, tilting her head to watch me as I watch her. "Are you looking for my tomatoes?" I ask. "Come back in a few weeks and I'll have plenty for you."

"I keep telling you, sugar, they're never gonna talk back," Huxley says with a grin.

I turn my head to watch him pass by, walking in the opposite direction. "It won't stop me from trying," I call after him.

He gives me a quick wink as he strolls on past, looking particularly rugged today. The scruff on his face is coarse as he grows it out and the flannel shirt rolled up at the sleeves is a bit of a new look for him. It's different, but it's a look that works, and one that I like very, very much.

Being here has changed him, too, and in all good ways. Not that anything needed to change within him—Huxley was always perfect to me.

But something freed within him the night we killed his mother. It's not something we talk about anymore, though we talked about it a lot back then. The first year was hard for us, but then…we found this place. We found this little piece of paradise nestled away in secret, and it was like the universe had aligned for us.

I step back from the fence and turn to face him as he

strolls away, carrying a stack of logs across the clearing beside the modest cabin we built on our own. I watch as he approaches the stump near the shed where we store our chopped wood—a shed that we also built on our own.

Ambrose is in front of the stump, lifting his axe high above his head and driving it down with force, splitting a log with one perfect strike. He sets it down as Huxley lays the logs beside the stump, swiping sweat from his brow with the back of his forearm. He smiles at Huxley when he stands back up, his teeth sparkling bright framed by his pillowy lips and thick black beard.

He lifts the bottom hem of his long-sleeved Henley to swipe over his face, revealing his sculpted torso beneath. I feel a shiver run down my spine and an ache springs from nowhere between my legs. It will never cease to amaze me the way that they *know*. We've found such perfect harmony, the three of us together here on this beautiful stretch of Earth, that they know intuitively when I have a need…any kind of need.

I wouldn't have to lift a finger if I didn't want to because they would happily do anything for me. I don't understand how I got so lucky to have that kind of love from them, but I know I'll never take it for granted. And because I know they would do anything for me, I let them do anything *to* me.

Sometimes they play together, sometimes I play with Huxley, sometimes I play with Ambrose. But the best times are when we all play together, and it's been more than a week since we have.

I want them now and they know it.

Huxley's head turns over his shoulder to look at me at the same time that Ambrose snaps his eyes to meet mine across the clearing. I take in a shuddering breath as a cool late-spring breeze whips around me, chilly as it skates across my bare arms, making my nipples harden beneath my T-shirt.

Ambrose's face morphs into something serious—that sinful dark look he gets when he wants to do terrible and beautiful things to me.

I want him to do terrible and beautiful things to me.

His eyes are locked on mine from forty feet away as he steps toward Huxley, grabs his cheeks to turn his head toward him, and leans in to kiss him hard.

A soft moan escapes me, blowing across the yard, echoing silently all around us. Ambrose spins Huxley around and pushes his back against the shed, pinning him there with his body as he kisses him urgently, roughly, deliciously.

I stand still as I watch, need pulsing between my legs.

Ambrose breaks the kiss and looks back at me, though he keeps Huxley pinned in place with his hard body. My gaze falls on Huxley's face to find his eyes closed in delightful shock, his lips parted, waiting for Ambrose to devour him.

But I'm feeling a little selfish, a little greedy. I want to be the center of their attention. We haven't been truly wild together for a while, and I feel the need for it rustling through the trees. It's an itch that demands to be scratched. Even the Earth insists that we let out our violence on each other in small doses—we use each other for all our needs, even the dark ones.

Especially the dark ones.

It keeps us balanced.

We unleash our primal urges safely on one another so we never have to unleash them on anyone else. We don't let anyone else into our lives. It would disrupt our discordant harmony.

Ambrose's eyes narrow on me predatorially and my

breath catches in my lungs. He knows what I need and he's going to deliver.

"Fuck," I mutter breathlessly.

Before he can even think about making a move, I smile at him, turn, and run.

I don't need to look over my shoulder to know he's coming after me…to know they're *both* coming after me. I dart past the tree line and sprint into the forest. My feet carry me quickly across the soft earth, my shoes crunching over branches as I leap over logs and dart between trees.

"Fly faster, little bird," I hear Ambrose call from behind me, "I'm coming to catch and cage you."

Desire sinks in my gut. I want them to catch me, but I won't slow down.

It's no fun if the chase isn't real.

I feel them both running with me, as our one soul travels through the trees, forever connected, never letting me slip away from them entirely.

In the distance, I see the fawn from before, her head dipped and rooting around the forest floor.

A smile touches my cheeks to see her there, but it's not just her. There's another—no, there are three of them.

Three fawns together?

How extraordinary.

But where is the doe?

I run in their direction for no reason other than instinct drawing me near them. When their heads snap up all at once, ears perking to stand tall, and all of them looking in the same direction, I feel it in my bones.

Danger.

I cast a glance in the direction of their collective stare.

A mountain lion stands ahead of them, crouched and creeping toward them, preparing to pounce.

Where is their mother?

Why aren't they running?

Without a second thought, I sprint straight for them, darting in front of them and slamming to a stop.

"Glory!" Ambrose shouts as I turn to face the cougar.

"Glory, get down!" Huxley shouts, and I hear the click as he cocks the handgun he always carries when we're outside— for this very reason.

I hold up my palm in the direction of his voice, though my eyes remain fixed on the predator in front of me, creeping in low, sneaking up on these innocent fawns who didn't know to look out for predators in their own home. Like Ambrose, Huxley, and I didn't know to look out for the predators in *our* own homes.

Fierce protective energy tears through my gut and rips through my body, burning rage through my veins.

"Get down. I've got the shot," Huxley insists, his voice a little closer now.

But I only shake my head as I widen my stance, plant my feet, and pull my shoulders back to stand tall and proud above the cougar before me. I spread my arms out to my sides, holding them protectively in front of the frozen fawn behind me.

I let the anger of my past—the rage against the predators who raised all of us and failed to protect our inner children— boil and bubble inside me. I let it rise in my chest and warm my voice. I let it wrap strength around my words, and in a deep, strong tone, I shout at the deadly creature in front of me, "Get back!"

I've finally found my voice, my strength, my power. I feel it pulse around me, like a protective force field.

And the mountain lion feels it, too.

She rises, her movement nearly imperceptible with how gradually she moves, but she rises, coming out of her aggressive stance.

"Hold steady," I hear Ambrose say softly, closer than before. "You've got her, little bird."

I feel him push into the force field and it strengthens me further. The front of his shoulder touches the back of mine, and more power ripples through me. I stare down the mountain lion as she slowly backs away, but I can see the movement of Huxley from the corner of my eye, circling around to her side, holding out his gun for a clear shot if he needs to take it.

But with them beside me, protecting me without stepping over me, giving me the space to take control while watching my back with all the fierceness of lions protecting their pride, I'm the most powerful woman in the world.

"Get back!" I shout again with confidence that spills down my insides and drips through my core.

The predator jumps up, turns, and runs away.

I let out a long-held breath and the power of what I just did—standing down a fucking mountain lion—sinks inside me. It's a dense ball of fear that mixes with lust, creating a tornado of need that rips through my belly.

I expect Ambrose to touch me first, because he's right there, pressed up behind me. But my attention is drawn to my side as Huxley puts the safety on, shoves the gun in the back of his waistband, and charges straight for me.

He reaches out for me as he shakes his head, his eyes

wide with the same fear-lust combination that intoxicates me. "That was terrifying…and so fucking hot." His hands slip beneath my jaw, grip my face, and hold me tight as his lips crush mine and he walks me backward.

My back slams into a tree behind me and the stupid, beautiful little group of fawn finally scatter, as if they sense more danger between the three of us than they did with the cougar.

They may be right.

Because I know this is going to be violent and dangerous sex.

It's what I want.

Huxley kisses wetly and carelessly across my mouth, my cheek, and down to my neck. His hips shift forward, digging in against my body as his head dips so he can nuzzle his face into the crook of my neck.

My eyes pop open when I sense Ambrose approach, and he comes in quickly. He grabs my wrist where it lays around Huxley's neck and pulls me away from him sideways. I gasp as he tugs me harshly from the tree, my back scraping against the bark as I slide along it. He tugs me forward, wrapping his palm around the back of my head and holding me steady to kiss me violently. His tongue slices across mine. His teeth nip and bite.

Then Huxley comes in behind me, closing around me, wrapping me in heat as he presses his thickening bulge to my backside. I whimper into Ambrose's mouth as Huxley kisses my neck, sucks and bites, and seeks more of me with aggression.

They break away from me to kiss each other, and my head falls back against Huxley's shoulder. I look over at their licking, lapping mouths as I sink between them, my knees growing weak as desire drips through my core.

"Fuck me," I breathe, begging them both.

They both grab for me, frantically working to undress me. Huxley peels my shirt off as Ambrose works my jeans. He tugs the zipper down, and then I feel Huxley's arm close around my bare waist before he shoves his hand down my panties and roughly gropes for my pussy. I gasp and arch my back as his walking fingers step across my clit, pressing in roughly and rubbing in careless, painful circles.

"You like that?" he breathes against my ear. "You want us rough?"

"Yes," I hiss. "Make me feel how desperately you want me."

Ambrose paws my breasts, tugging the cups of my bra down to expose me. He bends and licks across my nipples, making my body rock with pleasure.

"I always want you desperately," Huxley says. "Every fucking day."

"Show me," I whimper.

Ambrose twists my nipple between his fingers, as his other hand reaches up and combs back into my brown hair—I chopped off the dyed blonde a few years ago and I've been growing it out ever since. Ambrose likes it better this way, and Huxley doesn't care about the color of my hair as long as I like it.

They just want the realest, truest version of me.

Ambrose slips his hand behind my head, lifting it from Huxley's shoulder and dragging me away with him as he backs up. His fingers slip between the strands of my hair, and he twists his hand, wrapping my hair around his grip and jerking my head back. I yelp at the sharp sting.

"Take off your clothes, little bird." He runs his tongue

from the hollow of my throat all the way up to the point of my chin, making me shiver.

He releases me all at once and I whimper. Stepping back, I reach around behind me to unhook my bra and toss it aside. I stare him down as I kick off my shoes and push off my jeans and panties.

I stand proudly between them and their hungry gazes, knowing that they never see all the imperfections of my body that I so frequently name for myself. All they see is a woman they love endlessly, and in our moments like this, I'm able to see myself through their eyes—because their eyes are so insistent with adoration and devotion.

"Do you want to fight us?" Huxley asks from behind me, his voice heavy with lust.

The word slips out on a breath without conscious thought. "Yes."

I used to be weak. I used to let bad things happen to me without fighting back, always waiting for Huxley to save me. So sometimes we play dark games—games that help me remember my strength and how much power I truly possess.

And I have so much power over them.

I like the way it builds inside me when we play this game. I like the way it makes me feel stronger. It lets me act out who I was before when I was so weak and defenseless and rewrite the narrative...They try to take control of me, they let me fight back, and they let me win.

Though sometimes I like to lose on purpose.

Ambrose's eyes flash darkly at me, his hand dropping down to cover and squeeze the bulge in his jeans.

"Turn around," Huxley commands, and with a deep

breath, I slowly turn to face him.

He pulls the gun from his waistband and places it a safe distance away to avoid any accidents in the midst of passion. Then, he produces a small length of rope from his back pocket and my grin twists, watching him coil it around his hand. I'll bet he grabbed it before chasing after me into the woods, hoping it would end this way…knowing that it would.

"On your knees," he says.

I shake my head slowly, showing him without words that I won't just comply.

"On your knees, little bird," Ambrose repeats from behind me.

My eyes shift to the right, purposefully disclosing my next move, because I know what I want his to be. I lunge, starting to run, but I don't try too hard this time. As soon as I lean, they're both after me. Huxley's arms coil around my waist and lift my naked body from the ground. He spins around as my legs kick and I try to jab him with my elbows. But Ambrose is right there in front of me, forcefully grabbing my wrists and tugging my arms in front of me.

He holds both of my wrists in one of his large hands while the other grasps and pulls at the end of the rope, still wrapped around Huxley's hand. Huxley sets me down on my feet but doesn't loosen his grip on me.

And this is where the fun begins.

I bend my knees, twist, dip, and pull myself sideways to get away from them as they fight to keep their hands on me.

"Hold her arms," Ambrose says, and Huxley's hands leave my waist to grip my elbows, squeezing my arms together in front of me, holding me steady.

Ambrose wraps some of the rope around my wrists, but he fails to secure me as I tug hard, jerking back both of my elbows and jamming them harshly into Huxley's biceps.

His weight shifts back just a little and I take advantage of the sway, shoving my weight back against him and pushing until he stumbles. Ambrose lets go of me as Huxley's foot catches and he trips, falling onto his back on the ground. I tumble with him, falling on top of him. His hands grip my waist as he lands and he flips me over, slamming me face-first into the dirt, smothering me with his warm, hard body.

I want to melt, sink into the soil, and become one with the earth. For a minute, I forget the game we're playing, allowing Huxley enough time to reach between us, enough time to unbuckle and unzip and free his cock. I turn my head, letting my cheek press into the dirt as his fingers slide down my crack. He reaches down between my legs to find my pussy already wet for him.

"Fuck, Glory," he mutters, shifting behind me.

I spread my knees for him, desperately wanting him to sink inside me. I let him align his tip and thrust his cock inside me with a full, aching thrust. I let it shatter us both for a few blissful seconds where we both gasp out strangled moans.

And then Ambrose grabs my hands, wrenching them out in front of me, trying again to wrap the rope around my wrists.

God, yes.

I remember the game again and how powerful the orgasm is when I fight back and win.

I squeeze my thighs together and buck my hips as Huxley pulls out, climbing my knees forward along the ground, trying to scramble out from beneath him. He grabs the back of my neck and shoves my face down into the dirt, coating my cheeks with soil—it makes me feel like I'm a part of the earth, one with nature, perfectly aligned with all the best and worst parts of myself as one complete person.

I'm bad and I'm good.

I'm darkness and I'm light.

I'm violent and I'm peaceful.

I belong to me, and I belong to them.

I fight through the pain to take my pleasure.

I thrash until I can pull my arms away from Ambrose, until I've bucked Huxley off my back. I turn fierce and furious as they try to take me back down—as the whole world once tried to take me down.

But as it always did, my violence takes hold of me, though not in the way it did in the past. With them, my aggression is wanted, something that brings them as much pleasure as the release of it brings me. And when we mix it all together with our reckless carnality, it sends shockwaves through the entire fucking universe.

My eyes catch hold of Ambrose, and he knows with a single look that I'm no longer their prey, that my power is taking hold of me and I'm going to take control. I see the flash as he tries to switch gears and figure out how to subdue me before I take over and win…but he takes too long.

In his moment of indecision, I act.

Scrambling to my knees, I shove Huxley onto his back, slamming him down on the dirt as I fight to climb on top of him. He pushes back at me as I get my knee over him, straddling his waist and settling my weight on him. Our hands grapple as he fights to grab my wrists and I fight to grab his, grunting and panting in our struggle.

He bucks up and my pussy aches for more of that, for more of him moving against me. But as much as that, my hands itch to shove and hit and grab and squeeze.

Ambrose shifts with me, turning with me to fight against Huxley. His eyes catch mine for a brief moment of heat that connects our energy as we both direct our sparring passion to Huxley. Ambrose takes hold of his wrists for me, pulling them back and slamming them to the ground above his head. My lips part as my eyes burn with passion, watching Ambrose wrap the rope around Huxley's hands.

Huxley's body twitches beneath me, bucking and rocking and trying to shake me off, but I'm not moving.

I'm taking.

I'm winning.

I scoot back, reach between us to wrap my palm around his erection, and line him up to meet me. Then I sit down hard on his cock, and the whole world stops spinning. The three of us groan at once, and then I start to move, rocking my hips back and forth, fucking Huxley.

"Take his cum," Ambrose growls at me. "Take it, Glory. Fuck him."

I don't need the command, but fuck, his words sink inside me and pulse through my clit. I fuck him with quick hard thrusts, so wrought with tension that I know I'm going to explode hard and fast.

I lean back, reaching with my hand to rub my fingers over my clit. But Ambrose lifts Huxley's bound hands, shoving them down, making him move his fingers to rest perfectly against my clit as I rub against them. I moan as Huxley curls his fingers to let me fuck his hard knuckles, as I see his bound hands tied up for me, knowing how he likes it, how he wants to be bound for me and let me take from him.

"Glory," Huxley breathes. "Shit, Glory!"

I feel him swell; I feel how he's right there on the edge of climax, but I'm not ready yet, and for fuck's sake, I'm coming first. I slam my hips to a stop and look down at him. "Don't you dare come yet."

"Fuck, I need it," he begs.

"How badly do you need it?" I ask.

"Make me come, Glory. Fuck, *please.*"

I want to give him everything.

I want to give him the whole goddamn world for the way he's changed me…for the way he's made me the best version of myself…for the way he's made me happy.

I move my hips again, slowly at first, just for him. "I'll let you come inside me, but then I want your tongue on my clit while Ambrose fucks me."

His head bobs in a sort of nod and his fingers wiggle against my clit, making me moan. "Yes. Just make me come inside you."

I roll my hips, gradually picking up my pace, rubbing and thrusting and fucking his cock as his fingers rub against my clit. Ambrose kneels at my side and his cock is out now, too. I reach to wrap my hand around it as he leans in to kiss me, not softly but roughly, battling my tongue with his.

Inexplicably, I feel it.

I didn't think I was there yet, but suddenly, I feel it in the way Huxley's cock swells within me—the way he lets me win, lets me take from him, makes me feel like a goddess above him.

"How fast can you come?" I ask against Ambrose's lips.

"As fast as you want me to."

"Oh," I groan, my head rolling back on my shoulders as Huxley presses his fingers hard against my clit. "How do you do this to me?"

"How do you do this to us?" Ambrose asks before biting my bottom lip.

I snap my eyes open to look at him. "Get there. Get there right fucking now and come on his chest."

"Shit," he mutters, fisting his cock and stroking.

I press one hand down on Huxley's wrist to hold him in place as I hold Ambrose's cheek with the other, digging my fingertips into his flesh to hold his face close to mine.

My hips move faster, harder, driving us all to oblivion. We become one together on the forest floor, our moans and cries of desperation rolling together until we're panting as one, gasping as one, chasing pleasure as one.

As my pussy squeezes around Huxley's cock, the joy of our union overwhelms me, corrals the particles of my ashen heart inside my ribcage, and all at once, crushes them back together. It sends off a shockwave through my body. It forces every muscle to tense against the soul-deep climax. It flows out from my heart, travels through my body, bounces against my fingertips and the tips of my toes, and shoots back to my heart.

Huxley's warmth spills inside me, filling me up, as Ambrose splashes across his chest, as we all let out a single, unified sigh of pure relief and complete satisfaction.

I collapse onto Huxley's painted chest, unconcerned about the mess as he rolls me onto my side. Ambrose cradles his body around mine from behind, reaching around to pull the ropes free from Huxley's hands.

We lay there together in the soil and twigs that cover the ground beneath. I feel as though I could happily sink into the earth with these two.

"I want to be buried here with you when we die," I say without thinking.

Huxley chuckles, stroking the side of my head. "Is that what you're thinking about right now? When we die?"

I blink up at him as Ambrose runs his hand down my side, propping up onto his elbow to lean over and kiss my neck.

"I'm not thinking about dying. I'm just saying…When it happens—someday—I want to be right here between you, even in death. I want our bodies to go back to the earth. The three of us together, forever."

"Your mind is a morbid and beautiful place," Ambrose whispers against my ear before leaning across me to kiss Huxley.

His fingers trace lines down my hip and slip across my thigh. I feel myself already growing in need again and press my eyes shut to enjoy the feeling of being nestled between them.

"I love you. Both of you. I just wish we could leave our harmony behind in this place when we're gone. Give our peace back to the earth and let it flourish in this forest."

Huxley kisses my forehead. "Is that what you want?"

I open my eyes to catch his dark gaze on mine. "Yes."

"Then we'll make sure you have it," Ambrose says, running his hand over the curls leading to my sex.

"How?"

"Whoever dies last…" Huxley starts, peeking over me to look at Ambrose, and they take turns speaking as if they could read each other's thoughts…and I wouldn't be surprised if they could.

"Whoever dies last, buries the other two," Ambrose adds.

"Then ends their life in the grave," Huxley says quietly, his eyes narrowed intently on Ambrose.

"And we make sure Glory—"

"Glory can't be the last."

I turn my head so my eyes can glance back and forth between them, watching them make an unspoken promise that painfully and perfectly twists in my stomach.

"You mean that?" I ask them. "You would do that for me?"

They both shift their eyes to look at me, and I feel the power of their bond, their commitment to making me happy… even in death.

"I promise," Huxley says.

Then Ambrose follows, "I promise."

A true smile spreads brightly across my cheeks, knowing that neither would ever break a promise to me. I feel comfort in this morbid oath, knowing that a promise like this is more eternally binding than marriage, than any Earthly ritual one could make up.

"Then seal it with a kiss?" I ask.

They look at each other, then they look at me. And as their mouths descend on mine, I feel the weight of the universe press down on us, wrapping around us like a celestial embrace that recognizes that we belong here, together forever. We belong to each other in life, in death, and forever beyond. We've found our perfect balance together.

All the wrongs of our past have been righted.

All our pain is gone.

No more suffering.

No more abuse.

No more trauma.

No more.

All that remains for us is pleasure, peace, and the dark vow that binds us for eternity.

CONNECT WITH BRYNN

Author Newsletter
brynnford.com/connect

Goodreads
goodreads.com/brynnfordauthor

BookBub
bookbub.com/profile/brynn-ford

Instagram
@brynnfordauthor
instagram.com/brynnfordauthor

TikTok
@brynnfordauthor
tiktok.com/@brynnfordauthor

Facebook Page
facebook.com/brynnfordauthor

Facebook Reader's Group
bit.ly/brynnsdarlings

BRYNN'S BOOKS

The Four Families Trilogy
Counts of Eight
Dance with Death
Pas de Trois

The Four Families Spin-Off
King of Masters

Standalones
Jagged Line Paradise
Sugar Wood

ACKNOWLEDGMENTS

Writing this book was such a crazy, twisted ride and I'm so grateful for all the people who helped me finish it!

I have to thank my husband first—babe, you really came through in making sure I had the time and space I needed to get this done. I know it took away a lot of time from us, but I promise I'll give that time back!

To Danielle, Mary, and Maria…seriously, THANK YOU. Your constant support, love, guidance, and honesty keeps me going and makes me a better writer. I literally couldn't do this without you—you're the best!

Danielle, an extra thank you for all the work you do as my PA. You are literally AMAZING and I don't know what I'd do without you (so don't try to hide from me).

Rachel, aren't you proud of me? I wrote the MM part of MMF! I know I said I couldn't do it, but I did it! And I couldn't have done it without you. Thanks for all the sexy MM scenes you sent me to read as "book research" and for giving me the confidence and support I needed to stretch my writing repertoire.

To my street team and ARC eam, I absolutely adore you. Your support and love for my books humbles me. Thank you for sharing, reviewing, and helping other readers find my books!

Dez with Pretty in Ink Creations, the cover you made for this book is stunning—thank you so much for making such beautiful artwork for this twisted tale! Nada with Najla Qamber Designs, I'm so happy that I can always rely on you to make my manuscripts so beautiful—thank you for always doing such incredible work!

To my awesome editor, Silvia…How do you always manage to polish my words so beautifully? I'm so happy that I found you and I hope you're ready for all the crazy books yet to come!

My final thank you goes directly to you, reader. You picked up this book, you read the words I wrote, and for that alone, I am grateful. If you connected with the characters or the story and enjoyed this read, just know that you and I have met through these words, and I'm forever thankful you took the journey with me.

ABOUT THE AUTHOR

Brynn Ford is an author of dark and dirty romance for daring readers. She is a lover of the dark, twisted, and playful and strives to bring the unmentionable aspects of passionate romance into her stories.

Brynn lives in the Midwestern United States with her husband and sons, whom she expects will someday be embarrassed by their mom's books. When she isn't obsessively writing, you may find her binge watching favorite shows while eating far too much junk food or fanatically reading, always seeking to lose herself in the emotional roller coaster of a damn good story.

She is quite the idealist despite her fascination with the wicked and warped aspects of humanity. She's a firm believer that her characters continue to live on outside the pages in the minds of her readers. Stories don't just end because there aren't any more pages to turn.